The
Ordained

Also by Terence Faherty

The Ordained

Terence

—

Faherty

St. Martin's Press 〰 New York

Production Editor: David Stanford Burr

Library of Congress Cataloging-in-Publication Data

Faherty, Terence.
        The ordained / Terence Faherty.
                p.   cm.
        ISBN 0-312-16958-2
        1. Keane, Owen (Fictitious character)—Fiction.   I. Title
PS3556.A342073   1997
813'.54—dc21
                                                                97-23062
                                                                CIP

First Edition: December 1997

10 9 8 7 6 5 4 3 2 1

For Jesse Hubbard, Merritt Hurst,
and Jack Palladay

The
Ordained

Invisible Men

FORT LITTLETON. The name meant something. I knew from the moment I saw it on the turnpike sign. It hit me the same way a familiar face in a crowd of strangers can. Not the face of an old friend or even an acquaintance. Just a face you've seen before. One you can study at length and maybe even place, without any real danger that the person you're watching will remember you. That sense of security was a definite part of the feeling of recognition the name Fort Littleton conveyed. An important part. I wouldn't have stopped if I hadn't been sure that, even if it should turn out that I knew this place, there wasn't the slightest chance the place would know me back.

I paid my toll at the booth that guarded the exit ramp. There were two booths, but only one was staffed, which placed Fort Littleton low in the Pennsylvania Turnpike's hierarchy. I never determined if that slight was justified because I never saw the town. Like so many of the places that lend their names to turnpike exits, Fort Littleton was off hiding somewhere, behind one of the wooded hills. It was represented locally by two gas stations, an Amoco and a BP, set across from one another a hundred yards or so beyond the tollbooth gate.

I selected the Amoco because it was the older of the two and my experiment required a place that had been there twenty years before. The station looked familiar, but then every gas station looks a little like every other. This one was a long, low, gray block building with a black roof, set right up against a hill. There were three repair bays, all closed, and two gas islands, both self-service. I parked at the island closer to the building, got one of its mechanical pumps going, and then stepped away to take in the place, its smells and its sounds.

By then I was convinced that I had been there before, that I'd stopped at the station on my last trip west. See, I told myself, here you are again and nothing bad has happened. Nobody remembers you. You're invisible.

The old pump clicked off emphatically. I got the nozzle out of the Chevy without spilling more than a pint of raw gas on its faded paint. Then I went to examine the men's room graffiti, looking for my initials without finding them and smiling at the condom dispenser. It was an old machine, but it had a new name to go with its lofty new role: Health Station. The inside of the gray building had been turned into a convenience mart. I browsed the narrow isles, selecting cheese-filled pretzels for me and a plastic bottle of 10W40 for the Chevy.

Then I took my place in the checkout line. I was only number two, but it promised to be a long wait. The woman ahead of me was telling a story to the man behind the counter. She was wearing a football jersey over shorts. I recognized the colors of the jersey as Penn State's, but the player's name and number didn't ring any bells. Though unsmiling, the clerk was giving her the kind of attention storytellers dream about, turning away from her only to spit tobacco juice at a wastepaper basket lined with a plastic garbage bag. It was a tribute to his marksmanship that what I could see of the liner was still white.

I tried once to catch the counterman's eye. Then the woman

used the word "mystery." I stepped back and pretended to study a display of authentic beef jerky.

"I know he's sleeping with her," the woman said.

"Brandie Connelly," the man behind the counter said.

"Brandie Connelly," the woman said, "from down at the bottom of High Street. He won't say so, but he smiles when I ask him, so I know. He's daring me to catch him at it. I've tried. I can't 'cause it isn't possible. But I know he's doing it. I even know when."

The man behind the counter shot a fresh stream into the wastepaper basket. "When?"

"Tuesdays and Thursdays, our old days to do it, only now he's doing it with that tramp Brandie Connelly, who's got nothing to do all day but steal people's husbands. He gets off at the plant at four, but on Tuesdays and Thursdays he doesn't get home till quarter past five. You know the drive."

"Fifteen minutes," the man said, "from the plant to the top of High Street."

"At four every Tuesday and every Thursday I walk down the hill and watch Brandie Connelly's house. I used to hide or pretend to be going somewhere else. Now I just stand in the street and watch. There ain't no back way in, unless he's dug a tunnel. That house is built right against a hill, like this place. At quarter past four, her stereo comes on, loud. I don't see anybody. I don't see him get there and I don't see him leave. Then at quarter past five, my neighbor, Dawn, flashes her front porch lights. I can just see them from down at the bottom of the hill. That's Dawn's signal to tell me he's gotten home. Right about then, Brandie Connelly comes out on her porch smoking a cigarette and smiling at me."

"Whaddya do next?" the man asked.

"I go back up the hill. I go home and he's there, sitting and smiling at me, too. I can smell he's had a beer. I can smell he's had more than that."

"Maybe he's stopping off somewhere else," the counterman said.

"No," the woman said, stamping her foot. "I know the miles to the plant: twelve."

"Twelve, that'd be right."

"And I checked the miles in his truck. From the time he leaves on Tuesdays and Thursdays till the time I climb that hill, he drives twenty-four miles. And there ain't nothing between the town and the plant."

"Nothing," the man agreed, spitting for emphasis.

"So he's getting into Brandie's house, with me standing there. He's getting in and he's getting home again. You tell me how he's doing it, cause it's making me nuts."

The next voice I heard was my own. "Whose idea was it for you to go down and watch Brandie Connelly's house?"

The woman swung around to face me. She was missing a tooth, which increased her look of surprise exponentially. But she wasn't too surprised to speak. "It was Dawn's idea," she said. "Dawn, my neighbor. She knows all about Brandie Connelly. Dawn's husband took up with Brandie last year. Then he ran off and left them both."

"So Brandie owes Dawn," I said.

"Owes her?" the man at the register asked.

"How old is Dawn?"

"Twenty-two, twenty-three," the man said.

"Twenty-two," the woman said.

"What's she look like?"

"Nice," the man said. "Blond."

"Dyed," the woman said, and then her eyes doubled in size. I felt a moment's panic at not being invisible anymore. But the woman wasn't seeing me. She was seeing High Street, seeing the blond neighbor who signaled when it was safe for her to climb the hill.

Seeing the local tramp who was willing to play her stereo and smoke a cigarette in a good cause.

"Damn," she said. Then she was running for her car.

The man behind the counter was bug-eyed now, and he wasn't lost in visions. He was looking right at me. Seeing me. Memorizing me.

"Who are you?" he demanded.

I set down the oil and the pretzels and money for the gas and followed the woman out the door.

"Hey! Who are you?" the man called after me.

Someone they'd remember in Fort Littleton, I thought.

One

THERE HAS TO HAVE BEEN A TIME when the Indiana State House was something people traveled to see. The local equivalent of Egypt's pyramids or at least New York's Woolworth Building. Something worth the train ride from Terre Haute or Evansville or the buggy ride from someplace less grand.

In September 1993, when I found myself there, the Indiana State House was no longer a tourist attraction or even the focal point of Indianapolis, although a principal street, Market Street, ended at its steep steps. This approach was compromised by newer, taller buildings, which lined Market's last blocks, and by a series of bus stops spaced out along Capitol Avenue—the street at which Market teed. These stops, trash-strewn Plexiglas enclosures papered in handbills, made the big, copper-domed building behind them look like a glorified bus station.

I bypassed the capitol grounds, which boasted an example of every tree indigenous to Indiana, and climbed the steps presided over by Oliver Morton, Indiana's Civil War governor. Not that I'd ever heard of him. The bit about the trees and Morton's place in history was passed on to me by a guard stationed in the state house rotunda, a talking Adam's apple of a guy. He also told me that the building had just been restored, its old brass chandeliers—once fitted with gas jets—rehung, and its original color scheme—determined by scraping down through layers of second thoughts—repainted. The result was Victorian and dark, but that didn't bother me. I'd been called both things myself.

I was tempted to ask the guard what time the next tour pushed off, but I hadn't driven out from Jersey to study Hoosier archeology. So I asked instead where parole hearings were held.

The guard directed me out the back door and across Senate Street to a brand-new building, also limestone but less ornate. I wondered in my idle way whether some future restorers would scrape its walls someday to find what colors were popular in the last years of the twentieth century. If so, the beige they'd find would be a letdown and a half.

I followed the signs for the B wing hearing rooms, as the state house guard had instructed. I expected to pass through a security checkpoint and maybe even a metal detector, but I never encountered either. I came to a crowd of people milling around a double door of dark red wood guarded by a young woman seated at a small plastic table. None of the milling people looked familiar, but I stopped and recited my speech.

The woman told me that the parole board was meeting next door. "Yeah," a man from the crowd chimed in, "this here is a money hearing."

I never found out what he meant by that, but I did observe that money hearings were a bigger draw than parole hearings. There was no crowd outside the next hearing room, no one at all in fact except for another young woman at another plastic table. She told me that I'd found the right place at last.

"They're just setting the camera up now," she added.

"Camera?"

"We videotape parole hearings."

She was slight and dark and college age. Her dark red suit jacket lacked lapels and a collar and even buttons. Its ascetic lines were contradicted by the blouse beneath, which had more frills than a square dancer's petticoats.

"Has the, ah, prisoner arrived?" I asked, looking around again for some sign of security. As far as I could tell, the door to the hearing room didn't even have a lock.

"If you mean the subject of the hearing, he won't be here. This hearing is for the public. There'll be a separate hearing next week at the state prison. You're welcome to attend that one, too, but most of the time family and friends prefer to address the parole board at the public hearing."

I only had a second to enjoy my relief, as we'd moved right to the next point in the agenda. The woman pushed a clipboard across the table. "Will you be addressing the board? If you want to speak, you have to sign in."

I picked up a pen and then stood there, acting as though, after a week of debating with myself and seven hundred miles of driving, I hadn't actually decided whether I'd take a hand. Only it wasn't an act.

The door behind the young woman opened and a pair of rimless glasses popped out, propelled by a sleek blond head. "We're ready, Irene."

Irene, I thought, a nice, old-fashioned name. I would have stood there all day admiring it, given the chance. Irene had other plans. She pushed the clipboard an inch my way. "You don't have to speak if you sign up," she said. "You can decide later."

I scribbled my name, Owen Keane, on the first blank line. There were names above it, names I hadn't read because I hadn't been able to focus on anything but the waiting white space. Filling it up released my eyes, but Irene whisked the clipboard away so fast my terminal *e* stretched out across the page and down, like an ominous trend on a graph.

"Hurry in," she said.

The hearing room was tiny. I'd been hoping for something

large, in which I could distance myself emotionally from the business being conducted. I stepped right into the middle of that business, so thoroughly that the man operating the video camera turned the big blue lens my way, as though I were some late-breaking news. In the second before the camera flustered me completely, I noted that there were three rows of blue plastic chairs matching the table in the hallway. Four of the chairs were occupied. The parole board also numbered four, all men and all seated behind a long wooden table that faced the audience.

I hurriedly took a seat in the last row, next to the man whose phone call had brought me to Indiana. The man shook my hand and said one word, "Okie," a severe contraction of my name. Then we sat and listened together.

Three of the men behind the long table were young. Two were white and one was black, and all were fitted out like mannequins from Brooks Brothers' window. The fourth man was old, mixed his plaids fearlessly, and let his gray hair fall down across his forehead like a cowboy caught without his hat. He didn't look up from the table when the youngster next to him spoke.

"This is a public hearing on the subject of parole for one Curtis Morell, who is currently serving a life sentence for murder in the Indiana State Prison. Let the record show that four of the five members of the parole board are present."

He droned on, adopting a dry, official tone intended to give the video record the exact quality of a musty transcript, noting the date and naming the members of the board. I noticed that he was dividing his eye contact between the camera and the audience, more specifically between the camera and two women who sat together in the first row. The only other spectator was also up front, in the chair closest to the door. He was the first to stand when the speaker asked if there would be any public testimony on the parole.

He identified himself as the prosecutor of Huber County, the little corner of southern Indiana where Morell lived when he'd been loose and committing murder. The prosecutor was from the same college class as the junior board members, but he lacked their fashion sense. His blue suit was a shade too bright for anyone but a game show host. He buttoned the jacket, apparently just to demonstrate that it would button. He undid it immediately and stuck a thumb in his belt.

It was just as well that he was comfortable. His role, it seemed, was to recount Morell's crimes for the record, and it wasn't a short list. I knew it by heart already, so I only listened with one ear as he described the murder, the rest of my mind taken up with half-forgotten images of shallow graves and shotgun butts. The speaker then moved on to a second killing that had been plea-bargained down from first-degree murder for lack of hard evidence. I drifted further away, to a nursing home so real to me I could feel its sticky floor under my feet.

Eventually, the prosecutor worked his way back through Morell's history to one of his lesser offenses: criminal confinement. He mentioned my name and another, Mary Fitzgerald, that was much on my mind. I was sure I gave no outward show of emotion. Nevertheless, the man in the seat next to mine patted my arm. He had to be thinking that it made me sad to hear the name of my lost love, killed in an automobile accident years after I'd gotten her safely away from Morell.

Actually, hearing Mary's name bothered me because it revived the internal argument I'd been having over my whole trip to Indiana. My debate with myself had really been a debate with Mary, or at least with my memory of Mary and her view of the world, which was that no one was really bad. Scrape away enough layers, as Mary might have put it, and you'd find the goodness. My competing position—reinforced by years of life Mary had been denied—was that people only had layers in the first place because they felt the need to hide their darkness. Or to disguise an emptiness that was worse than any darkness.

Morell was one of the empty people, and he frightened me. Worse than that, he'd once threatened Mary. I was more than content to leave him where he was. Mary, I knew, had long since forgiven him. She would have spoken out for his release, for his second chance. Or his fifth or his ninth one.

So the question was: Should I testify as I wanted to or as Mary would have? Should I speak the words of her faith or reveal that I had none of my own?

I never worked it out, because I never testified. When the electric blue prosecutor finished, one of the women in the first row stood. She was short and wore her hair piled up in a style that had once been called a beehive. I couldn't see her face, but I knew her before she spoke.

"My name is Beatrice Crosley," she said, twice, because the old man behind the table asked her to speak up for the benefit of the video camera's microphone. He asked it kindly and leaned forward as Mrs. Crosley began again.

"My son, Michael, was murdered by Curtis Dwight Morell. Had he lived, Michael would be looking forward to the twentieth anniversary of his ordination as a priest. In those twenty years of service, he would have accomplished an incalculable amount of good, ministering to the poor and the sick, baptizing, joining couples for life, consoling lost souls on their sins and failings. I've brought a photograph of Michael I would like you to see."

She took a large golden frame from her companion and handed it to the leftmost member of the board, the man with the rimless glasses who had spoken to Irene. First he and then the next two men in line studied the portrait solemnly. The old-timer at the end barely looked at the photo before turning it around for the camera. It had been a hard twenty years for some of us, but Crosley was still a bashful high school graduate.

"I have come here today," Mrs. Crosley continued, "to ask you to deny Curtis Morell's request for parole. I don't ask this for the sake of my son and all the lost good he would have done. It would be wrong to ask for that reason. Keeping Curtis Morell in prison for a hundred years will not bring back one day of my son's lost life. It will not bring back a day of my lost happiness, either, so I am not making this request for my own sake or because I claim a special position as a widow whose only son was taken from her.

"Our consideration should be for the living, not the dead, for the mothers who still have their children, not for me. Please do not give Curtis Morell the chance to take another life, to create another chasm of devastation and pain where there should only have been good. Michael accomplished one great good for this world. His death exposed an evil man and allowed good men to put him away where he could do no more harm. Please do not negate that sacrifice. Please do not require another such sacrifice of another innocent soul. Thank you."

She sat down in a very quiet room. The old board member was still holding Crosley's photo. He placed it face down on the table and said, "Thank you, Mrs. Crosley. Is there any other testimony?"

The man next to me rose to his feet and identified himself as Dennis Feeney. "There are others who came to speak," he said, placing a heavy hand on my shoulder. "I came to speak. But I know I can't add anything to what Mrs. Crosley has just said. None of us can. I think we can only take away from it by trying, and maybe even distract the board from her testimony. I've decided I just want to say that I'm here to support Mrs. Crosley. I think we should all leave it at that."

"Amen," I said, but not for the record.

Two

AFTER THE PAROLE BOARD HAD THANKED US and paraded out, the only sounds in the room came from the video technician, who was packing away his camera, and Mrs. Crosley, who was crying. I'd looked for her to break down any time during her speech, but her voice had droned on with an edge that was painful to hear. Even now she was far from worked up. She was sobbing more than crying, a soft, spent sobbing appropriate for a graveside.

Before I could make up my mind to intrude, she stood and started for the door on the arm of her companion, a tall young woman with straw-colored hair. On her way out, Mrs. Crosley nodded her thanks to the man who sat next to me. I'd met her once, briefly, but she looked at me now without remembering me. I couldn't blame her. I'd been a college kid at our one meeting, and she'd been middle-aged. Now I'd all but caught up with her.

"She'll be okay, Okie," the man next to me said. "Those are old tears. They may even be old friends."

I turned to look at the speaker, himself an old friend. The only name I'd ever called him was Brother Dennis. I'd even taken to using it—omitting his last name—on the letters I wrote him once or twice a year. It seemed natural to me that everyone would know him by his first name, even the post office.

I'd met the monk when I'd attended a seminary in the southernmost part of Indiana, St. Aelred's, Michael Crosley's seminary. Brother Dennis had been the resident assistant of my dorm and my cheerleader during my unhappy attempt at the priesthood. He was still cheering for me, decades after I'd thrown the game.

Since failing to become a priest, I'd held many lesser jobs. None of them had been anything but a means of paying my bills. Brother Dennis didn't ask me about my current job, which would only have embarrassed us both. Nor did he ask about my replacement vocation, the obsessive pursuit of mysteries. If he had, I might have told him that I'd put that behind me finally. He might have believed me.

"I guess I brought you out here for nothing, Okie," the monk said. "Sorry. I don't know what made me stand up and say what I did. You probably had important things to tell the board. I had a speech all worked out myself." He showed me a pack of well-thumbed index cards. "So what do I do? I stand up and say, 'That's all, folks!' "

"I'm glad you did," I said, although I wasn't sure about that. I'd been spared the ordeal of testifying, but I'd lost something, too. It was the illusion of being in touch again with Mary. I could feel her slipping away.

To delay her, I tried to see Brother Dennis through her eyes, to remember the interest she'd once taken in the monk. I'd failed to solve his mystery myself. I'd recognized that he'd been damaged physically and spiritually by some event in his past, but I'd never researched it, preferring to imagine improbable, romantic explanations. Mary had identified the trauma as the Korean War, through the simple technique of lending the monk an ear. She'd learned that he'd been wounded and that a friend had died in his arms. The information had transformed my opinion of the gentle, scatterbrained man with the scarred face and hands of a prizefighter, ennobling him as none of my imaginings had done.

"At least I got a chance to see you again," I said. "You're looking great."

"My birthdays don't bother me," the monk said. "Other people's do. Yours do, Okie. I've been picturing you as a skinny, long-haired kid. You still could use a good meal, but your hair! You're grayer than I am. How did it happen? You can't be much past forty."

"I worry a lot," I said.

"About what, Okie?" He reached up to grasp the forearm I'd propped on the back of my chair. "What worries you?"

"Well, for one thing, I seem to have a lot of gray hair for a man my age."

The monk laughed. "One of those vicious circles. I know them well." He squeezed my arm and let it go. "We'll talk some more when you come down to see my pottery. I'll get the truth from you then."

"Your pottery?" I asked as Brother Dennis stood. He'd been a potter—a bad potter—as long as I'd known him, first at St. Aelred's and then at a less structured religious community in a little town called Oldenburg. A little town I hadn't planned on seeing. "I thought we could have lunch," I offered instead.

"We can have lunch or dinner or breakfast or whatever you want when you come down to Oldenburg." He grimaced as he straightened his back. Then he stooped over again, unconsciously. "I'm not taking no for an answer. You can't have come all this way and not see the place. Besides, we have to have a good talk. We can't talk in a restaurant."

I'd actually been visualizing a bar, but I let the image fade. "I'll come," I said.

"I knew you would. Today's not good, Okie. The place is a mess. You're tired anyway, after your drive. I can see the tired-ness."

In my hair, I thought. "I could stand an early night," I said. The abrupt ending of the hearing had burst the little blister of nervous energy that had kept me awake during the long drive west. I could feel myself slipping downward in my plastic chair.

"Good idea. Rest up. Come down tomorrow or Friday. I'll give you directions. Either day is fine. Take care of any other visiting you have to do first."

I had no other visiting to do in Indiana, unless I stopped by Rex Stout's birthplace to see if anyone had put up a historical marker. At least I didn't think I had any other commitments. As usual, I was less than fully informed.

I offered to walk Brother Dennis to his car. We made it as far as the steps of the building. There the monk stopped to examine a bench and a big metal ashtray that was shaped—appropriately enough—like an oxygen cylinder with its top cut off. The container was overflowing with butts.

"Where the office workers come to smoke on their breaks," Brother Dennis said. "They're not allowed to smoke inside, poor souls. It's the same all over. You see them out in all kinds of weather, huddled in little groups. You've kicked that filthy habit, haven't you, Okie?"

I knew he meant smoking and not huddling in little groups, a habit I'd never acquired. I remembered that I'd smoked quite a bit at St. Aelred's, "an outward, visible sign," as the Church might have put it, that all was not right with me. I'd given up cigarettes a few years later. Oddly, one sounded good right then.

Before I could shake the feeling, someone tapped me on the shoulder. "Owen Keane?" a woman's voice said.

It belonged to the tall young woman who had been supporting

Mrs. Crosley in the hearing. With my usual acumen, I'd classified her as a friend or relative of the sobbing woman.

"I'm Krystal. You remember. Krystal Morell."

Curtis Morell's daughter. I remembered an eight- or nine-year-old with the habit of popping up where I least expected her. That talent seemed to be the only thing the girl and this woman had in common. The face considering me now didn't need washing, as the girl's always had. It was an angular face, but a pleasant one, with a broad, flat forehead, sharp cheekbones, and a small nose that sprang up suddenly, well below the probing blue eyes. I remembered the blond hair—now short and squared off—as dirty and tangled and worn much closer to the ground. Several feet closer, in fact.

I couldn't examine the rest of her; she was watching me too closely. I had to make do with reading the expression of a young man who was checking Krystal out on his way into the building. He stopped short of whistling, but I got the message.

"Owen Keane," she said, pressing my hand. "And Brother Dennis." She hugged the old monk.

He held his hand down, the palm out flat, to indicate the height Krystal had been when I'd brought her to St. Aelred's for safekeeping one bad night. "Wow," he said. "Now I really feel old."

"You don't look a bit different," Krystal told him.

Before she could hand me the same line, I asked, "Where is Mrs. Crosley?"

"I just put her in a cab. She was all in, bless her heart. It took a lot of strength for her to come here today. But she wanted to keep faith with her son. What about you, Owen? Why did you come?"

My answer was standing next to me, but when I looked to him to field the question, he let me down. "I'd better write up those directions, Okie. I'll use that bench over there. You and Krystal visit for a minute."

"Directions?" Krystal prompted when the monk had shuffled away.

"To Oldenburg. He has a pottery there."

She paused for a moment, then asked, "You don't know where Oldenburg is?"

"I'm lucky I remembered where Indiana is."

"Where are you living now?"

"New Jersey."

I waited for her to ask me why I hadn't become a priest. She jumped past that question. "What happened to the pretty lady?"

"Mary?" I asked.

"Yes. I always think of her as the pretty lady."

I told her about the automobile accident in which Mary had died.

She pressed her thin lips together and nodded. "I thought something had happened to her. When I saw you come into the hearing, I knew things hadn't worked out the way I'd been imagining all these years."

They hadn't, but that had nothing to do with the accident. I let it pass.

"How have they worked out for you?" I asked. When I'd last seen her, she'd been on her way to a foster home.

"There were bad years. But things turned out well. I'm a doctor now."

"You were when I knew you."

She laughed. "My folk remedies, you mean?"

"Yes."

Krystal paused again, lost in thought. When she finally spoke, I had the impression that she had decided to file those thoughts away.

"My grandfather died in prison," she said, skipping ahead again. "My grandmother passed away last year."

I said I was sorry, though I remembered the pair mainly as her father's accomplices.

"They both paid a big price for the things my father did. I hope they'll keep him in prison. For my grandparents' peace and for Mrs. Crosley's sake."

"When did you meet her?"

"Just today. I guessed who she was when she came in. And I introduced myself. I've wanted to meet her for a long time. You probably don't remember, but I had a crush on her son."

"I remember," I said.

She looked down at the pavement. "It was just a crush. He never did anything to encourage it. Anything to take advantage of it. Nowadays you couldn't tell someone about a little girl being in love with a seminarian without starting them guessing the ugliest things."

"I never did."

"No," Krystal said, brushing my sleeve lightly. "You wouldn't."

Brother Dennis returned, having taken enough time to write out directions to Tibet. He tucked the folded envelope he'd used into the pocket of my shirt. "Tomorrow or Friday, Okie. Either one. Just call first. I wrote my number down.

"It was very nice to see you again," he said to Krystal, shaking her hand. "You two have a nice talk."

Then he was off, bumping into one passerby after another as he turned every few steps to wave.

"So you're staying in Indiana for a day or two," Krystal said between waves.

"It looks that way."

"The town where I live, Rapture, isn't all that far from Oldenburg. Maybe an hour away. Maybe two."

"Is Rapture where you practice?"

"It's one of the places. I make a circuit of the little towns around the county. 'Dr. Bowden and her traveling medicine show,' they call me. Bowden is the name of the family who finally took me in. I was happy to get a new name after everything that had happened."

"I understand."

"I was wondering if you'd like to visit me on your way down to see Brother Dennis." She read my expression and quickly added, "You might be able to help me."

I asked her how.

"We've got a little mystery," she said. "As I remember, you're good at untangling them."

Her memory was selective, it seemed. She had forgotten how much trouble my untangling caused. I hadn't, as I had more recent examples to remind me.

"I don't do that anymore," I said.

Krystal didn't believe me. "It would mean a lot to me," she said.

She didn't say, "And after all, I saved your life," but somehow I seemed to hear it.

I was already hooked, but she kept playing me. "There's a religious angle to the mystery."

"What would that be?"

"Not here," she said, looking around the sunny stone steps. "A story like this needs atmosphere. Come down to Rapture, and I'll tell you all about it."

Three

"YOU'LL NEVER FIND MY PLACE," Krystal said. "So I'll meet you in Rapture itself. Call me before you start out."

She reached up and took the envelope from my shirt pocket. "I'll add my directions to Brother Dennis's." She unfolded the envelope and read for a moment. "He's written something else here. He says it's a line from Psalm 68. 'God sets up the solitary in families.'"

Not being a correspondent of the monk's, Krystal didn't know about his habit of heading his letters and notes with lines of scripture.

"Is that a reference to me and my foster family?" she asked.

I thought it more likely to be Brother Dennis's idea of a pickup line, but I didn't say so.

Dr. Bowden figured it out anyway. "The old sweetheart," she said. "If you really are solitary, Owen, you'll take to Rapture. The town is like a family."

Rapture was a family that was fond of its privacy, as it turned out. I spent a long, uneasy night in a motel on the east side of Indy. The sounds of traffic from the neighboring highway should have been comforting echoes of Jersey, but they only reminded me of what

I would soon be giving up: a quick escape route back to the Garden State.

The next morning, Thursday morning, I started out in my little Chevy Cavalier, with the Styrofoam cups and hamburger wrappers of my drive west still along for company. I drove south on Interstate 65, following the signs for Louisville, Kentucky, where I'd once put Mary Fitzgerald on an airplane and sent her off to marry someone else. I was spared an actual visit to the scene of that debacle; Krystal's directions took me west on Highway 50 at a town called Seymour, well north of the Kentucky line.

My map showed big patches of pale green beyond Seymour, identified as sections of the Hoosier National Forest. The actual forest was dark green and less broken up than the map indicated. In a particularly dense patch east of Bedford, I spotted the turn for Rapture.

Highway 50 had been wide and well paved, with a surprising amount of truck traffic. The road to Rapture was narrow and rough. The local highway department intended to keep it that way, too. They had coated long stretches of the road with crushed stone on a tar base. It was a maintenance technique I hadn't seen in my home state since my grammar school days, and it reminded me of a fact regarding southern Indiana. It was a place where time moved slowly.

The forest overhung the little road. Only an occasional field, tall with dry summer grass and decorated with a sagging fence or barn, provided a break in the green. Smaller trees—redbud and dogwood—lined the road at Cavalier height, packed together so tightly in low spots that they looked like a hedge run wild. Soon though, the road ran out of low spots. It climbed and wound and climbed again, and then I was in Rapture, without so much as a stray dog or corncrib to warn me.

The town may have been lacking in suburbs, but it did have a reception committee. She was seated on the hood of a Jeep Cherokee that was parked in the only sunny spot along the town's main street, her face held up to the sun. I parked behind the Jeep and stepped out into dusty warmth and the sound of a power saw.

When the saw paused for breath, Krystal looked down from the sky and said, "Welcome to Rapture, Owen. You made good time. I just got here myself."

I was thinking that I'd wasted good time, not made it. "Don't you warn your patients to stay out of the sun?" I asked by way of sharing my mood.

"Not very practical advice for farmers, Owen. They wouldn't believe it anyway. No Aztec had a higher regard for the sun than a farmer does. So I preach moderation. Moderation in all things.

"Besides, I don't have any patients. Not today. I arranged for a colleague who owes me a favor to cover for me. Isn't that what Dr. Watson always did when Sherlock Holmes sent for him?"

"My name's Keane," I said. "And *you* sent for *me*. Otherwise, it's a pretty tight analogy."

"Moderation in all things," Krystal said and slid off the truck.

She'd traded her city clothes of the day before for a faded plaid shirt, its sleeves rolled up to her elbows, and jeans shorts. The arms and legs the outfit displayed were long and slender, but solid with bone. Her wrists were wide and her hands were muscular and cool to the touch.

I discovered that last quality when she took my warm, unmuscular hand and guided me toward a side street as narrow as an alley. It descended toward a grove of huge oaks and the scream of the reawakened power saw. We passed little houses of nearly identical design. They were narrow wooden structures with steeply pitched roofs whose unadorned front gables all faced the street. A few were obviously lived in—Krystal exchanged smiles with several residents who were enjoying the morning air on their porches or puttering about their yards—but many of the houses appeared to be deserted.

"Been losing patients lately?" I asked above the rising sound of the saw.

"I've lost one," Krystal shouted back. "I'll tell you about it later. First I want you to hear about Rapture."

"Are we going to your office?"

"Office? That was my office parked up there on the hill. My Jeep. I work for the county health department out of Bedford. I've got a desk up there, but I'm too busy making my rounds to see it very often."

The noise of the saw stopped suddenly, and Krystal shouted the last few words of her explanation before she caught herself. She stopped walking to laugh and to look around self-consciously. "Now that I can whisper," she said, "I'd like to ask you for a favor. A promise, really. None of the locals know about my past. About my father, I mean. I'd like to keep it that way. If anyone should ask how we met—"

"I'll mention Paris."

"Thanks, Owen."

At the bottom of the hill, the road entered the cluster of oaks. The trees formed a perimeter for a compound of wooden buildings, the largest one the size of a barn doubled in length. Above its big front doors was a hand-painted sign that bore the words RAPTURE COFFIN WORKS and a year: 1862.

The interior of the building was as vast as a cavern but nowhere near as cool. It smelled of hot machine oil, freshly cut wood, and glue. The sunlight coming in through the shed's high windows was dampened by dust swirling upward like snow. Along the left side of the main room, pairs of sawhorses held wooden coffins in various stages of completion. They were unlike any I had ever seen, narrow with high sides and rounded ends. Opposite them were saws and other pieces of woodworking equipment. All were driven by wide, flat belts that ran upward to a system of pulleys and shafts suspended in the dusty air below the ceiling beams. Even without the screaming saw, the power system, clattering on above us, provided enough noise to mask our entrance. None of the half-dozen men moving between the tools and the sawhorses noticed us until we neared a large workbench that stood in the center of the room.

Then the man seated behind the workbench, himself large enough to make the eight feet of rough planking covered with old tools seem no bigger than a standard desk, looked up. His face—broad and ruddy and fringed above and below with wispy gray hair—came to life at the sight of Krystal. He got up from his chair to greet her.

"Dr. Bowden, my good friend. Come with a cure for my arthritis?"

"I'm still working on that," Krystal said.

"Still working?" he asked, towering over Krystal—and me. "Work faster, woman, or God will beat you to it. His cure will be too permanent."

"You'll be asking me for a cure for deafness next," Krystal said. "Where is your hearing protection?"

The giant cupped a hand behind his ear. "What do you say?" he asked and laughed. "Who is this with you, a health inspector?"

"No," the doctor said. "This is an old friend of mine, Owen Keane. Owen, this is Emmett Haas, the mayor of Rapture."

"Mayor," Haas repeated derisively. "This town is too small to have a mayor. I am the dogcatcher," he said to me. "And the street cleaner. I used to be Santa at Christmas, too, but we do not have any young children at the moment. Now, if our lovely doctor would marry . . ."

"Don't hold your breath, Emmett."

"Oh well. I never fooled the children anyway." He held a finger across his bare upper lip. "Not even with a false moustache."

"Owen is visiting from the East," Krystal said. "He's curious about the town."

"I can see he is curious," Haas said, looking down at me through dime store reading glasses. "A blind man could see that about him. But this is Thursday, Doctor, a work day. We only dress up to entertain the tourists on weekends. Come back on Saturday. We will have apple cider for sale."

"I'm hoping Owen can help us, Emmett. With Prestina."

"Ah. That is different." He turned to the nearest of the workers scattered throughout the large room, a young man with a ponytail, whose sweeping had brought him close to Haas's workbench. "Willie, tell everyone to take some quiet time now. I will be back in ten minutes sharp."

Four

HAAS LED THE WAY OUT through the double doors of the factory, walking gingerly, as though the sawdust-covered floor were strewn with broken glass. Once outside, he brushed more sawdust from the shoulders of his coveralls and ran a hand through his beard for good measure.

"I usually start my lecture out here," he said when we arrived at the base of the largest oak. There was a bench there, but Haas didn't take advantage of it. "Not that there is much call for it nowadays. People today are content with their own beliefs, if they have any. If they have none, they are even more content. Either way, they lack the patience and sympathy one needs to understand the dreams of another time. Are you one of the content, Mr. Keane?"

"No," I said.

"No. I thought not. That makes you a worthy audience. You will make up in attention what you lack in numbers. Have you ever heard of the adventist movement?"

"Yes," I said. "Years ago. In school." I waited for Krystal to mention St. Aelred's, but Haas didn't give her the chance.

"You may remember, then," he said, "that the movement grew out of the teachings of William Miller and others who predicted that the Second Coming of Christ would occur in 1843. One hundred and fifty years ago this year; think of that. The prediction was based on a reading of the Old Testament—the book of Daniel—that convinced Miller the end would come two thousand and three hundred years after the rebuilding of the temple in Jerusalem, an event scholars of the day placed in 457 B.C.

"Miller and the others began preaching a warning of the approaching cataclysm and the message spread through the various denominations, capturing a convert here, a preacher there, sometimes a whole congregation. The movement slowly gained strength as 1843 drew near. To give one example that impressed me when I first heard of it as a child, an adventist named Himes had a huge tent constructed that could seat four thousand souls with room for two thousand more in the aisles. Amazing, is it not? The tent was used for camp meetings as far west as Cincinnati and Louisville."

Haas was impressed all over again as he pictured the great tent. He roused himself from the dream with a shrug. "Around the same time, a small group of Hoosier settlers broke away from a Shaker community and set out on their own. The Shakers believed in universal celibacy, as you may recall, and my ancestors and others—the group that broke away—could not hold with celibacy, luckily for me. They got caught up instead in the wave of adventist fervor that was sweeping down the Ohio Valley. They gave it their own peculiar twist, claiming that the faithful would be whisked up to heaven without warning on the last day, an event they called the rapture. They made up a name for themselves, too, the Ordained of God. And they founded this town, Rapture, in 1841. They planned to spend the time remaining in study and prayer and—this is my own theory, Doctor—in making up for the time they lost while they were celibate.

"Well, 1843 came and went and nothing happened. The

Ordained were not worried. They—and others around the country—had spotted an error in Miller's calculations. You see, he had done his figuring using the Christian calendar. Anyone with sense would see that an Old Testament prophet would base his prognostications on the Jewish calendar. This insight pushed the predictions into 1844 and even gave the adventists the most likely date for the Second Coming: the Day of Atonement, the tenth day of the seventh month of the Jewish calendar. October 22 to us gentiles.

"Imagine that, Mr. Keane. Knowing the date of your judgment. It would certainly focus your mind, would it not? Who could not remain faithful if they had an appointment set? And one that was only a few months away.

"The adventists of 1844 were certainly focused. But that caused friction between them and other Christian groups. The adventists could not understand why anyone would preach anything but the end-is-near warning. Everything else seemed trivial to them. Their relations with the newspapers were even worse, as you might imagine. Or maybe you would not. Maybe you think the press was different in the 1840s, less secular, less cynical."

"I would have guessed that," I said.

Haas nodded. "Living in the past, as I do, I see more of a connection between that lost time and ours. I am struck more by the similarities than the differences. Anyhow, the newspapers of the day had a good time poking fun at the adventists. They got away with it, too, because the other Christian groups were happy to laugh along.

"None of that affected the Ordained, tucked away here as they were. There were no newspapers in Rapture and no competing denominations. Nothing to disturb the watching and the waiting and the general lack of celibacy that preceded October 22, 1844.

"Just before midnight on the twenty-first, the whole community gathered in a field on the highest hill in the area. The hilltop had been specially cleared of trees and kept clear by the village livestock. It was called Rapture Meadow.

"The press said later that adventists around the country had gathered in high places wearing 'ascension robes,' flowing white garments like bridal gowns. That turned out to be a newspaper hoax. There is no evidence of any robes being used anywhere, but the image fit the popular view of the crazy adventists, so it stuck. Certainly the people of Rapture did not get themselves up like any pasteboard saints. I think they dressed in the best clothes they had—who would not?—and gathered to hold hands and pray."

"So what happened?" I asked.

Haas laughed. It was little more than a dusty chuckle, but it seemed to take a lot out of him. "I was right when I said you are a worthy audience, Mr. Keane. You really become involved in a story. You know what happened: nothing. Sunrise on the twenty-second was as beautiful an example as anyone could remember, the kind of crystal-clear morning we get in the fall, not a hint of a mist or a cloud, just a few stars lingering on like heart truths.

"Still the Ordained did not despair. They waited the day out, singing and praying. They prepared what in those pioneer times was a banquet. They ate it and waited. None fell away as evening came on and the stars returned. If anything, their emotions rose as midnight approached again. The first and most influential Adventist periodical had been called *The Midnight Cry,* after all.

"You remember the original midnight cry from your Bible, do you not, Mr. Keane?" Haas asked, almost playfully. "From the parable of the ten virgins in the Gospel of . . ."

He waited, not really expecting me to be able to fill in the blank. Krystal did, I could see. For her sake, I made the effort.

"Matthew. Chapter twenty-five, I think."

"Very good. You remember then that the virgins were awaiting the arrival of a bridegroom who was strangely delayed. He came when they least expected him, at midnight. The Ordained recalled that parable and held fast. Every dream of those hoping and dreaming souls became focused on the midnight hour. The moment the end *had* to come."

Haas took off his reading glasses, folded them, and put them into a breast pocket of his coveralls. Then he sat down on the bench at the base of the tree. Krystal crossed to stand beside him.

"I am fine, Doctor," Haas said as she patted his shoulder. "Just a little winded. You forgot to scold me for not wearing my dust mask in there. But that is not the real truth. The truth is I am not a very good tour guide. A lecturer should not be emotionally involved with his story. I don't know why it should bother me so today."

He looked at me as though it might be my fault. Then he said, "Midnight came and went, Mr. Keane, and the unredeemed world lingered on. Adventists around the country called it the Great Disappointment. Most drifted back to their various denominations, becoming 'indefinite-time believers' or forgetting adventism altogether. Forgetting all faiths altogether, some of them. A smaller group worked out a complicated explanation for the Lord's failure to appear. The 1844 predictions had referred to Christ's movement to the Holy of Holies in the heavenly sanctuary, there to begin the second phase of his work of atonement. This had actually occurred on October 22, 1844, they proclaimed—leaving it to the rest of the world to disprove. Their theory is explained in a pamphlet we used to have around here somewhere."

Haas looked down at the pocket where he had put his glasses, but it held them and the stubs of pencils and nothing else.

"Is that what the Ordained believed?" I asked.

"No. We have that pamphlet around for the tourists who are curious about later Adventists. A professor from Indiana University wrote it up. We do not have a pamphlet explaining what the Ordained believed after October 22, 1844."

"But they didn't disband."

"No, they did not. If anything, the community drew closer together. They were isolated here, of course, safe from the world's ridicule. Still, you would think their belief would be shaken. To have invested so much treasure—spiritual treasure—in a single tenet and then to have that tenet exploded absolutely." Haas shook his head. "What belief could seem secure after that?"

He stood up, gently passing Krystal's comforting hand back to her. He'd jokingly referred to himself as a tour guide earlier. Now, as he led us back inside, he sounded like one.

"The Ordained remained together, worshiping regularly at the meeting house they built and gathering every year in Rapture Meadow on October 22 to reenact the Great Banquet, as they called it. The population of Rapture held steady despite the deaths of some members during the Civil War. To supplement their farming, the Ordained fell back upon the woodworking skills that were part of their Shaker heritage. Instead of furniture, though, they set themselves to making these."

Haas ran his fingers along the unfinished wood of a coffin lid. When he spoke again, the practiced quality was missing from his voice. "Coffins. They might have picked tables or barrels or wagons. The official history of the sect suggests that the coffin factory had a Civil War connection, that it was built to help fill the endless government orders during the fighting. I've never believed that. There has to have been some significance to the Ordained's decision to make an item they once believed they would never need. Sometimes I think it may have been a gentle penance, that they may have been poking fun at themselves and their hopes. Other times it seems to me that they had simply found a direction for themselves in the failure of the rapture.

"It may have been as close to a theological insight as the Ordained ever got," Haas added wistfully, "the idea that the Lord guides us through our humiliations and failures, not through our successes."

If so, I thought, I was getting more than my share of guidance. I asked, "What happened to the Ordained after that?"

"Throughout this century," Haas said, his voice tired now and soft, "the population of Rapture steadily dwindled, as the wide world called to the children of the sect. Many small towns in Indiana have shrunk and some have disappeared, so what happened here is not unusual. It is sadder for us, though. Rapture was never just a place to live and work. It was a place to wait for the eternal. It was a belief, a hope.

"I am the last patriarch of the Ordained. I tend the church properties, run the coffin works—although my workers are all nonbelievers, exiles from the modern world. When one of my dwindling flock passes on, I make a coffin for him or her by hand, in the old way.

"I planned to make a coffin for Prestina Shipe," he said to Krystal. "If I was granted the time. Now I wonder if she will ever need one."

"What do you mean?" I asked.

"The doctor will explain, I think," Haas said. "Thank you both for stopping by."

Five

WE DECIDED TO TAKE KRYSTAL'S TRUCK. It had a standard shift that she yanked around with enthusiasm as we climbed out of Rapture on the main road before turning onto a rutted gravel tract that plunged into a little valley. As the trail dropped away, Krystal downshifted aggressively, hanging me up in my seat belt.

"You should see these roads in the winter," she said. "I'm happy to be on the gravel ones then, ruts and all. Last February—"

I reached out my hand, both to interrupt her and to grab the dashboard. "I'll come back some year for the skiing," I said. "Tell me about Prestina Shipe."

"Sorry, Owen. I have been stalling. I'm worried that once I explain, it'll stop being a mystery and start sounding like nothing. I've been afraid since I got the brilliant idea of dragging you down here that you'll end up patting my head and telling me not to worry."

"I don't often pat doctors' heads. They usually pat mine." I almost added that they sometimes rapped my head and listened for an echo, but I didn't want to diminish Krystal's opinion of me. Not yet. It occurred to me that her withheld story and I had something in common. Our attraction stemmed from a lack of information. Krystal could only have the vaguest memories of me, memories that had been gold-plated by time. If she'd known how my life had played out in the years since we rescued one another from her crazy father, she would have gone out of her way to avoid me after the parole hearing.

"I promise not to say your mystery isn't one," I said. "Unless I really believe that's true. Even then, I may lie to protect your feelings."

She laughed. "I'll start at the beginning then. Prestina Shipe is a member of the Ordained of God, as Emmett said. All the members are getting on; Prestina is seventy-two. She's one of my patients and a good friend. More than that, she's my business partner."

"She's a doctor?"

"Not exactly. Back in Indy you teased me about the herbs I used to grow, remember?"

I nodded.

"Prestina grows medicinal herbs at the little place she has down in the valley. She's grown them for years and sold them to the tourists who come through Rapture in the fall when the leaves are turning. But lately, the day trippers have been going to more trendy places, like Nashville over in Brown County, and passing Rapture by. Prestina's business was falling off, which worried me. It wasn't just income she was losing, Owen. It was also her sense of purpose, the reason she had for getting up every day and getting busy.

"So I talked her into starting a mail-order business."

"And you put up the money to start it," I said, as much to explore my new view of Krystal as to advance the story.

"Right, I did. I never expected to see the money again. But the business really took off. Our timing was accidentally great. People's interest in alternative medicine is higher now than it's been at any time since the seventies. We call our stuff Dr. Prestina's Miracle

Herbs, and every packet has a picture of Prestina on the front. The 'doctor' part is a veiled reference to me. Prestina insisted on it."

Krystal downshifted again and then stood on the brakes for good measure. "I got talking so much, I almost missed the drive. We're here."

We turned into an overgrown lane cut through a field of goldenrod and thistle and a dozen other weeds I couldn't name. The prettiest of those was topped with spiky purple flowers that were the exact shade of lenten vestments. The cottage beyond the field was a much paler version of the same color, a lavender weathering to light gray, and it had a slate roof crowned with a little cupola that was itself topped with a likeness of a running horse. All along the front porch of the cottage, bundles of flowers and herbs had been hung to dry.

"The herb gardens are out back," Krystal said. "Also the sheds where Prestina prepares the herbs and packages them. I'd show you all that, but you'd think I was stalling again."

I was already thinking that, but now that we were off the roller coaster road, it didn't bother me. Nothing was bothering me at the moment. I felt an odd desire to sit down on the front porch and close my eyes. "Does she run the whole operation herself?" I asked.

"No. I help when I can. At harvest time, we hire away a couple of Emmett's workers on a temporary basis. He doesn't mind. He helps sometimes himself. But Prestina oversees it all. The success of the business is taking the years off her, Owen. It really is."

She used the present tense self-consciously, as a declaration of faith, and I realized that we'd gotten to the point at last. "Until what happened?" I asked.

"Until she disappeared. Come inside."

She unlocked the front door—deep blue and decorated with tiny white stars and quarter moons—using a key hidden under a potted chrysanthemum. The inside of the house was warm and smelled like a potpourri warehouse. Krystal breathed in the jumbled fragrances with half-closed eyes while I looked around.

The front room was an office with no fewer than three desks: an open rolltop whose pigeonholes were jammed with long white slips of paper that turned out to be orders for herbs, an orderly partners desk with a chair on either side and a row of catalogs and books acting as a divider, and a computer stand on which a late-model Macintosh was humming away happily.

On the wall above it was a metal-framed color photo of a white-haired woman with a large aquiline nose and very pink skin. Her little eyes were popping wide and her lips were pursed, the combination suggesting that the photographer had asked her for a kiss before clicking the shutter. She was wearing what looked like a white lab coat.

"Prestina," Krystal said. "We had that picture taken at the mall in Bloomington, at one of those places where they doll you up first and do your hair. How do you think she looks?"

"High tech," I said, patting the humming computer. "Like this room."

"You were expecting rocking chairs and doilies?"

"Is the hot tub out back?"

I went looking for it, finding instead a small bedroom with both rocking chair and doilies, a sitting room squeezed around a wood-burning stove, a tiny bath, and a slightly larger kitchen whose enameled appliances made the computer in the front room seem like a fragment of science fiction.

Krystal joined me in the kitchen. "This is where it was," she said, crossing to a drop-leaf table that sat beneath a window dotted with stained-glass birds and butterflies held aloft by suction cups.

"Where what was?"

"Prestina's breakfast," Krystal said. Then, in a rush, she gave up her story.

"Two days ago, I came over before I started my rounds to help Prestina sort through her orders. We work together at the big desk you saw out front, the partners desk. It's Prestina's way of making me feel at home here.

"I knocked at the front door. I almost never have to, because Prestina usually hears my truck and comes out to meet me. Tuesday morning she didn't. She didn't answer her door either. I walked around back and looked in the sheds and the fields and didn't find anyone but the stray cats that are always hanging around.

"So I unlocked the door with the same key we used today and came in here, calling to Prestina. I was afraid she'd fallen or worse. I found every room looking exactly as they do now, except this one. This table was set for her breakfast. Oatmeal, buttered toast, and coffee, all of it stone cold. The toast was as hard as drywall. The meal could have been set out very early that morning or maybe even the morning before."

"When did you last see her?"

"I called her Sunday night to tell her I'd be by on Tuesday. She said she was anxious to talk to me and that was all."

"Nothing about going off somewhere for a visit?"

"No. Prestina doesn't own a car. She doesn't even know how to drive one. She has to call a friend whenever she wants to go somewhere. These days, it's usually me. I've phoned around; no one has heard from her."

"What else did you do?"

Krystal pushed her cropped hair upward and held it there while she thought. "I searched for a note. That meant going through all the slips of paper in the house and all the likely files in the computer. Nothing. Then I went down to talk with the police. Rapture doesn't have its own police. We share a sheriff's substation with three or four other towns. You passed it on your way in on Fifty. It's in an old filling station, and it's manned by exactly one deputy, a piece of work named Dix."

Krystal's eyes narrowed. She took her hands out of her hair and curled them into fists, planting one on each hip. "He didn't react fast enough for me and I let him know it. That was a mistake. Some men can't take anything from a woman but polite questions and meek answers."

"How old is this Dix? Maybe he's just prejudiced against young people. Or doctors. Or blonds."

"Sorry. I shouldn't jump to conclusions. For whatever reason, we tangled right off. He told me he wouldn't even treat Prestina as a missing person until she was gone for forty-eight hours. And he added that it wasn't a crime to skip your breakfast, the son of a bitch.

"Excuse my language, Owen. It's always at its worst when I'm around Dix or I think of him. Dix won't use a curse word himself. Not one. I don't know why. It may be a religious thing or it could be he used to have a problem with his language and now he belongs to swearers anonymous. It's my secret goal to get a 'damn' or a 'shit' out of him, but to date the best I've done is 'dag nab it.' " She pantomimed a left jab. "I may have to haul off and pop the guy."

"You said just now that you came into the house because you were afraid Prestina had fallen or worse. So you have considered— don't pop me for checking—the possibility that she took ill in some way."

"Of course," Krystal said, smiling again and disassembling her fists. "But the more I thought about it, the less likely it seemed. She's not on any medication, so she couldn't have accidentally taken anything incorrectly. A mild stroke might have left her disoriented, but she isn't a likely candidate. Her blood pressure is lower than mine. Besides, would a stroke victim lock up her house and hide the key before wandering away?"

"Maybe she had the attack outside."

"Why hadn't she eaten her breakfast, then? It doesn't add up. Still, I used the possibility of a medical emergency as a way of prodding Dix into action. He led a search of the woods around the farm using volunteers raised by Emmett. We searched until dark on Tuesday without finding a trace of Prestina.

"That was it for Dix. He told us that Prestina would most likely turn up visiting friends down in Kentucky or over in Illinois or in Moscow maybe. Then he quit. He used this big investigation he has going as an excuse."

"An investigation into what?" I asked. "Chicken rustling?"

"No. Our old nemesis, the thing my father was into. Drugs. Dix can tell you all about it himself. I'll take you down to meet him when we're through here."

I couldn't wait to hear how Krystal would explain me to Dix. That is to say, I could wait a lifetime.

"I would have searched again yesterday," Krystal was saying, "but I had to drive up to Indianapolis for my father's parole hearing. I went there thinking the timing couldn't have been worse. I changed my mind when I saw you."

The man who was two minutes away from disappointing her. "You told me yesterday that this mystery had a religious angle."

"I wanted to intrigue you. You were in the seminary when I last saw you, after all."

"So I'm intrigued. What's the religious angle?"

"Don't you see it? It's why I wanted you to listen to Emmett's story before we came out here."

"This is my blank expression," I said.

"I come into this locked house and find the bed made, the table set for breakfast, and no sign of the lady who lives here. The lady who is one of the last surviving members of the Ordained of God."

She turned to the table and sat down there, settling herself warily, as though she expected the chair to be yanked from under her. "Everything looked like . . ."

"Like what?" I asked.

"Like the rapture had finally kicked in, one hundred and fifty years late." She hurried to add, "The Ordained thought they could schedule it like a train, but the rapture, if there was such a thing, would sneak up on you when you least expected it."

Making me a sitting duck, I thought. I wanted to ask her who was pulling whose leg, but that might have fallen under the heading of not taking her mystery seriously. Worse, I might have seemed to her to be making fun of Emmett Haas and his tiny flock.

Before I could rephrase the question, someone knocked on the front door.

"I'll go," Krystal said, getting up.

"We'll both go," I said, not censoring myself this time. "I wouldn't want you to find the kitchen empty again."

The doctor caught me smiling at her and said, "I liked your blank expression better."

The man we found waiting on the front porch was even less pleased with me than Krystal was. He was tall and dark, closer to Krystal's age than mine, and dressed like a nature photographer on assignment, in immaculate hiking boots and a well-pressed combination of khaki shirt and pants that had button-down flaps on all their pockets. The two pieces that didn't fit were his narrow, very black sunglasses and his slicked-back, urban professional's hair.

"I've been looking for you," he said to Krystal while the black lenses remained locked on me. "Emmett told me I'd find you here."

"Steve," Krystal said. "This is—"

"Owen Keane. I know. Emmett told me. Any sign of Ms. Shipe?"

"No," Krystal said.

"Well, whatever happened to her is contagious. We just had somebody else plucked off the face of the earth."

Six

THE MAN IN KHAKIS LAST NAME WAS FALLON, and he was an agent of the Drug Enforcement Administration. Krystal told me that much as we followed his white Ford Explorer back out of the drive and onto the gravel road. The DEA man turned away from Rapture and headed deeper into the valley.

"Steve's here on assignment," Krystal said, "working the case I mentioned earlier, the one that has Deputy Dix so full of himself. Steve doesn't like Dix."

"Or me," I said. "Did he take me for a mobster?"

Krystal laughed at the idea, louder and longer, I thought, than was really necessary. "The truth is even sillier than that," she finally said. "Steve has a thing for me. I think you made him jealous."

"Do you plan to straighten him out on that? Or do you like him jealous?"

"I haven't decided whether I even give a hoot. Steve's okay. A little intense, but okay. The problem is he's a city boy. He fits in down here like Dom Pérignon at a pig roast. We went to dinner one time at this little country place that prides itself on its salad bar. The waitress took our drink orders and finished with the standard 'Help yourselves to the salad bar.' And Steve asks her if she wouldn't mind going for us!" Here Krystal shifted in her seat and batted her eyelashes at me. " 'Just make us up a little selection of the things you like yourself, sweetheart.' I almost walked home.

"And he has this attitude about rural Indiana that really bothers me, the idea that everyone around here is either a homicidal hillbilly or a drooling idiot. It's a prejudice I ran into when I was at Indiana University. A lot of my professors were from out of state, and they acted—some of them, not all—like they were living in a frontier outpost surrounded by hostile aborigines. A real *Heart of Darkness* mentality. They wouldn't stray a mile from Bloomington, except maybe to scurry up to Indy or down to Louisville for a concert or a play. They never got to know any real Hoosiers, just other expatriate snobs."

I was feeling fairly guilty by then over my own reluctance to visit southern Indiana. Krystal made it worse by adding, "I'm glad you're not like that, Owen. Although you'd have some reason to be after what my father did to you."

The white truck hadn't traveled a mile before it turned into a lane bordered by fields of corn, the stalks uneven in height but uniformly dry and brown.

"The Batsto farm," Krystal said. "I should have guessed. Steve's a little obsessed with this place. A guy named Clyde Batsto lives here alone."

"Another Ordained of God?"

"No, I told you, they're all ancient. Batsto's no older than you. Besides, he's too much of a loner to be a member of anything. His parents might have been, though. They're both dead."

"And buried, I hope," I said, but not loud enough for Krystal to hear me.

We parked next to the Explorer in a yard that already contained another four-wheel-drive truck—a Ford pickup—and a Sheriff's Department cruiser. Beyond the vehicles was the farmhouse, which was white and larger than Prestina's, though not as well kept. The roof had three different colors of shingles, and one end of the house had been stripped of its siding, revealing the insulation beneath. The siding might have been removed so the insulation could be added. If so, the project had been underway for some time. The plastic vapor barrier had come loose in spots, allowing pink fiberglass to poke through like runaway intestine.

"Great," Krystal said. "What a place to visit right after I've given my lecture on the simple dignity of rural Indiana."

Fallon told us to stay by the cars while he conferred with his "troops." I took the order meekly enough, but the doctor bristled. As we watched, Fallon greeted two men, also in civilian clothes, though wearing guns. Fallon was wearing one now himself. After every few words of their conversation, he'd look back to see if we'd made a run for it.

During one of these checks, Krystal surprised me by taking hold of my left arm. I was wearing a short-sleeved shirt, which had allowed her to spot a slight bump on the outside of my arm just above my wristwatch.

"How did you break this bone?" she asked.

Fallon looked around at us again and scowled.

"You wouldn't believe me if I told you," I said.

"When did it happen?"

Another glance from Fallon and another scowl.

"About three years ago."

"Whoever set it should have his license revoked." Fallon was no longer bothering to look away between scowls, and I realized that Krystal was holding my hand as well as my arm.

"If you keep using me to make Mr. Fallon jealous," I said, "you may get an opportunity to show off your own bone-setting technique. Or maybe just your stitching."

"I'll be good," Krystal said, dropping my hand. When Fallon crossed to us, she stepped out to head him off. "You may have gotten the wrong impression, Steve. Owen is an old friend of the family. I've known him since I was a kid."

"A little kid," I added.

"Sorry," Fallon said, extending his hand to me. It was no bigger than Krystal's, but a lot warmer. "I'm in a piss-poor mood this morning, as the locals say. I thought we were going to make some progress finally. Instead we seem to have stumbled into something out of Rod Serling. Did Krystal tell you what we're after in Rapture?"

"No," I said. "She was leaving that to Deputy Dix."

Fallon scowled again. "Deputy Aw Shucks? Somebody would have to explain it to him first. To nutshell it for you, my agency has reason to believe that the area around Rapture is being used as one of the midwestern distribution hubs for drugs coming up from Mexico."

"I keep telling him that there aren't enough people around here to support a decent grocery store, never mind a drug empire," Krystal said.

"And I keep telling her that the bad guys aren't selling the drugs around here, that they're very careful not to sell the drugs around here. They're receiving the bulk shipments, breaking them down, and sending them out to cities around the Midwest. There are operations like this all over the country, intentionally kept small and redundant to spread the risk. The ideal locations are thinly populated and remote, but with access to the interstate highway system. Rapture has that, thanks to Highway 50, which, not coincidentally, is just beyond the field on the other side of that barn.

"The proximity of this farm to the highway is what attracted me to Batsto in the first place. That and his arrest record."

"Steve means Batsto drinks."

"I mean that Batsto's been arrested for driving under the influence. The arresting officer found a bag of marijuana in his possession."

"A small bag," Krystal said.

Following their conversation was giving me a sore neck. To rest it, I asked Fallon, "How does the highway running past the farm figure in this?"

"It eliminates the need for a courier truck to ever come into a town or even to stop. Nothing would be easier than tipping a bundle off a moving truck if your target is seventy acres across. We figured Batsto would wait on the appointed nights and bring the stuff back here. We've had the highway under surveillance and we've raided the farm. No luck."

"No sense," Krystal said. "Ask him how Batsto intended to ship the repackaged drugs, Owen. He doesn't know."

I declined the opportunity to step between them, thinking at the same time that they sounded married already and then some.

"I know that it's nearly harvest time," Fallon said. "Batsto is close to moving truckloads of corn out of this place. And our information is that a big drug shipment is due any time."

"His anonymous tip, he means," Krystal said. "Batsto will be lucky to get one truckload of corn out of this worn-out farm. And he won't be shipping that farther than the nearest grain elevator."

"Batsto has acted suspiciously from the start," Fallon countered.

"That's because you couldn't keep yourself from looking down on him," Krystal fired back. "And treating him like a dangerous redneck. All he's guilty of is boozing and orneriness."

"And dematerializing," Fallon said. "Come inside."

We walked past Fallon's men, two more city boys, like their boss. They smiled at Krystal and scowled, loyally, at me.

Fallon was explaining as we walked. "I decided to change tactics on Mr. Batsto. Instead of rolling him up, I thought I might persuade him to work with us."

"To turn informant?" I asked.

"Yes. He knows what's going on around here, I'm sure of that. He's in on it or he knows who is. Even if Batsto's involved, he's not really a keeper. This kind of pissant operation is designed to be expendable, as I said before. But if I could get him to work with us, to help us backtrack toward the starting point of the distribution system, we could do some serious damage. We might put a dozen or more Batstos out of business."

He held the screen door of the farmhouse open for Krystal. I caught it before it shut behind them.

"So I stopped by unannounced this morning," Fallon continued.

"With a couple of bodyguards," Krystal said, nodding back toward the men in the yard.

"Actually, I came alone. When I found what I found, I called in backup, including the local representative of law and order."

That ironic afterthought was directed to a man waiting inside the house. I awarded myself no points for deducing that he was Deputy Dix, as he was wearing a uniform, unfashionable polyester in seventies tones of beige and brown. From that starting point, it was easy to fall into thinking of him as the stylish Fallon's mirror opposite, the DEA man's country counterpart. The two men were about the same height and appeared to be the same age, but Dix still wore his sandy hair in an early John Denver bowl cut, and he was sporting a gut that Fallon would have starved himself to erase. His face was square-jawed, with an artificially flattened nose and small, distrustful eyes. The deputy's complexion was as ruddy as Emmett Haas's, but I'd have to wait to find out if that was his natural coloring or a reaction to Fallon's condescension.

"No sign of Batsto anywhere on the farm," the deputy told Fallon, who nodded. "No sign of any drugs, either," he added, getting no nod.

Fallon had turned back to Krystal and me. He removed his sunglasses, revealing eyes that were nearly as dark. "I knocked, of course, but I didn't get an answer. The door was unlocked, so I came in."

Dix stirred, and Fallon addressed his unspoken objection. "I felt justified in verifying Batsto's health and well-being, given his potential value to our investigation. I identified myself as soon as I crossed the threshold, but no one answered me. Then I heard water running upstairs."

"So you went outside to wait politely in your truck," Krystal suggested.

"No," Fallon said, flashing her a guilty grin. "I didn't. But I didn't go upstairs to kick down the bathroom door, either. I waited right here, soaking up the atmosphere."

He gestured to the room's worn furniture, whose dark upholstery had a greasy sheen, to the water-stained wallpaper, or maybe just to the general aura. I was seriously missing Prestina Shipe's potpourri.

"I waited," Fallon said. "And I waited. Half an hour went by, and the water was still running. I decided something wasn't right, so I went upstairs."

He acted it out, stepping over to a staircase that ran up one wall of the room. We followed him, Dix bringing up the rear and sniffling steadily.

At the top of the stairs was a small room containing a single narrow bed. It was light and airy compared with the first floor of the house. Fallon and Krystal bypassed it, but I went in, attracted by the movement of something yellow suspended from the ceiling. It was a model airplane, an old-fashioned one made of balsa wood and paper. It was hanging over the bed, turning slowly in a breeze that passed between open windows.

Behind me in the doorway, Deputy Dix was blowing his almost nose. "The bathroom's this way," he said.

The bathroom turned out to be bigger than the bedroom that had distracted me. Its floor and the lower half of its walls were tiled in tiny octagons. They were grayish white, except for a patch near the tub's faucet, which must have been the location of an emergency repair. The tiles there were pink, and they looked like the scar of an old wound. The tub beneath the wound had claw-and-ball feet, but it was fitted with a modern showerhead—the kind that dispenses massages—and a trendy curtain, on which the logo of the Indianapolis Colts was repeated over and over.

"This is how I found the room," Fallon said, turning on the shower and pulling the curtain closed to give us the full effect. "I called to Batsto from the doorway, and identified myself for the fortieth time. No answer. I could see his things scattered about, but something told me he wasn't here himself.

"I was fed up by then anyway. I came in and yanked open the curtain." He demonstrated, reaching out for the shiny plastic without taking his eyes from us.

Emmett Haas had complimented me that morning on my ability to get into a story. He would have been proud of the way I did my part now, looking into the empty shower and feeling Fallon's own surprise and confusion.

"All I found," the agent said, "was a piece of soap dissolving on the drain." He pointed down to that small bit of physical evidence. "The only thing I could think of was that story you'd told me, Krystal. The one about Ms. Shipe and the rapture."

He thought of it again and smiled. I could feel Krystal stiffen beside me. Fallon went on without noticing.

"Think of getting all lathered up and then—pow—you're standing in front of the Almighty. That had to be a shock for old Batsto."

The feeling had surely been mutual, I thought as Dix held up Batsto's pajama bottoms. They were wider than Fallon's grin.

"What happened to Prestina is no joke," Krystal said coldly. "Neither are the Ordained." She turned on her heel and marched out.

I lingered as Dix said, "Batsto heard you coming and ran is all."

Fallon shook his sleek head. "Nobody hears me coming if I don't want him to. I'm thinking Batsto was tipped off."

The two men stared at each other for a long time. Then, without any apparent signal, they turned their heads in concert and stared at me.

"I'll just wait out front," I said.

Seven

I'D TOLD FALLON AND DIX I'D WAIT out front, but once downstairs I wandered toward the back of the house. I passed through Batsto's kitchen but didn't linger there. The sink full of unwashed dishes and the overflowing garbage can reminded me of my own kitchen and how I'd left it. For the first time since I'd crossed the state line the day before, I put New Jersey behind me with a mental wave and an unspoken promise to be back soon.

Not that I was thinking, as I should have been, of Krystal's mystery. I passed out through the back door of the farmhouse, noted with mild surprise and less interest that Batsto had built himself a sun deck, and then descended into the backyard, drinking in what was now early afternoon.

The day had turned into a beauty, the kind of late summer, early fall day when the full sun, beaming down from a deep blue sky, feels no warmer across your shoulders than a friend's arm. I would have followed Krystal's example and turned my face to the sun, but that would have cost me the view. To my right was Batsto's red barn, better maintained than his house, its open doorway patrolled by cousins of Prestina Shipe's cats. Beyond the barn was a corner of a cornfield and beyond that was a line of trees, perhaps marking the edge of Highway 50. If so, the green wall also cut off the road's noise. All I could hear was the buzzing of the insects who were happily chewing away on Batsto's corn. To my left, the forest was much closer. I could see fat brown squirrels moving about in it, and, high on a dead branch, a hawk with a speckled breast, who alternately watched the squirrels and me. I wondered if Clyde Batsto was in the forest somewhere, watching me, too. The question couldn't hold my interest.

My mind went back instead to the Ordained. The afternoon reminded me of the climax of Emmett Haas's story. The October day of the Great Disappointment had surely been very like this September one, just a touch cooler, probably. There would have been more color in the trees, too. Only a few of the ones before me had even begun to turn. I imagined the trees around Rapture Meadow as a riot of yellows and reds. It had been harvest time, after all, the most natural time of the year for a community of farmers to expect an accounting.

From that vivid picture of the day when the world didn't end, I moved to imagining its anniversaries, the long line of October afternoons on which the original Ordained and then their descendants had reenacted what Haas had called the Great Banquet. It was a strange event to celebrate, on the order of my returning to St. Aelred Seminary every year for homecoming.

St. Aelred's hadn't seemed so close to me since the evening I'd left it. It was close physically, of course, less than fifty miles away, but it felt much nearer than that, as near as the line of trees that marked the highway. If the school had really been there, just beyond the field of brown stalks, would I have crossed to see it? That morning, my answer would have been no. Now I stood and wondered.

I was still wondering when Krystal found me. "What are you doing?" she asked.

"Thinking about what's beyond the corn."

"Highway 50," she sighed. "Steve's really fixated on that road."

"And on you," I said.

That cheered her up. She laughed as loud as she had at the idea of Owen Keane, mobster. "We'd make a great pair, wouldn't we? The drug agent and the daughter of the man who used to grow pot in his lower forty. What a crazy life it is, Owen. You think you're headed somewhere and then you end up back where you started, like a person lost in a snowstorm who walks in a big circle because one of his legs is shorter than the other. We've all got one short leg, that's our problem."

"I know," I said.

I looked at my watch, and she said, "Time to go visit Brother Dennis?"

"If I go at all. I could do that tomorrow if you'd like me to stay."

"How close are you to an answer?"

"I haven't figured out the question yet."

"Do you think the two disappearances are related?"

"I don't see how they could be. Unless you're right about the rapture."

"Don't you start teasing me, Owen. It's easy to scoff at a belief. I should know, I've done it often enough. Cheap and easy. Back in Bloomington, I would have laughed as loud as anyone at the silly Ordained. It's just that now . . ."

"Now what?"

"Nothing. Go and see the pottery. Maybe something will come to you on the drive. Come by as early tomorrow as you like. You're welcome to stay with me tonight if you can't find a bed in Oldenburg."

She raised her voice when she made that offer, the hairs on the back of my neck going up at the same time. I knew without looking that Agent Fallon had walked up behind me.

"You're not going to get me on that one twice," he said.

Krystal smiled her curly smile, and I relaxed again. "Sorry," she said.

"I'm sorry," Fallon said. "I was making fun of myself and my efforts just now, not the Ordained. I certainly wasn't making fun of Ms. Shipe's disappearance. In fact, if you'd like, my men and I can help you look for her this afternoon. We should be searching these woods for Batsto, but there's no reason we can't search in the direction of her farm."

"I'd really appreciate that, Steve," Krystal said.

It was a nice little reconciliation scene, but there was one character too many on stage. I cleared my throat and asked Fallon a question. "What kind of drugs are being smuggled through this area?"

"Methamphetamine," he said. "Familiar with it?"

"It's called crank, isn't it?"

"Or meth or speed," Fallon said.

"It's mostly used out West, I thought."

"That's where the problem is biggest, but it's spreading east. Meth is already figuring in a significant number of emergency room cases in St. Louis, which is only six hours west of this very farm."

"Methamphetamine has been around for a long time," Krystal said. "They think Hitler used it."

"And JFK," Fallon said. "It gives a high energy rush that's very popular with movers and shakers. You might say the times have caught up with the drug. Unfortunately, meth users develop a tolerance. Then they develop depression, insomnia, and paranoia. Modern problems for a modern world."

He picked a long blade of grass and stuck it in his mouth, smiling at Krystal as though it represented a dare. "You make meth in a laboratory," he said, "which gives it considerable advantages over stuff you have to grow. The trade used to be controlled by motorcycle gangs. They were small-timers, so the trade was small. Now the big Mexican traffickers have moved in, and the meth trade is soaring. And spreading. It's a get-in-on-the-ground-floor opportunity for any bright boy with a new idea on how to move the stuff around. So we're getting new wrinkles like these back-woods distributorships."

Krystal reached up and took the grass from his mouth. Fallon kept smiling. "Speaking of woods, we're ready to start searching these whenever you are, Doctor."

"Let me run Owen to his car. I'll be back in fifteen minutes."

Fallon shook my hand. "We'll be here."

Krystal offered to show me her property on the way back to Rapture. She was certain I wouldn't find the place otherwise. I decided not to take her concern personally. Prestina Shipe's place and the Batsto farm were almost due south of Rapture as Krystal laid it out for me, drawing meaningless lines in the dust on her dashboard. Her home was a little to the southwest of town, just below a ridge that ran between Rapture's hill and the next one in line. The last quarter mile of our trip was on Krystal's own driveway, a lane so narrow that trees brushed the Jeep on both sides as we passed. The drive ended at a clearing in the woods that held a house trailer, one still new enough to shine in the filtered light.

"I thought you doctors were rich," I said.

"The ones whose patients have insurance do okay. I'm going to build a house back here someday, but I want to wait till I can do it right. The trailer is plenty good enough in the meantime."

"Pretty isolated, though," I said.

"You're from New Jersey. Anything with grass around it seems isolated to you. Besides, I have a guard. Come and meet him."

She led me around to the back of the trailer. Near a prefabri-cated shed, a large gray dog was chained to a tree. The chain may have been intended to discourage dognappers. A restraint didn't seem necessary for the sleeping dog, who barely lifted his head when Krystal petted it. He took no notice of me whatsoever, a quality I always admired in large animals.

"Do you remember Blue?" Krystal asked, naming the dog that had guarded her grandparent's farm.

"He'd be about one hundred and fifty in dog years," I said. "This one doesn't look a day over ninety."

"This is Blue the third. He's sixty-three in dog years, which is about the right age for Rapture. He's still worn out from helping me look for Prestina on Tuesday. Aren't you, boy?" She ruffled his floppy ears again and then stood up.

I was surprised to see that her cool blue eyes were wet. "I love this place, Owen. I love these people who believe in something that didn't come true. I haven't felt this at home anywhere. Not since I lived with my grandparents. Back before I met you. Now I'm afraid of something that's hard to describe."

"Nutshell it for me."

That echo of Fallon's newspeak brought a smile to her face. It went away as she said, "I'm afraid my world is about to explode again."

Eight

I KEPT MY EYE OUT FOR DRUG COURIER trucks on my drive east on Highway 50, but I didn't see any. Or maybe I saw a dozen; it was impossible to tell. At a town called North Vernon, I switched to a road identified on my map by a single digit, a three. It was more of a road than its humble designation implied, especially the last stretch, ten miles of divided highway that deposited me in Greensburg. That town advertised a tourist attraction, a tree growing out of the roof of its courthouse tower, but I didn't stop to gawk. Instead, I picked up Interstate 74, the road Brother Dennis had assumed I'd take down from Indy when he'd written my directions. I spent fifteen minutes on its quality pavement, and it brought me within a few miles of Oldenburg.

No town had been better named. It was small and situated on a hill as high as Rapture's but far less wooded. The few large buildings along the town's principal street were brick and European in design, their facades topped with stair-step gables that looked German or Swiss. I decided that the town's founders had been homesick and that they'd taken it out on Oldenburg's architecture.

That guess was confirmed by Sister Gisela Weise, the person who answered the bell at Brother Dennis's address. Whenever I'd written that address on an envelope, I'd pictured an isolated house with a pottery shed out back. What I found wasn't a house at all. It was a compound containing half a dozen buildings, large and small, surrounded by a brick wall, six feet high.

Sister Gisela, a short, round-faced woman with happy eyes and a slight lisp, showed me through an iron gate, giving me an abbreviated history of the place as we went. "The town was founded by German Catholic immigrants in the 1850s. They built our beautiful church, which I'm sure you saw on your way into town. Did you stop and make a wish? You should always stop at the church when you visit a new town. It entitles you to a wish.

"The town's founders, as a way of giving thanks for the richness and beauty of their new home, built a big convent here." She gestured around the compound. "Now the convent has become a home for retired religious. In the Middle Ages, the male and female religious often lived together in one building, or common house. We've returned to that, though we have separate buildings for the priests and the sisters. We also have retired monks, like your friend.

"Not that Dennis is really retired. We don't let him retire, not our famous celebrity."

"Celebrity?" I asked as she guided me across a cobblestone courtyard.

"Well, a local celebrity. You know about his pottery. We've sold it for years here, even when he was working down at the seminary, at St. Aelred's. I have to admit that, back then, I thought his things were . . ." She paused, embarrassed.

"Eccentric?" I suggested.

"Yes, that's it. Eccentric. None of his plates were flat and the bowls weren't exactly round. I used to wonder how you could work on a pottery wheel and not turn out something round. I didn't realize that he was making a statement."

"A statement?"

"Yes, about the imperfect nature of this world and the futility of human attempts to create perfection here on earth. A gentleman from Indianapolis explained it to me. He was the one who discovered Dennis's work a few years ago. He set up the exhibition in Indianapolis and the one in Cincinnati. He believes that Dennis is trying to work out some old loss through his art."

That was one safe bet, I thought. Who wasn't trying to work out some old loss? Dr. Krystal Bowden was. Her friend Emmett Haas was. I was.

"I've tried to talk with Dennis about it," the nun was saying, "but he always laughs and changes the subject. I guess you have to make the choice if you're an artist: either you spend your time talking about art or creating it. We're glad that Dennis chooses to create it."

It didn't sound like any choice Brother Dennis would make or even acknowledge, but it was too late to discuss the point. We'd arrived at the pottery, one half of a building that had once been a greenhouse. The other half was still set up with racks for plants and an overhead watering system. The racks were all but empty, but the glass roof and walls were in good repair. At the pottery end of the building, many of the panes in the walls and most of the ones in the ceiling had been painted gray, creating a oxymoron: a glass house with a lousy view.

"Must be cold out here in the winter," I said.

"It is," Sister Gisela replied. "Even with the kiln going. But summers are worse. I don't know how Dennis stands the heat."

The monk poked his head through an open window. "That's easy," he said. "I work in the nude."

The monk and the nun enjoyed a good laugh over that picture, while the representative of the laity smiled indulgently. Then Sister Gisela left us.

Brother Dennis was leaning on the window's narrow sill. His

arms were clay-covered to the elbow, and he wore random streaks of the pale gray stuff on his face, looking like an Indian warrior who had risen above symmetry.

"Okie," he said. "Thanks for coming. It's a dream come true to have you down here."

"I had to come to find out what's really going on," I said. "Sister Gisela told me you've been discovered. Why didn't you mention that in one of your letters?"

"I didn't want you to laugh at me. Some temptations are just too hard to resist. Can you think of a funnier joke than the idea of me as an artist?"

Me as the finder of Prestina Shipe for one, I thought. I said, "I'm proud of you."

"Don't you start with me, Okie. I'll throw you out."

I reminded him that I wasn't in yet, and he tapped his forehead with an open palm, a gesture that brought St. Aelred's back so strongly I could almost feel the Roman collar around my neck.

"Right," he said. "There's a door around the corner. Meet you there."

Despite its protective coating of paint, the little glass building had made the most of the afternoon's heat. I couldn't blame the kiln, a brick beehive squatting in the far corner; it was dark and empty. The focal point of the shop's single room was the pottery wheel. Its position of eminence at the center of the floor was emphasized by a circle of pale gray—the same dried clay that decorated the monk's face—radiating from the wheel across the bare concrete. This corona had a gap, which told me where the potter normally placed his stool. The wet clay that had most recently been sprayed in that direction now coated the full-length apron the monk wore over a T-shirt and ancient trousers, whose sheen reminded me of the vanished Clyde Batsto's lived-upon furniture.

"You get the nickel tour for driving all the way out here,

Okie. This table over here," he said, pointing to one where the missing stool now resided, "is where I do most of my work, where I shape a piece to begin with. I don't use my wheel as much as I used to. The kinds of things the tourists like—the artsy-fartsy things, excuse me, Okie—don't always need turning. If they do, though, it's over to the wheel next. Then it might be back to this first stop where I add handles maybe or legs. Then we move over here"—he led me to another table, a two-tiered one, its top step packed with jars and brushes—"for the glazing step. One of the good sisters usually helps me with that. She has beautifully steady hands. Then it's into our electric kiln, and that's it. We ship the piece to some crazy person who thinks he's bought himself the *Mona Lisa.*"

Characteristically, the monk had ignored the room's most interesting features, the many examples of his work in various stages of completion that were scattered about. Though forewarned by Sister Gisela's tossed-off references to artistic statements and exhibitions, I was amazed by the pieces I saw. There were a few examples of the creamers and jam pots I remembered from the monk's early work—"the St. Aelred period," his Indy patron might call it. But most of the works in progress were much larger and only vaguely functional. The tall, square-cornered towers of clay with jagged, open tops might have served as vases if it hadn't been for the holes of various shapes that had been punched in their sides. As it was, their dark glaze made them look like the ruined battlements of a burned castle. They shared a table with less easily pigeonholed objects, rough triangles of clay standing on flat bases. At first, these looked like sails on a fleet of rafts, sails picking up the reddish brown of a sunset. Then—disconcertingly—they suddenly looked more like half a dozen rusted knife blades thrust up through a black floor.

I asked Brother Dennis what they were. He waved the question away.

"Who knows? I only make them. Some critic will tell me what they are. It's a game I play with them. I turn out the most outlandish things I can think of, and they come up with some way of explaining them. Talk about creativity! Those guys have it sitting around in gallon jugs. Never mind that stuff, though. What I want to show you is over here."

He led me to the far corner of the glazing table, where a large, lopsided bowl stood on squat legs. The bowl had been glazed a dark green that shifted randomly to black and back again, and it had an exaggerated lip that rose and fell like a closed-circuit roller coaster.

"You inspired that, Okie. Instead of coming back here yesterday to clean up this place like I said I would, I made this. I kept thinking of vicious circles after we talked about them. Remember when I was asking you about your gray hair and you said you got it from worrying and I said about what and you said about having so much gray hair? That was a good one. So I decided to make you a vicious circle as a souvenir. It's only a punch bowl, really. I didn't even get all the legs the same length. Sorry about that."

I'd called Brother Dennis from Rapture to warn him that I was on my way, so he knew I'd been to see Krystal. I told him now of her fear that we all traveled in circles, reminded of it—and her image of a person lost in the snow—by the uneven legs of my souvenir bowl.

"You see?" Brother Dennis said, slapping his forehead again. "That's what always happens to me. I foul something up, like the legs on this thing, and it ends up being a symbol of something. You could be a critic, Okie.

"But I'm sorry to hear that Krystal is hurting. It seemed to me when I saw her yesterday that she finally had everything going her way. Tell me about it."

I shouldn't have wasted more of my visiting time in Oldenburg with Krystal's problem, but I did, spilling out the story of the Or-dained and Prestina Shipe and even Clyde Batsto. The monk lis-tened patiently, only interrupting me once, just after I'd described the Ordained's odd dream of being plucked off the earth without warning.

"But that's the reality for all of us," my host said. "You could be in heaven before you draw your next breath. Not your body, but the rest of you. It's always a possibility. You've got to be ready to go at any time. You're ready, aren't you, Okie?"

"Not quite," I said.

When I'd finished the story, my audience scratched his head. For the first time, I noticed that his grizzled hair was thinning. I could see old scars winding their way across his scalp.

"That's a puzzler for sure," he said. "We need a beer to help us think. There's a tavern down the street where we can get one. Just let me wash up first."

"You told me yesterday we couldn't have a decent talk in a restaurant."

"I meant an Indy restaurant. Too noisy. That won't be a prob-lem in this place. Not on a Thursday night. They grill a good steak there, too, on an applewood fire. It'll be my treat. I'd invite you to eat here, but that might be dangerous for you. Everything on our menu assumes a really lethargic digestive system."

Nine

I WAITED ON THE STREET IN FRONT of the compound for the monk, enjoying a cool breeze that was blowing through the town as evening came on. Somewhere upwind, someone was burning leaves that had gotten a jump on the fall. It was a smell I remembered instantly, though I hadn't experienced it in New Jersey for a decade at least. I closed my eyes and pictured little, turtle-shaped mounds of beech leaves burning in a lost backyard. I could see each delicate brown leaf, with veins as regular as ribs and edges that were perfectly serrated. I remembered how each one turned to white-gray ash the second the flame reached it, ash that contrasted with but also perfectly complemented the remaining golden brown of the pile, the way the spent tip sets off the color of an expensive cigar. Or was that bit of the memory, the vivid color contrast, really the memory of a cigar and not a pile of leaves? The breeze couldn't tell me.

Like the rest of Oldenburg, the tavern we eventually found was a carefully preserved antique, a little shoe box of much-varnished wood hung with advertisements for dead breweries. We sat in a well-partitioned booth, drank German beer by the pitcher, and talked—but not of the Rapture mystery.

Brother Dennis told me stories of my classmates from St.

Aelred's, men I couldn't remember as clearly as the burning beech leaves that still haunted me. One exception was a guy named Swickard, who had gotten himself classified as a prig—not an easy thing to do in a society of priests and would-be priests. If Brother Dennis had asked me to guess how Swickard had turned out, I would have said he was the pastor of some fat, happy eastern parish that gave him a new Riviera to drive every year. The monk shocked me by saying that Swickard had become a missionary, that he'd gone to Africa after his ordination and had never come back.

I ended up drinking more beer than I'd intended to, motivated somehow by the news of Swickard the missionary. Brother Dennis's mood also sank as the evening slipped by, but for a very different reason.

After we'd pushed away the remains of our steaks and passed on dessert, he asked, "Are you going to go down and see St. Aelred's while you're in Indiana?"

"No," I said, though I hadn't been sure earlier that afternoon.

"I think you should, Okie. I'll go with you if you like, or you could go alone. Just go and see the place and maybe say good-bye. The way you snuck off back in '73, you never got a chance to say good-bye. Maybe it would help you with closure. They talk a lot about closure these days."

"They do," I said.

"It isn't all bunk, either. Letting something fester is no good. I should know."

"You?"

"Yes, me. I have a confession to make, Okie. You're just the man to hear it. Will you?"

"Yes," I said.

The monk sipped his beer. "Here goes, then. I went to Indianapolis to testify at that hearing out of a desire for revenge."

"So did I."

"I don't believe that. And even if it were true, you have good reasons to want revenge against Morell, reasons that related to that hearing. My reasons don't have anything to do with his crimes, but I was going to use that hearing to get back at him. I pretended I was there because of what he'd done to you and Mary and Krystal, but it was really because of what he'd done to me. I realized that while I was listening to Mrs. Crosley speak. Thank God I did."

For the second time that day, I was surprised by tears. The monk pressed his eyes with his broken knuckles and went on.

"I made a big mistake with Morell, Okie. After his trial, I got in touch with him. Don't hate me for that. I didn't write you about it because I was afraid you might think I was being disloyal to you. Or maybe I didn't tell you because I knew I was being disloyal.

"Morell was down in the southwestern part of the state then, at Wabash Valley Prison near Carlisle. I had the idea I could reach the guy. Do you believe that?"

I said I did.

"I think it was because he was the same age as the guys at St. Aelred's. I thought I had a special way with you, a talent. I thought if I just spent time with Morell, I could turn him around. Save him. I didn't believe in the possibility of an evil person then. Not even after Korea and all that horror.

"Before I visited him that first time, I'd only seen him at his trial. And he didn't testify there. He just sat and stared straight ahead. God help me, I felt sorry for him. I kept asking myself: How could he have done these horrible things? What pressures or—you know—experiences could have bent him that way? As much as anything else, I went to Wabash Valley because I couldn't answer that question.

"I kept going because Morell poured his heart out to me. He was terrified, Okie. At first I thought it was just the prison that scared him. Then I decided that it was more than prison, that he saw the future as a black pit and himself teetering on its edge. He'd gotten himself mixed up in college, gotten his head filled with a lot of nonsense about a strong man's will being the only moral force in the universe. When he lost that, he was left with nothing.

"It scared me just to listen to him, Okie. I felt like a little kid again, crouched next to the radio, listening to *Inner Sanctum,* too frightened even to reach up and turn the dial."

He froze again now, his gaze fixed on a spot beyond my shoulder. His left eyelid, which always drooped a little, was drooping seriously now. "Did you reach him?" I asked.

"I thought I had. I thought I'd saved his soul. I brought him a Bible and dozens of other books. He ate them up. He always had a new question to ask when I'd make a visit. Most of them I couldn't answer, but there was always someone at St. Aelred's who could. We talked a lot about his baptism, but he was slow to set the date. He was busy with his appeals." The monk shook his head and added, "I helped there, too.

"Then there was trouble at Wabash Valley. There was a fight and a man got stabbed. Morell told me he'd acted in self-defense, but the prison people didn't believe it. They transferred him to Michigan City, the toughest prison in the state.

"Driving to Wabash Valley was an effort, but it was a breeze compared with Michigan City. It's way up on Lake Michigan, Okie, over three hundred miles from St. Aelred's, however you drove it.

"Still, I'd make the drive once every two or three months, and Morell would always be waiting, hungry for any news and gossip from the outside world and anxious to discuss some theological brain twister. He was anxious for the things I'd bring him, too, the magazines and the little treats for his sweet tooth.

"I made those drives on and off for years. Once I stopped going for over a year—from late 1983 through all of '84. But he kept begging me in his letters to come back, and finally I did. During all that long time I could never pin him down on his baptism. He'd have some doubt. He'd fall away. And I'd have to win him back over the course of a year's worth of visits and letters. Then he'd doubt again."

The monk poured the last of our beer into his mug, signaling to our waitress with the empty pitcher. "I thought Morell was dependent on me. Now I see it was really the other way around, that I'd fallen in love with the idea of saving him and I couldn't give it up. Finally, though, I'd had it. For his own sake, I got tough with him. I told him he had to make a commitment or I wouldn't be back."

He drained his mug and sat staring at it. "What happened?" I asked.

"He laughed at me. It was laughter he'd been holding back for years, and when he finally let it go, it came out of him like an eruption. He'd been stringing me along, Okie, playing me—and not just for the favors I did him. He played me for the sport of it, for the challenge. Now that I'd wised up, I didn't amuse him anymore and I could go to hell.

"I was in shock, even though I'd been waiting for that laughter—without realizing it—almost from the start. I was so dazed that I only remember one of the terrible things he said to me. He said that the only thing sillier—no, he said more absurd—the only thing more absurd than the idea of worshiping a dead Jew nailed to a cross was the idea that an omnipotent God would send an old stumblebum like me around to speak for Him. He was right about that much at least."

"I don't think Morell has ever been right," I said.

Brother Dennis patted my hand. "He knew enough to teach me something, Okie. He taught me that evil is a force in the world, that there are people who are sworn to it, the way you and I are to the light. I could have done without that lesson."

We sat for a long time after that, but made no more than a dent in our last pitcher of beer. Then Brother Dennis slapped the table-top with both hands.

"I won't let you drive back to Rapture, Okie," he said. "I've had too much to drink."

"Me too," I said.

"You'll stay with us tonight. I'll find you a room. Come on."

Oldenburg didn't have enough candlepower to dim the stars. There was a sky full of them waiting for us outside. We stood unsteadily in the center of the street, gazing up at the show.

I wanted to ask Brother Dennis when his final visit to Morell had been. I was guessing it had occurred sometime before the monk had been discovered as an artist. But I never brought it up. He might not be aware of the connection between his art and his glimpse into Morell's heart, if there even was a connection. Maybe it was important that he didn't know. Or important that he didn't talk about it. Whatever the balance, I didn't want to upset it.

The monk took the floor in any case. "You're sad, Okie. Why?"

"Your story," I said as we began our walk to the compound.

"No. You were losing steam before that. What was it?"

I had to think back. "Seeing your shop and the work you're doing. And hearing about Philip Swickard. You two have accomplished so much. And I have so little to show for the past twenty years."

He stumbled on a manhole cover and I caught his arm. "There," he said, "you see? You accomplished something just then. Don't be so hard on yourself. Your life is your accomplishment, Okie. It's your art."

"The life that's been me wandering in a circle?"

"Are we back to that again? To Krystal's poor soul lost in the snow, traveling in a circle because his legs are different lengths? Dr. Krystal's one smart lady, but she may be wrong about that. She may be wrong that it's such a terrible thing, I mean. Here's a guy who thinks he's walking a straight line, but where's that line taking him? What's he walking into? He doesn't know. He's just plain lost. He could be tracing any kind of meaningless scribble in the snow. Instead, his tracks are creating this perfect shape. The symbol of the eternal. The circle."

He drew one in the air for me. "What seems to the man to be meaningless wandering is really a perfect design—if it's seen from the right perspective."

"Whose perspective?" I asked.

"The perspective of the one who made the lost man's legs different lengths to begin with," the monk said. And he pointed up to the stars.

Ten

I LEFT OLDENBURG EARLY THE NEXT MORNING. Very early. So early that my good-byes with Brother Dennis were muted and fuzzy-headed. Or maybe our hangovers caused that. I know I had no desire to share the retirees' bran flake breakfast. My hair was hurting, which was my body's way of calling out for sweet coffee and greasy food.

I found those things at a franchise restaurant at the I-74 exit for Greensburg, the town with the tree in its tower. I sat in a corner of the restaurant's funhouse dining room, well out of the way of the happy, Friday morning customers. There I sipped my coffee, ate a croissant stuffed with fried egg, bacon, and cheese, and dipped potato poker chips into paper thimbles of ketchup.

As I ate, I calculated and recalculated how far east I could drive that day if I got an early start from Rapture, arriving at a different answer—Wheeling, West Virginia; Somerset, Pennsylvania; Jersey itself—every time I did the math. That was my real reason for rising so early, for doing Brother Dennis out of the last hour or two of our visit. I wanted to end my dreamy sightseeing and go home. My plan was to drive to Rapture, give Krystal my apologies and a worthless promise to call if I thought of anything, and then head north until I picked up I-70.

After breakfast I retraced my route of the day before, nursing my third cup of coffee and wording the excuses I'd use with the doctor. The words came slowly. Lying is harder when you're not sure of the truth, and I hadn't figured out the real reason for my panic. I only knew my mood had something to do with my sadness of the previous evening. Or rather, it had something to do with Brother Dennis's challenge to that sadness, his idea that my random moves were part of someone else's grand design.

I'd awakened with the irrational feeling that everything that had happened since I'd set foot again in Indiana was part of someone's plan. The bucolic, beautiful day I'd passed in Rapture and Oldenburg now seemed like a setup, something intended to lull me to sleep, to make me drop my guard. I felt like I was standing with one foot poised above a snare, one I couldn't even see.

It was still early by my standards when I drove through Rapture. Even so, I listened for the scream of the saw as I passed the coffin works road. I was thinking about stopping to say good-bye to Emmett Haas, but his little factory was quiet and, apparently, deserted. That was just as well. I didn't want my excuses to sound stale when the time came to use them on Krystal.

Finding the doctor's trailer was more of a job than I'd thought it would be. If she hadn't driven me right to her door the day before, I don't think I could have pulled it off. As it was, I had to explore a bit. I blamed my confusion on having approached her place from a different direction, down from town instead of up from the Batsto farm. My other excuse was even more desperate. It was based on the height of my Cavalier. The terrain had looked different from the vantage point of Krystal's truck. Certainly the foliage had. I'd looked down on the weeds and scrub bushes that lined the road, looked beyond them, easily. Now I was right down amongst them, looking up at them even, when the Chevy bottomed out in a particularly deep rut.

This diminished perspective and the feeling of being pressed upon from all sides intensified my unease. When I finally found Krystal's drive, I crept along it, my right foot hovering above the brake pedal.

Even at that pace, I made enough noise to raise Blue III from the grave. The old dog was feeling peppier than he had the day before, or else the approach of a strange car warranted more of his attention. He barked five or six times as I parked next to the Jeep. The dog had a deep, raspy bark that made me wonder whether, like me, he'd once been a smoker. I looked for him to settle back in the dust after that, but he didn't. He sat down at the extreme limit of his chain, staring me in the eye and whining.

The high-pitched pleading ran right through me. I scanned the tiny yard, thinking that if I'd had a gun tucked under my arm, it would have been one great moment to draw it. Instead, I called out Krystal's name, both to quiet the dog and to settle myself. It didn't accomplish either end.

My greeting also failed to produce Krystal. I crossed to the front door of the trailer. The actual door stood open, but my way was blocked by a screen door. I knocked on its aluminum frame, calling Krystal's name again. Then I listened, hearing only the faintest rattle, which I took to be the work of the breeze on some remote part of the trailer.

I told myself that Krystal had gone for a walk. She'd elected not to take Blue along, which accounted for the dog's whining. That story satisfied me until I tried the screen door and found that it was locked. There was no keyhole on the screen door, no way to unlock it from the outside. If Krystal had gone for a walk, she would have left the trailer open or locked the real door. Only someone staying inside would set the catch on the screen door.

I knocked again, louder, and only succeeded in raising Blue's whining an octave. I went back to the Cavalier, dug around in its glove compartment, and came up with my pocket knife. With it, I cut a corner of the screen door's plastic mesh away. Then I reached through and unlatched the door.

Once inside I had a choice of directions, left to the kitchen or right, into a miniature living room. I turned right, passing sofa and chairs piled with medical journals and textbooks and coming to a closed door. I knocked and then opened it. There was a bedroom beyond the door, but Krystal wasn't using it for that. Instead, the little room was serving as a warehouse. The bed and the scant floor space were stacked with boxes marked "Dr. Prestina's Miracle Herbs."

I backtracked to the kitchen. There I found Krystal's ring of keys, hanging from a hook near the door. I also found the source of the muted metallic tapping I'd heard from the door. It was the death rattle of a teakettle that was sitting on an active burner of the gas stove. The kettle was shaped like a stylized apple, and it had once been red. The upper third of it still was. The rest was blackened and blistered. It had boiled itself dry, but when? An hour ago? Ten minutes ago?

On the counter beside the stove was a mug that held a virgin tea bag. In a toaster next to that, an English muffin patiently awaited its fate. There was a stick of butter to keep it company, still in its silver wrapper but soft to the touch.

I moved the kettle to a cold burner, turned off the stove, and continued my search, finding first a bathroom, the curtain on its tiny shower still damp. The final room was the master bedroom. The queen-size bed was expertly made, and the window curtains above it were open to the morning sun.

I went back to the kitchen and listened to the ruined tea kettle crack and pop as its bottom cooled. The only other sound inside the trailer was the whisper of a hungover man with an East Coast accent.

"Raptured," he said.

_____

Eleven

THE RAPTURE COFFIN WORKS was still peaceful and, it appeared, unmanned. As I crossed the packed dirt courtyard where Emmett Haas gave his lectures, I had a vision of an empty workroom, hand tools dropped about randomly, the big power saws and drills turning silently, with no one left to feed them wood. If I'd found the factory that way, I think I would have headed east on foot.

But I didn't. As I approached the building's big barn doors, one of the workmen stepped from the shadows beyond. It was the broom pusher Haas had addressed the day before, the one he'd called Willie. He was carrying the same broom today, which helped me place him, the broom being more memorable—three feet wide at the base with coarse bristles grouped like shocks of corn—than the man driving it. The broom was also taller, I noted, when Willie held it upright so he could lean on it. He was slight and maybe twenty-five, with stubble on his narrow jaw and a bandanna tied around his head—tied so it covered his hair but let his ponytail escape. His single earring caught a little arrow of sunlight that had found its way through the courtyard's canopy of leaves, and I remembered Haas saying that he was now forced to hire outsiders to keep the works going.

I asked for Haas, and Willie spat. "Damn sawdust," he said. "Old

Emmett ain't here. Got the tingles this morning about some tree being cut down, a black walnut. He took the truck and the crew and went out after it. Old Emmett, he likes black walnut trees."

I took a few casual steps to my left, so I could look past Willie and confirm that the works were empty. As I sauntered, I asked, "What are the tingles?"

"The things these hicks get from the forest or wherever. The tingles tell 'em things, like there's going to be a frost or rain or the fishing's good here and not over there." He mimicked casting with a tiny motion of his wrist. "Things nobody who ain't a hick can figure out. Some of the guys think Emmett is on some kind of old-timers network, that he gets a call whenever anybody's going to cut down some tree he wants. I think it's just the tingles."

"Ever discuss this theory with your boss?"

"Yeah, right," Willie said. "Like he'd tell me. I don't know none of his secret handshakes. Do you?"

"No," I said.

"You're from back East, right? You talk that way."

I said I was.

"I've been there. I miss it sometimes."

That made us soul mates, which didn't buck me up. I asked Willie when Haas would be back.

"What time is it?" he asked.

"Nine-thirty."

"Old Emmett will be back in half an hour. He told me ten o'clock, and you can set your calendar by Emmett."

Half an hour was too much time to waste sitting around. I drove down to Highway 50 to look for the filling station turned sheriff's substation. It was a newer building than I'd visualized when Krystal had first told me about it. Swayed by Rapture's general antiquity, I'd pictured something in white ceramic block with rounded corners, maybe with a faded sign over its front door featuring a red, winged horse. The actual building was made of cement block, painted olive, with a flat roof trimmed in a broad band of brown aluminum siding, heavily dinged. It was another survivor from the seventies, I thought, like Dix's earth-tone uniform. Like me.

The deputy was seated behind a metal desk in a room that was too big to have been part of the original design of the service station. I didn't have time to look for traces of the walls the remodelers had knocked down. As I walked in, Dix looked up from the massive stacks of paper he was shuffling.

When the door had closed itself behind me, he said, "Don't tell me. Dr. Bowden's been whisked up into the sky."

"You know?" I asked.

"I know how this joke is going," Dix said. "And I know who it's on. I just don't know why you people think it's so blamed funny." He took a tissue from the box on his desk, started to sneeze, and didn't. "There are people around here who are actually starting to believe that something supernatural is going on. Old people. I think scaring old people for laughs stinks."

"I'm here to report Dr. Bowden's disappearance," I said. "If it's a joke, it's on me, too."

"Why don't you start by telling me who you are. The doctor skipped over our introduction yesterday."

"Are you planning to write any of this down?"

He pushed his piles of paper aside, spilling part of one on the floor. "Golly Moses," he said, the words silly but the tone angry, and then, "Leave the darn things," when I stepped forward to help. He banged around in the desk and came up with a blank form and a pen. "Shoot."

I gave him my name and address. Then I described how I'd found Krystal's place: the whining dog, the Jeep, the screen door locked from the inside, the blackened kettle. That part of the story caught Dix up a little. He paused to picture it. Then he shook it off and continued his block printing.

When he'd finished, he asked, "When did you last see her?"

"Between one and two yesterday afternoon, just after we left you at the Batsto farm."

"She came back after that to play in the woods with Fallon and his men. They didn't find anything, by the way. I last saw her about two. Fallon must have been with her till four or five o'clock. Maybe a lot later. Which means she won't be legally missing until tomorrow evening.

"I tried to explain that concept to the doctor when she came in the first of the week fretting over Miss Shipe. We can't treat an adult as missing just because she hasn't been seen for a few hours. Not unless there's some evidence of foul play. You've got the right not to be seen if you don't want to be."

He paused, giving me the opportunity to exercise the right. I said, "Prestina and Batsto haven't turned up, have they?"

"No. But that doesn't change the law as far as the doctor is concerned. Speaking of the law, how did you get inside her locked trailer?"

"I broke in."

"Huh. So what we have here," he said, tapping the form on his desk, "is a confession of breaking and entering."

"I had reason to believe that Dr. Bowden might need my help." It sounded just like one of Fallon's rationalizations, which wasn't lost on Dix.

"Don't you really mean you had reason to believe she'd been taken bodily into heaven? Out of a locked trailer, no less. How does that work? There wasn't an open skylight, was there? And how was Batsto levitated out of that shower yesterday? The bathroom window was painted shut. There was no hole in the ceiling, either."

"Now who's making jokes?" I asked.

"Fair enough," Dix said. "We'll get back to business. You've given me your name and address, Mr. . . . . Keane. But you haven't told me yet how you came to be in Rapture."

"I met Dr. Bowden when she was a kid, when I was out here going to school. I came back to Indiana . . ."

I stopped, having run up against my promise to Krystal not to tell the locals her family history. I finished the sentence with "on business," but not quickly enough to fool Dix. He knew I'd held something back. I watched his expression curdle as I stumbled on.

"Dr. Bowden looked me up. She asked me to come down here to talk about something that was worrying her. It turned out to be Prestina Shipe's disappearance."

"Why you?" Dix asked.

It was a question I'd been asked before, a question I'd often asked myself. While I thought about it yet again, Dix completed the familiar litany of things I was not and never would be.

"You're not a policeman. No cop would give the legend about the Ordained the time of day. And you don't look like any private investigator I've ever met, either. But I'm not what you'd call experienced in that area. Are you one?"

"No," I said. "I'm just someone the doctor trusted. Someone she knew would take her worries seriously," I added.

Dix caught my meaning. "My pay raises, small though they be, are based in part on who I take seriously and who I don't. I'm not some old friend with time to spend on a girl who grew up pretty."

It was an odd thing for him to say. Like his earlier reference to the evening Krystal and Fallon might have spent together, the remark made me wonder whether Dix might be another jealous suitor—one Krystal hadn't spotted yet herself. If so, he was remarkably indifferent to Krystal's welfare, but the jealousy angle might have accounted for that.

"Are you going to take *me* seriously?" I asked. "Or do I have to call the sheriff?"

"Good luck with that," Dix said. "I've already tried this morning. I found out he decided to take himself a long weekend. By pure coincidence, this happens to be the weekend of the big drug delivery, if the feds are right."

"Your sheriff doesn't want to have his picture taken next to a pile of confiscated methamphetamine?"

"He might—if he thought there was going to be any pile. But the sheriff knows that Fallon and his boys couldn't track a freight train with a metal detector. Fallon's been all over this county, up to Zelma, over to Bono. Everywhere he's been, he's been sure he was in *the* place. Now he's sure about Rapture. The only thing the sheriff is sure about is that Fallon's lost him votes in the next election."

"Sounds like I'll have to try the state police."

"You're welcome to. There's a trooper post down in Jasper you could call. Or you can just hang around Rapture till the troopers come to you. They'll be plenty of them sniffing around here this weekend. Agent Fallon will see to that."

Fallon. He was the man to tell about Krystal's disappearance. He'd turn Rapture upside down looking for her. And maybe get Deputy Dix out of his chair while he was at it.

The deputy had had the same thought. I could tell by the way he almost smiled. Had he mentioned Fallon by chance or to take my mind off the state police or just to get rid of me? I couldn't tell.

"Would you like Fallon's number?" he asked.

"Please."

He wrote it on an index card. "Got a car phone?"

"No."

"Use this one." He turned his desk phone around to face me. I stepped over and punched in the number. While I listened to the other phone ring, Dix asked, "Where'd you get off to yesterday when you left Rapture?"

"Oldenburg."

"Pretty town. Stay there last night?"

"Yes."

"Did you make any arrangements to meet the doctor this morning?"

I'd counted seven rings. Fallon wasn't home. "She knew I was coming back, but not when exactly."

"But she knew it would be this morning?"

I hung up the handset. "What are you getting at?"

"Just wondering if the doctor might be using you. She may have staged her disappearance, knowing you'd be by to report it. It might be her way of getting me to take the Shipe business more seriously. Dr. Bowden put one over on me earlier this week. She told me that Miss Shipe had a health problem that could have caused her to wander off. That was just a story the doctor made up. I called Dr. Stanger over at Brookside. He was Miss Shipe's doctor before Dr. Bowden came to town. He said Prestina Shipe would outlast most of the hills around here."

"How does Batsto fit in?"

"He's a coincidence. He plain skipped out yesterday and Fallon can't bring himself to admit it. Batsto may have given Dr. Bowden the idea of faking her own disappearance. She might have figured with three in a row I'd be forced to do something."

"You showed her," I said. I held up the index card. "Where's this phone?"

"The Double Nickel Motel, ten miles west of here on Fifty. If Fallon's not out chasing today's hot tip, he should still be there. He doesn't keep farmer's hours."

"Thanks," I said, turning to leave.

"Tell him I'll be stopping by the doctor's trailer in an hour or so when I do my next circuit. If that doesn't satisfy him, he can come by and try to kick my keister into gear."

Twelve

I ALMOST MISSED THE DOUBLE NICKEL MOTEL. It was set well back from the highway on a treeless rise, an old-fashioned one-story motor court whose office was a neat little house built of the motel's tan brick. The buildings also shared pale gray shingles, their roofs as bright in the morning sun as the gravel drive I nearly drove past.

The problem was the motel's sign. I'd been looking for the words "Double Nickel" done in neon script, maybe, or chiseled into a slab of the ubiquitous limestone or hand painted on a fragment of barn. Instead I saw a small white square on which the number 55 stood out in bold black. I saw the sign but didn't observe it, because I took it for a speed limit posting. At the last second, I noticed the tiny "Motel" beneath the numbers and remembered that "double nickel" was dated trucker slang for the fifty-five-mile-an-hour limit.

Every room of the motel opened directly onto the same gravel parking lot. I spotted Fallon's Explorer there as I pulled in and, parked next to it, the white Ford pickup Fallon's flunkies had driven to the Batsto farm. As I climbed out of the Chevy, one of the flunkies appeared. He was carrying a heavy leather case, which he lowered carefully into the pickup's bed. Their metal detector, I thought, the one Dix said they used to track freight trains. I got that joke, belatedly, and smiled in spite of my errand. The smile displeased the man who was stowing the case.

He was a weightlifter with a GI haircut and a squint so pronounced it had to be affected. He screwed his eyes down to blue slits as I asked for Fallon.

"Breakfast room, sir," he said. He didn't salute, which was just as well. The "sir" made me feel rickety enough. "Third door down, next to the ice machine sign."

I asked him how he liked the Double Nickel, thinking, with a sinking sensation that wiped the remains of the smile off my face, that I might be checking in soon myself.

"Not the worst place we've been on this tour, sir," the large kid said, focusing on the tip of my nose.

I thought about asking him to explain the game that was going on between his boss and Deputy Dix, but I didn't have much hope that he'd tell me. And I didn't want him to put an eye out while he thought it over.

The breakfast room was actually the motel's vending area. Squeezed in between a soda machine and a droning bin of ice were four tiny tables, one of which was the buffet. It held a coffee maker, jugs of milk and juice, and three or four varieties of breakfast cereal, stacked in plastic containers that doubled as bowls.

The room's only customer was Fallon. He'd selected denim for today, or maybe it was just too early yet for regulation khaki. The cuffs of the long-sleeved blue shirt had been turned back exactly one time each for no reason I could see. It had to be the way men in the know were wearing them this year. Exposing his wrists did show off a heavy gold bracelet, which in turn showed off his tan. So maybe there was planning involved. Some had certainly gone into the selection of his table. He was seated in the far corner, where no wild Hoosiers could sneak up behind him.

Not that he was relaxed. His dark eyes had been on me from the second I'd crossed the breakfast room's picture window. He nodded as I closed the door behind me.

"Mr. Keane. Morning. If you're looking for Krystal, she's not here. I wish I could say she was."

"So do I," I said, putting so much into those three words that they told Fallon most of what I'd come to say.

"What's happened to her?" he demanded.

I told him, admiring his professionalism as he sat like a coiled spring and heard me out. He reached the limit of his cool when I passed on Dix's message about stopping by Krystal's trailer sometime during his next rounds of the chicken coops.

Then the man of action in him took over. He pushed his table aside abruptly, rattling the soda machine. "Come on," he said.

Having no man of action to speak of in me, I stayed where I was, blocking the doorway. "First tell me when you last saw Krystal."

Fallon checked his momentum and gave me a concise report. "We searched the woods between the Batsto farm and Shipe's place, my men, Krystal, and me. It took us two hours, and we didn't find so much as a bent twig. Afterward I talked Krystal into driving over to Bedford for dinner."

"Did you stop to see Dix on the way?"

"No. I called him from Bedford. How did you know we'd talked?"

"He told me you hadn't found anything in the woods. Go on."

"That's it. After dinner, I drove Krystal back here to Rapture where she'd left her truck. I didn't see her home. Were you thinking I had?"

"Dix was."

"That bastard. I'll give him a briefing he won't forget."

He took another step my way. It brought us very close together, as I had held my ground. "Dix also thinks that Krystal might have faked her disappearance as a way of getting his attention," I said. "Any thoughts on that?"

"Would I be ready to kick somebody's butt up between his ears if I knew this was a joke? Or am I supposed to be acting?"

I wanted to take a step back, but there wasn't any room. So I stood there not answering him.

"I told Krystal she shouldn't have handed Dix that line about Shipe's health being dicey," Fallon said. "I knew if he found out the truth he'd never trust her again. As usual, she knew best.

"Listen. This is straight: If Krystal's trying to put one over on Dix again, it's news to me. But that possibility is sure as hell no excuse for him to sit around and do nothing."

"I don't think Dix is stuck in first because of that," I said. "I think it has more to do with the trouble between you two."

"There's no trouble, Keane. We just don't get along. That's not an unusual outcome when one law enforcement officer has another one land in his lap. In the DEA, we often encounter resentment and even resistance from the locals. It's part of our NWE, our normal working environment. It almost never means anything."

"Almost never?"

"Well, there's always the possibility that the local law is deliberately looking the other way where a local crime is concerned. The temptation would be especially strong in a case like ours. Like I told you yesterday, our smugglers are very careful not to let any of their product hit the local market. A cop in that situation, especially one as autonomous as Dix, might consider it all somebody else's problem.

"I'm not saying that's the case here. All I know is that Dix hasn't been very cooperative. It might just be the way he's built. Or he may have picked up on the attitude of his boss, the sheriff."

"He hasn't been cooperative either?"

"Not very."

"Not even in Zelma and Bono?"

Fallon actually drew himself back, as though I'd cuffed him on the chin. "My operations in both those areas were fully justified by the information I had in hand at the time."

"More anonymous tips?"

Fallon butted chests with me. It would have been a mismatch even if I hadn't been taking shallow breaths to filter his cologne. "Why are we standing here talking? We're wasting time we should be using to search for Krystal."

"We're not going to find her hunting through any forest," I said.

"How then?"

"Do you believe in the rapture?"

"Of course not," Fallon said.

"Then discussing the drug smuggling isn't a waste of time. It can't be a coincidence that three people have disappeared within a few days of that big meth shipment you keep talking about."

Fallon hadn't gotten by me physically. But now he leapfrogged me mentally. "Batsto," he said. "Batsto's behind all this!"

"I don't—"

"Shipe must have gotten wind of something going on down the road from her place. That fits! During her last phone call to Krystal, Shipe said she was anxious to talk to her about something. Batsto notices Shipe snooping around and snatches her. Then he gets word somehow that I'm coming for him and he makes himself scarce. Why leave the shower on, then?"

He conveyed the fact that the question was rhetorical by placing a hand on my chest. "Wait a minute," he said. "Wait a minute. He does it because word has gotten around about how Prestina's place was left—the breakfast sitting there untouched—and it tickles Batsto to think he's accidentally revived the local superstition. So he sets up something similar when he runs out.

"But he doesn't go far. He's there somewhere watching when

I come by. He would be, wouldn't he? So he could laugh at his joke. And he's still there when I come back with Krystal and you. He sees me together with Krystal, and he decides to snatch her, too. Or maybe he's afraid that Shipe has told her business partner something."

I was dizzy by then. Fallon had no trouble brushing me aside. "We've got to get moving, Keane. If we're right, Krystal's in up to her neck."

"If *we're* right?" I would have said if Fallon had given me a chance to speak. But he was already out on the sidewalk, calling to his men.

"Saddle up! We're paying a call on Deputy Dix."

"I'm not," I said, so loud I startled myself. Fallon jerked around—this time as though I'd kicked him.

"I'm going to see Emmett Haas," I said.

"Good idea, Keane. The mayor will raise the town. What's left of it, that is."

Thirteen

FALLON WAS WRONG ABOUT EMMETT HAAS. Far from rais-
ing Rapture, the last patriarch of the Ordained, when I finally lo-
cated him at the coffin works and passed on the news about
Krystal, seemed barely able to raise himself.

Compared with my visit earlier that morning, the works was a
beehive, the air alive with dust and noise and with a sweet, spicy
smell I hadn't noticed before. Haas caught me sniffing the air as
he crossed to me, walking in big, bow-legged strides like a movie
cowboy.

"Recognize that, Mr. Keane? It is sassafras wood. Wonderful,
is it not? We cut two sassafras trees last week over in Spencer
County. Two!

"It was a favorite trick of the Ordained: the use of aromatic
wood in the lining of the better coffins. It was a nice touch in the
olden days when they could not do much embalming. Nicer for
the mourners. Cedar gives you a stronger fragrance, but sassafras is
more authentic."

He gestured me over to a worktable where one of the strange,
round-ended coffins was being fitted with its sassafras lining. When
I didn't step up for part two of the lecture, Haas frowned. "Is
something wrong?"

For the third time that morning, I described what I'd found at Krystal's trailer. I felt that my earlier renditions had only been rehearsals for this one. I pressed on with the telling, even after Haas had begun, physically, to slip away from me. His watery eyes never left my face, but his legs bowed more and more. He slowly settled, coming to rest finally on a little wooden bench.

"The doctor," he said over and over again. "The doctor."

He was so devastated that I found myself borrowing lines from Deputy Dix. "She may be back already. She might have been called out on an emergency, maybe by somebody who drove there and picked her up. She might have just forgotten the stove."

"Not that one," Haas said. "I have never met anyone so sharp. And I have lived a long life. For her to be here, serving the people of this county, is such a blessing for us. It could not last, I knew, but every day I counted as a blessing."

"Why couldn't it last?"

"Because this place is too small for her. This county is too small, for one so talented. She has the world to choose from, that one. This town would not be the choice of anyone who has the whole world before her."

"But she did choose Rapture."

"She chose to stop here. She has some knots to untangle, knots tied for her in the past. She will not discuss them. I respect that, but I know they are there. She is untying them by working here in Rapture. Then she will move on."

It seemed to comfort Haas to speak of Krystal's future. He settled back, resting his grizzled head against the unfinished coffin.

"I have seen it many times," he said. "The young people moving on. Once, when I was young myself, I resented them for throwing aside their heritage. It seemed to me that the whole world couldn't balance the scale that held little Rapture. Now I see that I was unfair. A man has only one life. He must make what he can of it.

"So the young leave us. Only the unthinking and the frightened stay."

"And the believers," I said.

Haas smiled. "And the believers."

"That can't have described Clyde Batsto. So he must have been one of the other types, unthinking or frightened."

Haas brushed sawdust from his beard with both hands. "The unthinking type, I would say. But Clyde's decision to stay on in Rapture was no victory for the Ordained. He never really joined us. There were Batstos in the group that waited in Rapture Meadow in 1844. And Clyde's parents were believers. I made their coffins myself, both in the same year. But Clyde went his own way.

"I always expected him to leave. He was never a happy boy. Never interested even in the worldly things that this area has to offer: the farming, the hunting, the fishing. Always looking off somewhere but never going. Maybe I am wrong. Maybe he was one of the frightened after all."

"Did he once want to be a pilot?"

Haas looked puzzled. I told him about the model airplane that hung in Batsto's room. "I do not recall that, but it would not have surprised me if he had left to follow such a dream. The surprise was that he hung on, working the farm after his parents died. It seemed to happen not so much through a conscious choice as through an indifference that settled on him. I have seen it happen to a child when the parents are taken."

I'd seen it happen to promising young people for another reason. "I've heard that Batsto used drugs. Is that true?"

"Now you are asking me about things I do not pretend to understand. Clyde Batsto is the bad fruit of good vines, that is how I think of him. I am afraid that I have believed from the start that Clyde may be the man behind Prestina Shipe's mystery. But I did not voice my fears until last night, when the doctor stopped by to tell me that Clyde was missing, too."

"You saw Krystal last night?"

"Yes. After the government man, Mr. Fallon, brought her back from Bedford. She saw my light burning here and stopped in to give me the news."

"How did she seem?"

"Tired, but not discouraged. That is the great thing about being young: the ability to be physically tired but spiritually fresh. Mr. Fallon may have cheered her up. I remember wondering if he might be the call from the wide world that took her away from us at last."

That thought reminded Haas of Krystal's disappearance. I watched him fight against his emotions, the battlefield his big, weathered face. The deep groves cut around his eyes narrowed. He bared his teeth a little and set his jaw. Then all the lines softened at once, and he let his breath out slowly.

"Maybe it was you who made the doctor happy, Mr. Keane. By coming down here. The doctor has great faith in you, the kind of faith the people in Rapture have come to have in her."

It was Haas's turn to watch an emotional reaction. What he saw worried him. He stood up, grunting with the effort. "Come out back with me," he said. "It will be more private."

There were two doors in the back wall of the workroom. One was set left of center and bore the word OFFICE in ornate lettering. The second door was dead center and unmarked. Beyond it was another enormous room, made to seem even larger than the workroom by the complete absence of its far wall.

Haas led me past the biggest circular saw I'd ever seen, the kind of saw heroines were fed to in silent movies. Beyond that, near the missing wall, was a diesel engine mounted on a concrete pad, looking like the remains of a bulldozer that had been stripped by thieves. Haas patted its yellow hood as he passed it.

"The heart of our works," he said. He pointed up to the rafters, to the system of belts and drive shafts I'd noticed on my first visit.

"It powers everything. Once, when I was a boy, a steam engine sat in that spot. It had the word FAITH painted on it, because it drove everything the Ordained did."

I looked for an inscription on the diesel but saw only the name of its maker. Haas was outside by then. Backed up to the open end of the shed was an elderly flatbed truck. In it lay Haas's prize from the morning: the remains of the black walnut tree. The giant had had its branches removed, but it was still wearing its bark. It was held in place, like another Gulliver, by totally inadequate chains.

Haas rubbed the smooth butt of the log affectionately. "We will get many board feet of lumber from this beauty. We will make many folk art collectors and museums happy."

He looked me over—evaluating me for board feet, I told myself, although I knew it was for something else. "You are not happy, Mr. Kane," he finally said.

"It's been a bad day."

"When I first saw you, you were troubled. Is it something you would like to talk about?"

It wasn't. Not directly at least. So I asked, "You said this tree would make folk art collectors and museums happy. What did you mean by that?"

"We sell most of our work to them, collectors and museums. The doctor did not tell you this? Oh yes, we have become folk artists, my workers and I. Rapture is a tourist attraction and our coffins are art. Is it not a strange world? How does a person display a coffin, I always wonder. They are so big."

His honest bafflement reminded me of Brother Dennis, another artisan who had been promoted to artist when he wasn't looking. But the monk had seemed bemused by the transformation, while Haas was almost resentful.

"It provides money for the town, so I should not complain. The Ordained have no pension fund. There is no retirement plan for old, tired patriarchs. Still I feel sad for the sake of the old Ordained, the founders. Once a faith, now a curiosity; their precious meadow, a picnic ground; their meeting house and their town, roadside curiosities. Things never worked out for the Ordained as they hoped they would. Always a jog in the road for them. But they took their jogs and bumps with grace and so must I."

It was an opening for the question I'd been wanting to ask Haas since he'd told me the history of the sect. "How did they do it?" I asked. "How did they manage to stay together after the Great Disappointment?"

Haas put a hand on my shoulder, moving me backward gently until he could focus on me more easily. "That is it, is it not?" he said. "That is what I see in you. A kinship with my forebears. You have had a great disappointment of your own, have you not, Owen? You have lost your way. You need not talk of it. I will respect your silence.

"On the subject of the Ordained and their response to their own disappointment, I am afraid I cannot help you. I do not know how they overcame their crisis or what sustained them afterward. There is no record of that in the writings of the time."

He patted the walnut tree. "Here we have a witness to that October morning. Unfortunately, it is dead now, too, and mute. One of these rings actually corresponds to 1844. One of them here approximately." He pointed a thick finger at a spot near the center of the pattern of concentric circles.

"I have counted rings on other trees," he said, "so I can make a guess. This beauty was just a sapling on the morning when the world did not end. Just a child, so maybe its testimony would not help us very much."

He laughed softly at the idea, so softly that the deep rumble seemed to come from his chest rather than his throat. "I stand in awe of those people. More than anything else, my awe has kept me here, year after year. But it is an awe mixed with jealousy and, sometimes in the quiet moments of the night, with anger. I have often wondered why they took such pains to pass down their instructions for working wood but were so careless about the secrets of their faith. It had to have been that believing was as natural to them as breathing. You do not teach a child to breathe, do you, Owen?"

"No," I said.

"No," he repeated and turned back toward the workroom. "I will wait here until I hear from Deputy Dix and Agent Fallon. Then I will give them all the help I can."

"What should I do?" I asked.

He turned and considered me from the gloom of the shed. "You should go and talk to a woman of our town. Her name is Marietta Feasey. She lives in a little pink house up at the head of this street. You will find it easily."

"Is she a member of the Ordained?"

"Not anymore. She can tell you about that, if it pleases her to. She has her own ideas about Prestina's disappearance. I do not understand them, but you might. They are modern, scientific ideas, the kind that took the place of the things the Ordained believed in."

Fourteen

AS EMMETT HAAS HAD PREDICTED, I had no trouble finding Marietta Feasey's house, the only pink one in Rapture. Of course, if I'd simply stopped at every house that still looked occupied or questioned the few shuffling residents I passed, I would have found Feasey within a few minutes of leaving Haas whatever the color of her house. There just wasn't that much left of the town.

Feasey's little cottage showed it was a going concern by more than its bright pink siding and its even brighter white trim and picket fence. The little yard had a manicured look that was more out of place in rustic Rapture than fresh paint. And there were flowers, beds of them everywhere, still lush and full of blooms now, in this last, lazy moment of summer.

One of the beds was decorated with a wooden board cut in the shape of a broad woman's backside. She wore a white dress with black polka dots and appeared, when viewed from the right angle, to be bending over the bed.

More folk art, I thought, remembering Haas's lament about his caskets and feeling his embarrassment. I pictured one of his fancy coffins in somebody's front yard, filled with dirt and planted with petunias.

I was still picturing it when I heard metal being scraped against metal in the side yard. I followed the sound and found a woman kneeling on a piece of towel next to yet another flower bed.

Feasey was narrower than the lawn ornament lady out front and less formally dressed, in old blue pants, older sneakers, and a wheat-colored smock with a flowing waistline and sleeves and a tightly gathered neck. The woman's own neck was loosely gathered, and the tanned skin of her forearms and face had wrinkles that crossed and recrossed one another, forming a moving pattern of tiny diamond shapes. In contrast, her hair—cut short and combed straight down across her forehead and the tips of her ears—was an unremitting chocolate brown.

I was standing next to her before she noticed me. She looked up without alarm. Her dark eyes were all but hidden by large square lenses tinted brown and mounted in heavy plastic frames. Just before she turned back to her work, I noted a hearing aid in her right ear.

The work Feasey turned back to was cleaning mud from a little trowel using a second implement, a pronged weeder that resembled a claw. Beside her was another piece of toweling and on it something that looked like a clump of onions.

"Bulbs," the woman said. She startled me by adding, "Not onions. Day lily bulbs. You end up with too many in one spot, so you separate the bulbs, spread them around. Pretty soon you've got yourself a garden."

"Pretty soon?" I asked.

She cupped a gloved hand behind her ear. I repeated the question.

"Ten or fifteen years will fill up a little yard like this. That's pretty soon as nature goes."

She removed her right glove and gestured to me to help her up. Up turned out to be five feet one or two. She took off her second glove and dropped them both at her feet. "Help you?" she asked.

"Emmett Haas sent me," I said. "I'm interested in Prestina Shipe's disappearance. He told me you have a theory about it."

"Old Emmett told you that?" she asked, using the nickname for Haas that Willie, the broom pusher, had favored. It sounded strange coming from Feasey, who had to be at least as old as the patriarch mayor.

"It's odd for him to be recommending me," she said. "He usually tells folks I'm something of a nut."

"Because you left the Ordained?"

"No. He's used to that happening after all he's seen. No," she said again. But instead of explaining, she asked, "Who are you, anyway?"

"My name is Owen Keane. I'm a friend of Dr. Bowden's." For some reason, I didn't mention what I'd found and failed to find that morning at Krystal's trailer. After seeing what the news had done to Haas, I was afraid to mention it.

"The doctor?" Feasey asked. "She's good people. She has an open mind. Sometimes a lot of education can close a person's mind as tight as no education. Hasn't happened with Doc Bowden. What's your interest in Prestina's abduction?"

"You think she was abducted?"

"It isn't polite to answer a question with another question, Mr. Keane. You go first."

"I'm interested in mysteries," I said, understating the case more than somewhat. "Dr. Bowden asked me to come to Rapture because she's worried about Ms. Shipe. If you have reason to believe that Prestina's been abducted, you should talk to Deputy Dix."

"Ha," Feasey said. "He wouldn't be much taken with my reasons or my evidence. I've beaten my head against that wall before. You say you're interested in mysteries. Do you mean big ones or small ones?"

"I've never been able to tell the big ones and the small ones apart," I said.

"Ha," Feasey said. "How about your mind? Is it open?"

"Try me."

"Test you, you mean? I will. Tell me what you know about alien abductions."

My heart dropped down to the height of Feasey's damp knees. I would have left her to pull her bulbs apart in peace if it hadn't been for a word she'd mentioned in passing: evidence. No would-be detective could walk away from a promise of evidence, however unlikely that promise seemed.

I ransacked my mental files for any information I'd stumbled across on alien abductions, mumbling something after a deadly pause about flying saucers and operating tables and the Bermuda Triangle.

Feasey had to lean my way and cup her ear to hear me. Her unsmiling attention took me back to grammar school. I felt I'd been caught daydreaming and unprepared again by a humorless nun. Before I'd finished, Sister Marietta straightened up and dropped her hand to her side.

"Unbelievable," she said. "A body could learn more than that reading the *National Enquirer*. The biggest issue of the day, and you don't know anything about it. You're no more a man of your times than Emmett Haas! You should grow a beard like his and practice talking like the Old Testament! Have you hidden yourself away like him in some musty dream of how the world should work?"

I could have denied that charge at book length, but I wasn't there to defend myself. "Let's hear your dream of how the world works," I said.

Feasey considered me while she waved away a bee that was trying to land in her hair. "Something comes over bees at this time of year," she said. "It's as though they realize the flowers are going and knowing makes them desperate and pushy and rude. Sometimes I think it may be senility coming on at the end of their lives, suddenly turning them into nuisances after they've spent the whole summer being useful and polite.

"Emmett Haas and I have known each other all our lives. For most of that time, we saw the world the same way. Even when I stopped seeing it that way, we stayed friends. Now we're suddenly as quarrelsome and awkward around one another as autumn bees. I didn't mean to speak sharply just now."

"I'd like to hear your theory," I said.

"Would you?" Feasey asked, batting at the bee again and nearly hitting me. "Come inside, then."

Fifteen

THE FRONT ROOM OF THE LITTLE PINK HOUSE looked like it had been laid out by a well-to-do teenager. The focal point was a twenty-six-inch television in a black plastic case set atop a stand that contained a VCR and a stereo. The tower was flanked by black speakers more than half as tall as the woman who owned them. A single reclining chair, upholstered in a gray-on-gray plaid, faced the television. Behind it, in an alcove created by a bay window, a computer hummed away happily. It was the twin of Prestina Shipe's, as near as I could tell. Two portraits hung on opposing walls. One was a famous forties painting of Jesus Christ that was all browns and golds and flattering light. Christ the matinee idol, it might have been called. The other was an enlarged publicity still of Mr. Spock, the Vulcan character from *Star Trek*.

Feasey stopped at the computer and tapped a few keys. "Still no messages from Prestina," she said.

I passed up the chance to make a smart remark about aliens and the Internet. The emotional tension of the morning—the initial shock and now this endless waiting for news—was getting to me. I was afraid if I so much as smiled I'd start giggling and never stop. If I had broken down and laughed, it wouldn't have been at Feasey and her little command center. It would have been at Owen

Keane, the man even unworldly types like Emmett Haas singled out for fool's errands.

"Lemonade or Coke?" Feasey asked from the doorway to the next room.

I ordered the cola, my breakfast coffee having long since worn off. When Feasey returned, she also brought cookies, and I warmed to her.

She scored more points by giving me the recliner and taking for herself the little swivel chair that went with the computer. She wheeled it so close to me that our knees almost touched when we sat down.

She munched at a cookie, which was shaped like a flat windmill, and stared at me, suddenly reluctant to speak. To get her started, I pointed to the fancy television and asked, "Do you get cable way out here?"

The question drew her back from a great distance. "Cable? No. I have a satellite dish. You didn't see it because it's hidden away behind my shed. I couldn't stand the sight of the ugly thing. I'd be lost without it, though. As cut off from the world as . . ." She stopped, embarrassed.

"As Old Emmett?" I asked. "Or me?"

She committed the social lapse she'd called me on earlier, answering me with a question. "Have you ever seen a UFO, Mr. Keane?"

"No."

"I've read polls in which seven percent of the participants admit to seeing one. If that percentage held true across the adult population of this country, it would work out to over twelve million people. How about periods of time you can't account for? Have you ever experienced lost time?"

Years of it, after St. Aelred's. But no UFO drivers were responsible for that, unless they were also scotch importers.

The unspoken joke didn't bring me closer to a fatal giggle, and that surprised me. I realized that I was suddenly in danger of falling asleep. I tried to rally myself with thoughts of Krystal, missing and in trouble. I should have been bouncing off the walls with impatience, I told myself, but picturing that only made my fatigue worse. Above Feasey's head, the photo of Leonard Nimoy seemed to be staring down at me. The actor and his fan shared hairdos, and I felt an irrational desire to brush Feasey's hair off her ears so I could see whether their tips were pointed.

I took a deep drink of my Coke and tried to remember the last thing Feasey had said. "Is missing time a symptom of alien abduction?"

"A classic symptom, along with unexplained burns and rashes and cuts. Lost time is the most intriguing mystery, though. A person looks up, sees a strange light in the sky, notes the time or simply knows what time it is. Then the light is gone, and the subject—who has no sense of time having passed—looks at his watch or the alarm clock and sees that hours are gone. One to eight hours usually."

"Prestina Shipe's been missing for three days," I said.

"I know. I'm worried about that. Some abductees report being told that their time aboard alien spacecraft is kept short to protect their health. An abduction like Prestina's that lasts for days is very rare and potentially very dangerous."

"Just being abducted isn't dangerous?" I asked.

"That depends on whom you read. Have another cookie, Mr. Keane. You almost inhaled the first one. Some abductees report terrifying experiments, the forcible removal of genetic material, artificial insemination, even the termination of a pregnancy the subject wasn't aware of. The insertion of electronic implants is another possibility, but I'm skeptical about those."

My mouth was full of maple-flavored windmill, so I couldn't second that.

"Those are the negative experiences," Shipe said. "They fascinate people as lurid tales always do. Most movies and television shows about abductions pander to that hunger. But the latest research in the field is concentrating on the positive, therapeutic aspects of abductions."

I swallowed. "Therapeutic?"

"Yes. There's a school of thought that maintains that the alien contact is intended to heal, not hurt. That abductees are the wounded of the world, people in need of restoration and renewal. Lost souls like Clyde Batsto."

"You know about his disappearance?"

"Of course I do, Mr. Keane. Rapture is a small town, after all. When I heard about Clyde, I thought yes, he'd be just the person they'd pick, a lost, lonely young man. Just the type who needs the expansion of consciousness a glimpse of the larger universe can provide." She gave me a long look, sizing me up for a little consciousness expansion of my own.

"How about Prestina Shipe?"

"A lonely old woman," Feasey said. "Another natural candidate for spiritual renewal. You certainly wouldn't abduct a seventy-year-old woman if your intention was to breed a new hybrid species."

"I wouldn't," I said.

"There is the possibility, though, of genetic research. Age wouldn't be an obstacle to that. In fact, there are cases in the literature in which the same individual has been abducted several times over a span of years, presumably to provide comparative tissue samples for some kind of ongoing study. Prestina's current disappearance may only be the latest in a series.

"Then there's the issue of cross-generational abductions. Abductions tend to run in families, you know. There are known cases affecting three generations. The Shipes and the Batstos have lived in this corner of the forest for many generations."

"Since the Great Disappointment," I said.

"You know about that? Emmett told you, didn't he? I've advised him against trotting that story out for tourists the way he does. The most plausible story in the world would begin to sound doubtful if it was repeated over and over like that. And the tale of the Ordained is a long hike from plausible.

"I've tried to apply my science to it, to use my research to explain some of the puzzling aspects of the history of the Ordained. Old Emmett won't even listen to me."

"I will," I said, forgetting for a moment Krystal and my slight justification for being there, the unlikely possibility that Feasey had some evidence about the disappearances. The story of the Ordained had that kind of pull for me.

Feasey removed her glasses and cleaned them with a paper napkin she'd been holding, shaking cookie crumbs from the napkin onto the now empty plate as a first step. The skin around her eyes was so wrinkled it looked as though she had several sets of overlapping lids. The eyes beneath the lids examined me now in a way that made me think the glasses had been obstructing their view.

"In my reading," she began, still squeaking away with the napkin, "I've come across some peculiar cases. You think everything I've told you is peculiar. Of course you do. Don't bother to be polite about it. If you'd read as much as I have, though, you'd have recognized certain patterns, recurring themes.

"For example: the beam of light that levitates the subject, enabling him or her to pass through closed doors and windows and even walls; the little gray aliens who are so common in the ships and sometimes so dangerous; the taller, fairer ones who may be captains or doctors or priests; the communication by telepathy. In fact, the uniformity of the abduction experience is one of the most compelling things about the literature.

"But every so often there's a story that's different, one that's arresting because it is different. I remember happening across the testimony of a thirty-something woman whose name was Lois. Lois's abduction began conventionally enough. Under hypnosis, she remembered seeing blue and white lights outside her bedroom window. She was taken into a ship, into a circular metallic room, where she met a tall fair-haired alien. So far, so routine. If he had given her a physical examination or even a hug, it would have been just another case history."

She stopped to slip her glasses back in place. "What did he do?" I asked.

"He showed Lois a movie. It was something like a movie, anyway, a movie without a screen. The images appeared in the air in the very center of the circular room. They showed the end of this world. First there was a nuclear cataclysm, brought on by our own foolishness. It triggered every kind of natural upheaval imaginable. It was as though the planet was sick and tired of us and our shenanigans.

"Lois was told—through telepathy, naturally—that these things were going to happen."

"As a warning?"

"No," Feasey said, shaking her head so emphatically she almost removed her glasses again. "No. There was nothing of that 'Ghost of Christmas Yet to Come' stuff about it. No call to reform. No chance for reform. This was going to happen. Period. There was no avoiding it.

"But," she added, holding up a single mummified finger, "there was a promise, too. The alien told Lois that a small number of humans who met certain criteria would be saved. At the last moment, just before the fatal buttons were pushed, the elect would be whisked up to the sky and carried off to a place of safety and happiness. Now, what does that remind you of?"

"The Ordained of God," I said.

"Exactly. I was sitting where you are now when I read Lois's testimony, and I had the very same reaction. It's the Ordained all over again, I thought. The whole Adventist dream all over again. The world ending, but the chosen ones saved. Could that be a coincidence? I wondered long and hard about that."

She handed me the empty cookie plate. Then she stood up abruptly and began to pace the small room. I set the plate on the floor and pushed myself forward in the recliner, but her rapid passing to and fro didn't give me a chance to stand.

"Then it came to me," Feasey said. "Suppose, I thought, that the story that has come down to us from the Ordained is really another abduction report. A report that was only vaguely understood at the time and further distorted as it was passed from generation to generation."

Up until now, Feasey had been selling me the story, telling it slowly and carefully and watching my reaction. Now she was caught up again by the excitement of her insight. The words poured out of her, and she forgot me entirely.

"They had only a rudimentary knowledge of hypnotism back then. Mesmerism, they called it. So they had no way to unlock experiences their conscious minds could not accept. It would have been natural for them to have recast their vague memories of an alien's prophecy of doom and promise of rescue into a religious revelation. Damnation for the many and redemption for the elect."

"But the Adventist movement was nationwide," I said.

"Why shouldn't it have been? Why not worldwide? The aliens would have selected those to be saved from the entire population of the planet. So there would have been pockets of them everywhere, awaiting the end time.

"It couldn't have involved a nuclear disaster, not in the 1840s, but there could easily have been a natural threat. An asteroid, perhaps. I've read a great deal about the danger of rogue asteroids. Some scientists think they killed the dinosaurs."

Feasey and I had both read too much of the wrong things, detective fiction in my case, pop science in hers. She was making me feel better about the way I'd wasted my youth, but not about the way I was wasting my day. I settled back in my chair, feeling tired again and cheated somewhat, too.

"But the aliens never came," Feasey was saying. "Maybe they were able to avert the catastrophe and save the earth, maybe by destroying the asteroid."

"Maybe there never was an asteroid." I said, my head lolling backward. "Maybe that's just a story the aliens cooked up to collect a bunch of likely specimens in one place and keep them there and their children and their children's children after them so the aliens could go on collecting fingernail clippings or whatever."

Feasey picked up on my weary sarcasm—she could hardly have missed it—but it didn't offend her. She seemed almost apologetic, sorry that her big revelation had let me down. Or perhaps she was just feeling sorry for me, because I hadn't been able to appreciate it.

"I think the promise made to the Ordained—whatever it was— the vision vouchsafed them, as they might have expressed it themselves, was real, Mr. Keane."

"Why?"

"Because they stayed together. They lived on happily in this place. They celebrated the Great Disappointment every year, although no one could say exactly why they did, why they celebrated the loss of heaven as though it was some happy deliverance."

It was an answer to the question I'd put to Emmett Haas: Why had the Ordained remained in Rapture? It was a question he hadn't been able to answer, perhaps the question that had caused

Marietta Feasey to doubt the faith of her childhood. Now she had an answer that satisfied her. She made one last attempt to satisfy me.

"I said before, Mr. Keane, that abductions run in families, that Prestina and Clyde Batsto may only be the latest links in a chain of abduction running back to the founding of the Ordained. I don't really believe that's true."

"Why not?"

"Because of the way the faith of the Ordained dropped away, generation to generation. Whatever experience the founders had, it wasn't repeated. Once that first group passed on, there was only their imperfect teaching, their misinterpretation of what had happened to them, left to sustain the community. It grew hazier with each retelling, until it finally passed into legend. And the descendants of those first Ordained dropped by the wayside one by one."

"Lately they've plain disappeared," I said, to remind myself as much as Feasey that there really was a point to all of this.

"Yes," Feasey said, pressing her hands together until they shook. "Finally there have been other signs. All over our planet, contact has been made again, just as the memory of that first contact was flickering out. They're back, perhaps because they knew they were almost forgotten, perhaps because of some new threat. They came back, and they came to this place, to Rapture, where they knew the faithful had gathered before."

I willed myself out of the chair. "You said earlier you had some evidence. What is it?" I'd paid my dues. Fork it over.

"I've seen them," she said.

I sat down again. "Aliens?"

"No. Their ship. The lights of their ship. Circling over this town. Don't say it was an airplane. I've heard that answer before. I know what airplane lights look like. These were different, brighter.

There's no reason for a plane to circle around here anyway. Or to come back like a train. We don't have an airport."

"Did you hear an engine?" I asked. It was a silly question, given that I was hoarse from speaking loudly enough for Feasey to hear me.

She shrugged and smiled. "I may have. I'm not sure."

"What do you mean the lights come back like a train?"

"I mean as regular as a train. On a regular schedule. I've worked it out. They come every third Saturday. They're due again tomorrow night."

Little Rapture was in for a busy weekend, it seemed. "You didn't see the lights around the time Prestina disappeared? Or Batsto?"

"No," Feasey said. "But they were both taken in the early morning, so I wouldn't have been out doing my stargazing. I'm going to be out tomorrow night. Will you join me?"

I said I would. I would have agreed to anything to have gotten out of there. I wanted to find Fallon in a hurry.

"You needn't be anxious, Mr. Keane," Feasey said, reading my mood. "They'll be back. Prestina and Clyde. They won't be the same, but they'll be back."

I hesitated, my hand on the front door knob. "They won't be the same?"

"No," she said sadly. "They'll be changed. I'm not sure why." She started to tell me something else, shook her head, and then continued in the impersonal tone she'd used back in the early part of her lecture. "It may be nothing more than the trauma of their experience, their rebirth. Or it could be a sign that those who believe in the sinister nature of abductions are correct after all when they insist that the purpose is not to soothe or instruct us but to alter and perhaps even replace us. You and I should take precautions, so we can be sure, when we meet again, that we really are who we seem to be. I know! We'll use a password."

"A password?"

"So we'll know we can trust one another. I'll say 'Neil' and you'll answer what?"

"'Diamond?'"

"'Armstrong!' You answer 'Armstrong.' For heaven's sake, Mr. Keane!"

Sixteen

THE SOUND OF A CAR HORN checked me before I'd reached Feasey's front gate. It belonged to Fallon's white Explorer, which was just pulling out of the courtyard of the Rapture Coffin Works. I waited by the gate as the truck climbed the hill, but that didn't satisfy Fallon. He continued to sound staccato blasts, until I wondered if his message was directed at someone other than me. It turned out that the horn playing had ceased to be communication and had become a creative outlet.

"Keane," Fallon said through the truck's open passenger window. "God damn it. What do you think you're doing? I thought you were going to stay with Haas."

"What's happened?" I asked, picking up on Fallon's anger but not understanding it. He'd been angry when I'd last seen him—at Dix and his casual attitude—but that hadn't even been a warmup for his present state.

"Get in," he said, his hand still tapping the horn, but too lightly now to sound it.

"What—"

"Shut up and get in."

We dug twin ruts in Feasey's road as we took off. I had an impression of Feasey standing at her front window looking frightened, but it may have been my own reflection, my own wide eyes, my own hand half raised in parting. Then we were on the main road, heading west toward Krystal's turnoff, scattering mourning doves that had been pecking at the gravel in the middle of the pavement.

"Are you going to tell me now?" I asked, just before we made the plunge down into the valley.

"I'm going to show you," Fallon said.

I started to tell him about my talk with Feasey, but he cut me off again. "No gossip, either. Nothing else. Nothing but this."

"Has something happened to Krystal?"

He ran my side of the Explorer into a ditch, either because I had distracted him or because he was tired of words. The ditch was filled with a tumble of rocks, and the jarring I got before Fallon let me back onto the road shut me up for the rest of the drive.

The white DEA pickup truck was parked in Krystal's little clearing. So was Dix's cruiser. Fallon's men were waiting in front of the trailer. I looked around for the deputy and spotted him out back, filling Blue's water dish from a garden hose.

Fallon ignored him. "It's inside," he said.

I took comfort in both words of that short sentence. I'd grown desperate thinking that Krystal had been nearby that morning—hurt or worse—that she'd needed me and I'd somehow missed her. Missed her and gone off to talk about dead cults and UFOs. But Fallon had said "it," not "she." And "inside." I couldn't have overlooked Krystal if she'd been in the trailer. There wasn't room to hide a cat in there.

Not a cat, but something. Fallon led me through the living room library and into the guest bedroom warehouse. It was still filled with beer-case-size cardboard boxes of herbs, but they were no longer neatly stacked. Several of the boxes had been opened. The rest looked like they'd been kicked around for exercise. Or spite.

"Here," Fallon said, the word choking him. He picked up a box of the herbs. It was designed to double as a display case. The inside of the lid was decorated with the photo of Prestina Shipe I'd seen in her house, the Dr. Prestina picture. There was a cartoon balloon coming out of her mouth. It contained a promise: "They're good for what ails you."

The box contained dozens of little cellophane packets of dried herbs held together at the top with folded cardboard tabs and staples. Prestina's picture was repeated in miniature on the tabs. This time, the cartoon balloons held the name of the herb contained in the packet.

I got no more than a glimpse of the packets before Fallon reached into the box and swept the top layer onto the floor. Beneath it was a plastic bag bigger than a whole row of the herb containers. It had neither a picture or a label. It was filled to bursting with white powder.

"Guess what that is," Fallon said, forcing the words out one by one. I didn't think he was really expecting an answer until he hissed "guess" at me again through clenched teeth.

I was looking at him, watching the muscles in his jaw work and thinking how much more intimidating his wide white eyes were than any Hollywood-inspired squint. I looked back with an effort to the box he held. The box was trembling, sending a steady stream of the surviving cellophane packets onto the floor.

"Methamphetamine," I said.

"Right," Fallon said. My acknowledgment seemed to be what he'd been waiting for since he'd found me in front of Feasey's house. The tension left him in a rush, his eyelids drooping first and then his head. He dropped the box back onto the pile.

"Right," he said again and slumped back against the trailer's tin wall. "Did you come in here when you were looking for Krystal?"

"Yes," I said.

"How is it you didn't find this stuff yourself?"

"I forgot to bring my search warrant."

It was an answer that doubled as a question, and the DEA man understood that. "We had reason to believe the occupant of this trailer was in danger. And there was evidence of a break-in. The screen on the front door had been slashed by persons or persons unknown. That was enough to justify a search of the premises."

"Did Dix agree with you this time?"

"To hell with Dix," Fallon said, but his heart wasn't really in it. "To hell with his search warrants. No judge is ever going to second-guess us on this one. We're never going to find anybody to take before a judge. They're all gone, everyone connected with this operation. Batsto, the man who received the drug shipments via highway drops. Shipe, the little old lady who supplemented her pension by breaking down the shipments, repackaging them, and shipping them out again. And Dr. Bowden, the mastermind.

"I would have expected something slick from Krystal, if I'd suspected her at all," Fallon said. "And this herb idea is Teflon squared. 'Dr. Prestina's Miracle Herbs.' It's so obvious it's innocuous. And it's the perfect way to ship the stuff. No drug-sniffing dog is going to find it. Not when it's buried in all that potpourri shit.

"Oh, the doctor is a smoothie. Much smoother than her rhubarb father. But just as morally flexible when it comes to the subject of illegal drugs. What do these hicks like to say? That apple didn't fall far from the tree."

I'd tensed up the second he'd mentioned Krystal's father. It was my standard reaction whenever I tried not to react. As recumbent as Fallon had become, he spotted it.

"Come on, Keane," he said. "You know all about Papa Morell. You told me that you and Krystal go way back, back to when she was a little girl. So you must know she grew up on a farm where her daddy raised bug-eaten pot for the local kids to smoke."

"How do *you* happen to know that?" I asked.

"I get it. Krystal swore you to secrecy, right? Said she didn't want any of the locals to know. Wanted to put her past behind her. She made me take the same blood oath, after she told me.

"It was just last night, on the drive back from dinner. I was trying to find out why she'd hidden herself away down here. You want to ask why I cared, right? Sure you do. You're one big question mark, Keane. A goddamn, badly dressed question mark."

"Am I?"

Fallon almost smiled. "Touché. I asked her because I was trying to talk her into leaving Rapture." He rephrased the sentence in the language of sensitivity. "I was suggesting that she consider leaving. With me. When my job here was done. She said she couldn't leave. She made it sound like living out here was some kind of moral obligation. Like she was repaying an old debt."

Untying old knots, the genuinely sensitive Haas had called it.

"I pressed her on it," Fallon said, "so I could understand what she was saying. I thought I was entitled to understand. What I was suggesting was pretty important. She finally told me about her father. It was his debt she was paying off in Rapture. It had something to do with her grandparents, she said. Their lives had been destroyed by her father. She didn't say how. I remember thinking that it would explain why she'd picked old people to take care of, when she'd be a natural with kids.

"But even when she was telling me about it, I was thinking something wasn't right, that something else was going on inside Krystal's head. You know how it is, Keane. You're having a conversation about something with somebody. You think it's about topic A, a ball game or the how the laundry got folded. And it's really about topic B, I hate my life, or get out I'm tired of you."

I reassessed Fallon's sensitivity and asked, "What was Krystal's topic B?"

"I thought she was trying to scare me off. Telling me about her father was a preemptive strike—a goddamn nuclear strike. She figured a guy who worked for the Drug Enforcement Administration would start running and never stop if he hears his woman's father was a druggie. That he'd be so worried about his next promotion he wouldn't have any time left to think about her."

"Was she right?" I asked.

Fallon shrugged. "What difference does it make now? We know that wasn't her topic B after all. There was something secret going on in her head, but it wasn't any scheme for letting me down easy. It was just another way for Krystal to laugh at the whole lot of us. She was thumbing her nose at me, Keane, the way she did with the 'Dr. Prestina's Miracle Herbs' name. She was waving at me and then laughing to herself because I couldn't see her."

He waved at me in slow motion. " 'Here I am. I'm the one you've been chasing all over the county. And you never even suspected me.' Who the hell would have suspected a doctor?"

A doctor gone bad makes the first of criminals, I thought, paraphrasing a very wise man. I didn't cite him aloud. I wasn't ready to accept Fallon's judgment of Krystal. I'd jumped to more than my share of conclusions in my career, jumped as easily as any pedestrian on the moon. For once, I kept my feet on the ground.

"Why would Krystal have invited me down here to look into Shipe's disappearance, if she was Shipe's accomplice?"

Fallon pushed himself off the trailer wall, causing the last intact tower of herb cartons to tumble. "Haven't you been following any of this? She did it to laugh at you. You had something to do with putting Krystal's old man away, right? She told me that much about you. That entitled you to be mocked like the rest of us. Hell, it probably moved you to the top of the list.

"This whole setup is the product of one warped sense of humor. Look at the town she picked: Rapture, Indiana, for Christ's sake. What better name could you have for the home of a drug distributorship? Krystal's provided more than a little rapture for people around the Midwest with this shit.

"And these phony disappearances. Tell me they don't point to some sicko comedian. Krystal whisks her two flunkies right out from under my nose and stirs up the ghosts of the Ordained while she's at it, just for fun."

"Why whisk them away? You didn't suspect Shipe."

"I had Batsto cold, though, and Krystal knew it. He was the weak link. If I'd gotten my hands on him, he would have handed me Shipe and the doctor. So poof, they're all three gone. There wasn't any reason for them to stay. With us sniffing around, it would have been too risky to go ahead with another shipment. So Dr. Bowden decided to pack up and move on to the next stand— Happy Days, Ohio, maybe, or Bliss, Illinois.

"She yanked her people out one by one and then herself. They're all off somewhere laughing at us."

At him, Fallon was really saying. He was only including me and the rest of the boys to make the insult less personal. And it wasn't working.

As we stood looking at one another—one of us glaring, the other blinking more than was necessary—I became aware that Blue was barking. He'd been barking for some time, I realized, but the noise had changed in tone, becoming the desperate sound of a dog who wasn't sure there was anyone else left in the world.

Dix entered the trailer after scraping his feet on the front doorsill like a man coming in from a snowstorm. He stepped into the spare bedroom, noted the scattered cases, and sniffed.

"What?" Fallon demanded.

"Found something else. The dog did, I mean, when I walked it out back. Dragged me to it."

"Show me," Fallon said, as though something in Dix's terse report had already told him what the dog had found. I'd missed the clue, but I didn't ask about it. I followed the two lawmen out of the trailer and—after Fallon had detailed the weightlifter to guard the place—into the clearing that was Krystal's backyard.

Blue was chained up again. As we trooped past him, the dog settled himself with the air of someone who has successfully passed the buck. I felt encouraged by that. Whatever Blue had found in the woods, it couldn't have been Krystal. He would have been inconsolable.

The forest started just beyond Krystal's shed. It started big, with an oak as old as Emmett Haas's dead walnut. A faint trace of a footpath circled the base of the tree. It turned out to be the tributary of a dry creek bed. The gully was lined with exposed limestone, big flat pieces of it, set like gray-green steps. Half a flight down, the way was blocked by a fallen tree, riddled with woodpecker holes. It had broken off four or five feet above the ground, leaving a jagged stump.

The grave was next to the stump. It was so shallow that it was as much mound as hole: a pile of dirt, stones from the creek bed, and fallen limbs.

"The dog did a little digging before I could stop it," Dix said. "Then I picked around enough to be sure."

Just visible at one end of the pile was the head of a bearded man. The skin of the face was incredibly white against the black beard, and it looked almost unmarked. The hair on the left side of the head was thick with something that looked like mud but probably wasn't. The eyes were closed.

Fallon crouched next to the body for a moment. Then he said, "Step on up, Keane. I'd like to introduce you to Clyde Batsto."

Seventeen

I WAS A SPECTATOR for most of the afternoon. I watched from the edge of the clearing as the men and women called in by Dix—the resources, Fallon called them—photographed, measured, and poked at Clyde Batsto. When they actually disinterred him, I managed to be somewhere else, up at the trailer giving a statement to a state trooper.

The trooper was another displaced New Jerseyan, a transplant from Bayonne. We chatted a little about our home state, the trooper telling me the things he missed: steamed clams, trips to Yankee Stadium, decent pizza.

"You wouldn't believe what passes for pizza out here," he said. "Frozen crusts with so much meat and cheese on them you can't find the sauce, which is just as well, because the sauce comes out of a can. Maybe out of a drum. The edible tray school of pizza making, my wife calls it. And she should know, because her dad made pizza all his life, starting out in a booth on the boardwalk at Asbury Park. Say, you're from Trenton, right? Do you remember what they call pizza there?"

Batsto's second funeral procession had made it to the top of the creek bed. Two attendants held bushes back so the litter bearers could squeeze past the giant oak. I wondered how many people

Batsto would have to tend him when the time came to put him back in the ground.

"Tomato pie," I said.

"Right," the trooper said, so happily that I gave up the idea the question had been intended to verify my credentials.

Deputy Dix was nowhere near as friendly when he took the time to talk to me at all. I put it down to his current situation. Everyone who arrived at the little trailer appeared to outrank the deputy. Dix just seemed to be someone who got outranked naturally, and he was sensitive about it. If that wasn't enough, his allergies had reacted badly to his time in the woods. When he climbed the creek bed for the last time and found me visiting with Blue, his eyes were streaming and his nose was running. He could have passed for Clyde Batsto's dearest friend.

"Let's drive back to my office," he said. "I need a pill. And you and I should talk."

I looked at the other officers milling about—maybe for Fallon, though he and his men had disappeared hours before.

"We *are* going to talk, Mr. Keane," Dix said. "Just you and me."

I must have reacted to that on some animal level, because Blue raised his head and licked my hand.

Dix added, conversationally, "There's nothing left to do here but search the woods. They're bringing dogs down from Bedford for that. Though this old boy would probably do as well." He ruffled Blue's ears the way Krystal had. "There's no reason we shouldn't be comfortable while we're waiting."

The front seat of Dix's patrol car was as soft as an old sofa, but I never got comfortable. The deputy's first question saw to that. "Why are you out here in Indiana, Mr. Keane? You almost told me this morning. You're going to tell me now."

I did, after telling myself that I'd find another way to keep faith with Krystal. I told Dix about the parole hearing in Indianapolis. That meant telling him next all about Curtis Morell and Krystal's connection to him. I then ratted on myself, describing my reason for being in Indiana in 1973, my vocation, and the mess I'd made of it.

We were pulling up in front of Dix's service station office when I finished. If any part of the storytelling had touched Dix, he didn't let on. Even his watery eyes had dried up on me.

"How can we verify all that?" he asked as he unlocked the station's front door. He held the door open for me, and not as a courtesy. I finally admitted to myself that I was officially a suspect. In the drug smuggling and the murder and who knew what else.

"Is this where you read me my rights?" I asked.

Dix was at his desk by then, trying to peel the foil backing off a sheet of allergy pills. "Darn this tamper-proof stuff," he said.

"Your Miranda rights?" he asked after he'd freed two of the pills and swallowed them. "That's the kind of nicety your buddy Fallon walks all over. From what I've heard of his reputation, he's made a career of playing fast and loose with other people's rules. You get away with that if you're successful. Fallon hasn't been, not lately. The way I hear it, this case may be his last chance to make good."

Mentioning Fallon turned out to be bad luck for Dix. Before I could deny any relationship with the DEA man, his white Explorer slid to a halt in front of the building.

"Speak of the devil," Dix said, taking the words out of my mouth.

Fallon came in at the double, his denim shirt soaked through, his sunglasses pushed up atop his slick hair. "I see you got him, Deputy," he said. He winked at me, but didn't smile. "The only guy in the county who isn't involved. I just missed you two out at the trailer."

"I was about to find out how involved Mr. Keane is," Dix said. "Have a seat."

Fallon sat next to me on the suspect's side of the desk and closed his eyes. Dix picked up his phone. First he called the Indiana Department of Corrections and verified that Morell's hearing had actually taken place. He then called Brother Dennis using the number I provided and listened to the monk's version of my last days in the seminary. During the same call, Dix determined my whereabouts on the previous evening. The deputy even made a long distance call to New York, to Harry Ohlman, a lawyer friend of mine who had vouched for me so often over the years he kept an intern on staff just to log the inquiries.

Near the end of that call, Dix put his hand over the mouthpiece. "He wants to talk to you," he said.

I shook my head. "Tell him I'm in solitary."

Fallon sat up while Dix was passing on my regrets. "I just came from the Shipe place," he said to me. "My men and I searched it top to bottom. With a fresh, new warrant, by the way."

Dix was trying to listen to the phone and Fallon both. Despite having the correct number of ears, he couldn't manage it. He said "Thanks" into the phone and slammed it down.

Fallon pretended not to notice. "We were looking for the one thing we didn't find at the trailer. Besides the lady who lived there, I mean."

He was still addressing me, so I played straight man. "What was that?"

"A customer list for the Miracle Herbs company. You didn't see anything like a mailing list when you were out at the trailer this morning, did you?"

I said I hadn't.

"We didn't find it at the Shipe house, either. I left one of my men there to search the computer files, but he isn't going to find anything. That little item's long gone. They were careful to take it with them."

"I'm more interested in what they didn't take," Dix said. "The drugs and Batsto."

"The drugs they left were just a sample," Fallon said. "They write that much off to petty cash. Batsto was another matter. He was their one vulnerable point, like I told Keane here. Batsto was a diseased limb, the one likely to kill the whole organism. So Dr. Bowden amputated him."

He tapped his head at about the spot where Batsto's injury had been. I had time to consider Fallon during the long silence that followed. Like many another rejected lover, he seemed to have found a new use for the former object of his desire. He couldn't keep the hatred out of his voice whenever he mentioned Krystal.

On the plus side, Fallon seemed to have classified me as a brother-in-suffering. Another man taken in by Dr. Krystal Bowden. I risked a little of the goodwill that went with that by asking another of my questions.

"Why did they go to the trouble of faking their disappearances and then spoil it by leaving the drugs and Batsto's body behind?"

"The faked raptures had served their purpose. They'd given the ladies a head start. It was time for the topper. The punch line."

"If you're right," Dix said, "Dr. Bowden's got one compulsive sense of humor. Satisfying it meant setting herself up for a murder charge. There are places around here where a body could stay hidden for years. They barely bothered to cover Batsto over."

"Naturally," Fallon said. "She wanted us to find him. What's the point of a punch line if nobody hears it?"

Dix sniffed. "She wouldn't have laughed just as hard thinking of us all worried to death about her?"

Fallon shook his head, the motion as subtle as a tremor. "Not quite as hard," he said.

"There's another possibility," I said. "Someone could be framing Krystal."

Dix didn't seem surprised by the idea. Unfortunately—to judge by his expression—he still considered me likely casting for the part of framer.

Fallon proved he couldn't read minds by asking, "Who would do that? Who do we have left? Are you telling me Prestina Shipe set all this up?"

"What do we really know about her?" I asked.

"We know she's seventy-two fucking years old," Fallon said. "And we know someone killed Batsto with a blow to the head. Do you see Shipe doing that?"

"We're not sure that's how Batsto died," Dix said, scrapping for points. "Ten to one it is, though. A blow to the head with something heavy and narrow, like the butt of a rifle."

This time I was the one who reached up to finger a spot on his head. A spot that had once been caressed by the butt of a shotgun.

"Shipe could have an accomplice, of course," Dix added. "Someone we haven't identified yet."

"Haven't identified yet?" Fallon repeated sarcastically. "The goddamn phone book for this place is printed on a matchbook cover. Who could this accomplice be? Mayor Haas?"

"How about somebody who works for the mayor?" I asked. "His men are all outsiders."

"So are you, Keane," Fallon said. "You should think about that before you help Deputy Dix cover up for the locals."

I expected Dix to blow up at that. So did Fallon, tensed in his chair like an astronaut waiting for zero. But the deputy only blew his nose for the tenth or eleventh time.

"It may be worthwhile talking to those guys," he said. "I'll handle that, Mr. Keane. Not you. Understand? From what I heard just now on the phone, you can't be trusted around any kind of a mystery. You just naturally start nosing in, and to hell with the police and everybody else."

I wondered who had filled Dix in, Brother Dennis or Harry. My money was on the lawyer. Then again, it might have been both of them. Dix sounded that sure of his ground.

"I don't want you getting hurt," he said. "And I sure as heck don't want you getting anyone else hurt. But I don't want you wandering away, either. Not just yet. How about we get you a room at the Double Nickel? I'll set that up right now. You can stay put there for a day or two so I'll know where you are. How's that sound?"

It sounded a lot like a cell door slamming shut. "My car is over in Rapture," I said. "Or am I allowed to have a car?"

I think Dix was actually going to suggest leaving the Cavalier where it was. But Fallon jumped in. "I'll run you over there to pick it up. A man can't survive at the Double Nickel without wheels. They don't serve lunch or dinner. And it's a long walk to the Kentucky Fried Chicken in Huron."

Dix sneezed and shrugged or maybe just sneezed extra hard. "Enjoy your stay," he said.

I was already thinking of what I had to do next, which was find out more about Prestina Shipe. I could have asked Emmett Haas or even Marietta Feasey, the woman who corresponded with Shipe via computer. But would either one, Shipe's patriarch or her friend, give me a straight answer? Dix had mentioned another possible source on my previous visit to his office: the doctor who had treated Shipe before Krystal came to town, the one who told Dix that Krystal had exaggerated her claims about Shipe's health problems. The deputy had even given me the doctor's name, but I couldn't recall it now.

At the office door, I turned back to Dix. "What's going to happen to Krystal's patients?"

Fallon said, "They'll be okay. She told me she arranged to have some local quack cover for her."

I would have shoved the DEA agent out the door, if he'd been unarmed. Luckily, Dix couldn't let Fallon have the last word.

"That would be Dr. Stanger over in Brookside."

I managed to bite my tongue before I could say, "Bingo."

Eighteen

I FIGURED I HAD TEN MINUTES—the time it would take Fallon to drive us to Rapture—in which to complete an impossible task. I had to turn the DEA man, as a character in a spy novel might have put it. Or rather, I had to turn him back. Return him to my side, to Krystal's side. Ten years might not have been enough time to get that done.

I didn't waste a second on a sidelong approach. While we were still in Dix's parking lot waiting for a truck to clear the lane, I said, "You're judging Krystal too fast. You tend to do that. A few hours ago, you were sure Batsto was behind all of this. You were wrong then. I think you're wrong now. Krystal could still need our help."

"I'll give her plenty of help if I ever find her again," Fallon said. He was staring at the truck—a big semi—as it passed us, staring as though he hoped to see through its corrugated side.

"I thought of something else," he said as we pulled onto the highway, "while I was listening to Deputy Dix yak on the phone back there."

"What?" I asked.

"Wait; it's a question. Think about this. Who first suggested to you that there might be a tie between Shipe's vanishing act and the old Ordained legend about the rapture?"

"Krystal did," I said, remembering the embarrassed way she'd brought up the idea in Shipe's kitchen and the promise that had lured me down from Indy in the first place, the promise that the mystery had a religious angle.

"Good," Fallon said. "That confirms my own experience. Now tell me how she could not be involved in those snatches when she was the one running around mumbo-jumboing them up with that Ordained bullshit."

I thought about it—out loud, because the clock was ticking. "Krystal's fascinated by the Ordained. They're part of what she loves about this area. She's attracted to them because they believe in something. She didn't have anything like that growing up."

Fallon grunted. "She was so fascinated by the rapture that she wove it into her own slicko sicko scheme."

"Everybody around here knows that history. Anyone could have used it deliberately as a way of throwing Krystal or Haas or the whole town off track. Prestina Shipe could have."

"Are you referring to Prestina Shipe, part-time cookie baker and the evil genius of Rapture? If you're not careful, you're going to start to sound obsessive."

"That would make two of us," I said.

Fallon braked hard and pulled the Explorer onto the shoulder. I'd won an indefinite time extension, but I didn't congratulate myself just then.

One of Fallon's rolled sleeves had come undone. He folded the cuff back while he steadied himself. "Look," he said. "If I'm a little bitter about Dr. Bowden, I'm entitled to be."

"You haven't known her all that long."

"What's time got to do with it? How long did you know this Mary Fitzgerald woman before you decided you loved her?"

I opened my mouth, but that was all.

Fallon leaned into me. "What's the matter? Don't like having your feelings analyzed by every amateur head shrinker who stumbles in? Welcome to the goddamn club."

He settled back, pulling his shoulder harness away from his chest with a clenched fist. "Krystal told me about the woman you were with when she first knew you. Pretty fast company for a boot camp priest, the way Krystal described her. What happened to her, Keane? I don't see any wedding band. Whoa, did I hit a sore spot? Let me guess, she dumped you for another guy."

"Yes," I said, thinking of the New York lawyer who had just had a phone slammed in his ear.

"Well, you're lucky," Fallon said. "That kind of thing happens every day. It hurt, I'm sure, but it didn't kill you."

"What's killing you?" I asked.

"The idea that I could love something rotten. Wouldn't that finish you off, Keane? If you found out that Mary Fitzgerald was guilty of the worst crime you could think of, the thing you'd dedicated your life to stamping out, wouldn't that ream out your insides?

"All day I've felt like somebody in a horror movie. A guy who finds out he's in love with some kind of zombie or vampire. What do they call them? The living dead? That's the way I feel about drug dealers. They're the soul dead." He slammed the truck into gear.

I tried to put the idea of Mary out of my head. "If you really cared about Krystal, if this were really about more than your ego getting kicked around, you'd wait until you were absolutely sure before you condemned her."

Fallon started to say that he *was* absolutely sure. Then he stopped and watched the road ahead. We were already on the turnoff to Rapture. I was running out of miles.

"There is that business about her Jeep," Fallon said. "I keep thinking about that. Why did she leave it behind? I don't mean why, really. I mean how. The why is brain optional. Her gag wouldn't have worked if the truck hadn't still been there. You would have just thought she'd gone off somewhere, maybe on her rounds. You never would have broken in and found the dead teakettle.

"So the Jeep had to stay. But then how did Krystal and Shipe get away? Shipe doesn't own a car. How could Krystal have had a second car stashed in a little place like Rapture without anyone noticing it?"

"The person who kidnapped her had his own car," I said.

Fallon wasn't even listening. "It had to be that a confederate came and collected her. Shipe, too, probably. I thought for a minute that they might have arranged to be picked up down on Fifty by the drug courier. But according to our information, the next shipment—the one that's being diverted to God knows where as we speak—wasn't due until the weekend."

"According to your anonymous source?"

"Yeah," Fallon said.

"How did that work?"

He shrugged. "It couldn't hurt to talk about it now. The tips came by mail to the DEA office in Indy."

"Addressed to you?"

"No, to whom it may concern. Typed, unsigned, and mailed from various locations around this county."

"But the first two tips were phonies."

"That's not hard to explain, whatever the sheriff and his top deputy may think. I believe the tipster was testing us. Testing his ass cover, I mean. He wanted to be sure we couldn't or wouldn't trace the letters to him. When he was sure, he gave us the real goods."

We were in Rapture, descending the grade into the coffin works lot. Fallon seemed to have said all he had to say.

"Suppose Krystal was your anonymous source," I said. "How do things figure then?"

"You tell me," Fallon said, but he was interested.

"Say Krystal found out that Rapture was being used for drug smuggling. So she contacted the DEA."

"Anonymously," Fallon said as we pulled in next to my Chevy. "Why?"

"Because of her past. She didn't want that coming out. So she couldn't get involved publicly. She mailed letters to you from various spots around the county when she was out making her rounds."

"That would fit," Fallon conceded. "And the wild-goose chases she sent us on to Zelma and Bono. Those were to test her cover, right?"

Agreeing would have been politic. But I'd spotted another possibility. "Maybe. Or maybe they were meant to frighten somebody here in Rapture: Prestina Shipe. If she was allowing her herb shipments to be used to distribute drugs, she was implicating Krystal. Krystal put up the money for the mail-order company. And the doctor part of Dr. Prestina is a reference to Krystal. If she informed on Shipe, she'd be turning herself in. With her father's record, who would believe she wasn't involved?"

I paused to give Fallon the chance to recant, but he wasn't quite ready. "Go on," he said.

"Krystal couldn't expose Shipe, so she tried to scare her straight. She brought you guys into the county. When that didn't work, she brought you to Rapture."

Fallon sat for a full minute. Then he shook his head. "I'll say this for you, Keane. You don't quit. But it just doesn't hang together. If Krystal is the tipster, why did she raise such a ruckus when Shipe skipped out? She had to be considering that possibility when she frightened the old broad. And if Shipe wasn't the one Krystal was trying to scare, how did the drugs get into the herb boxes?"

"I don't know."

"Well, you've got two things going for you. You don't give up and you're honest. At least those things used to be virtues, back in olden times. Now the only one that matters is getting results." I thought he would tell me about his career troubles then. That turned out not to be my business. "Climb out now and let me get back to work," was how he put it.

I got out of the Explorer, but I didn't shut the door. Through the trees that lined the street, I'd caught a glimpse of a pink house.

"I've been meaning to ask you," I said. "Have you considered the possibility that the drugs have been coming in by plane?"

"Plane?" Fallon asked. "What brought that up? Oh yeah, I forgot. You've talked with the UFO lady. She give you any windmill cookies? I was a good boy. I got two. I've heard all about people being levitated out of their beds by beams of light. And getting gynecological exams in space. Compared with her, old Emmett Haas is evening news credible."

"I'm not talking about her theories. I'm talking about what she witnessed, the lights in the sky."

Fallon cupped a hand behind his ear and shouted, "What? You've got mites in your sty? Oh yeah, she's a great witness. I can see that old get-a-life Trekkie on the stand now. The defense attorney asks her to read what's printed on the lenses of her glasses. And she says, 'Coca-Cola Bottling Company. Five cents deposit.'"

Fallon had almost worked himself into a laugh. He gave up the attempt with a sigh, dropping his hand from the gearshift. "We've looked into it, Keane. Even with Feasey's shortcomings as a witness, it was worth a look. It didn't pan out. The forest has reclaimed a lot of the old farmland around here. What's still being worked is planted right now. Corn and soybeans. You can't land a plane in a planted field. Not if you're hoping to get it out again. The few unplanted fields nearby aren't big enough."

"How about a helicopter?"

"Not right for this kind of work. Too conspicuous. Not enough range. It would be a plane if it were anything. A plane or a flying saucer. The county is dotted with little airports. We've checked around, had them watched. Nothing."

He slammed the truck into reverse and let it jerk backward. I got the message and shut the passenger door.

"See you at the Double Nickel later," he said. "I assume you're going over there directly."

The way he smiled as he said it led me to assume that he was only covering himself. "More or less," I said.

"Keep this in mind. I'm certain of one thing: Prestina Shipe didn't crack anybody's skull open with a rifle butt. If the doctor didn't do it, there's someone else around here who did. Watch your back."

"I will," I said.

Nineteen

FALLON WAS GONE, BUT I STILL STOOD there, breathing in the dust of his departure. The golden afternoon had turned a little cooler. I dug around in the back of the Chevy and came up with an almost respectable sports coat to wear over my golf shirt and jeans. Dr. Stanger of Brookside would take me more seriously now, I thought as I put the jacket on. He wouldn't be able to help himself. He'd be overawed.

That is, the doctor would be overawed if I ever made the drive to Brookside. And if I got there before the doctor's office closed. I was facing yet another deadline, but I just stood there, a formally attired hitching post in the coffin works lot.

The old factory was the thing holding me in place. By that I mean the possibility of talking the mystery over with the factory manager, Emmett Haas, was holding me. It was a temptation I often felt: the desire to pass the buck, to unshoulder my burden as a preliminary to getting the hell out. But I couldn't get out this time, not with my "client" unaccounted for. I didn't have many principles as a detective, because, as Dix had pointed out, I wasn't really a detective at all. But not losing a client had become all ten of the commandments to me. So a talk with Haas would not have freed me. It would only have been therapy, which is another way of saying a waste of my time.

And it might have been dangerous for Haas. The news that Krystal had disappeared had nearly floored him earlier that day. I'd forgotten to ask Fallon whether he'd told the patriarch about the drugs in Krystal's trailer when he'd stopped by the coffin works looking for me. Fallon likely hadn't, given the nonverbal mood he'd been in, and I didn't want to be the one to give Haas that shock.

My thoughts turned to Haas's employees, the outsiders Dix had promised to interview, the men he'd told me not to interview. Could I trust the deputy to do it? More to the point, could I trust Dix not to blunder in while I was doing the interviewing? I decided that I couldn't risk giving Dix an excuse to lock me up or to shoo me over the border. Not until Krystal was safe.

I climbed into my Chevy and looked up Brookside on my map. It was roughly northwest of Rapture, so if I headed out of town opposite the way Fallon and I had come in, heading west along the ridge line, I was bound to find the road to Brookside eventually. That or never be heard from again.

I had just passed Krystal's turnoff when I spotted someone walking along the ridge road. The slight figure wore a knapsack and carried a fishing rod. It sported a ponytail, too, which fooled me for a moment. Then I recognized Willie, one of the less skilled members of the coffin works team.

I tossed my earlier caution in the direction of the passing forest. Deputy Dix wouldn't object to me taking advantage of a chance encounter. Especially one he'd never hear about. I pulled up next to Willie and leaned out my window. "Want a ride?"

"Where you headed?" Willie asked back. He was a different man away from work. Cheerful. Energetic even. He kept up a good pace while I answered him.

"Brookside. If I can find it."

"The big city," Willie said and laughed. "There's a shortcut for it up ahead. I'll show you where to turn." He put his rod and knapsack in the backseat and then climbed in beside them, making a chauffeur of me.

"What the hell is this thing?" he asked, pointing to a newspaper-wrapped parcel that shared his seat. It was Brother Dennis's ceramic sculpture, the Vicious Circle. "You planning to mail your spare tire back home?"

"It's a punch bowl," I said.

"A punch bowl," Willie repeated. "Where's your candelabra? In the glove compartment? Never mind. Just get this here party wagon moving."

I started forward, but slowly, asking him how the fishing was.

"Not real great. The tinglers say you have to get up at dawn to do any good. But I'll be damned if I'll do that for any fish."

"The tinglers?" I asked his reflection in the rearview mirror.

"The hicks. I told you about them this morning."

"Right," I said. "You mean the people who can feel the tingles from the forest, like your boss."

"The tinglers," Willie said, drawing the last syllable out and ending it with a hiss. "I envy them. I surely do."

"You said this morning you wished you were back East."

"I do sometimes. But wishing ain't getting. I'd go back in a minute if it was safe, but it ain't."

"Not safe for you?"

"Hell, not safe for anybody. Not for maw, paw, or the little ones. Not safe for their dogs or cats or tweety birds, either. Not to mention their fancy punch bowls or cereal bowls or toilet bowls. Here's your turn."

I pulled over as close to the omnipresent ditch as I dared and shifted into park. I was afraid Willie would jump out before I could get another question in. He didn't stir.

"Why isn't it safe?" I asked, turning in my seat.

"Got a cigarette?"

"No," I said.

"Just as well. I'm trying to quit. Can't be hooked on something that ain't going to be around. It ain't safe back East because the whatchacallit, the social fabric is coming apart."

He repeated "social fabric" a few times like a wine connoisseur swishing a choice vintage around on his tongue. Then he asked, "Don't you ever go to the movies?"

"Not very often," I said.

"Can't get a date, huh? Been there. Hell, I *am* there. Rapture ain't no singles bar. But you give up to get in this life."

What I'd given up was any hope of directing the conversation. "What do the movies have to do with the social fabric?"

"They show you what it's going to be like in a few years. The movies about the future do. A dark, scary time, man. That's what the new millennium is bringing. Wars and rumors of wars. The big cities will be battlegrounds. Hell, they're halfway there now. Past halfway. But as bad as they are today, they'll seem like Disney World to people looking back a few years from now. After the big crash, I mean. It'll be dog eat dog then. Man eat man, some of the movies tell us."

The New Revelation, I thought. Suddenly I had an opening for the question I'd wanted to ask from the start. "Is that why you came out here?"

"Exactamundo," Willie said. "The people who survive the longest will be the ones in quiet spots like old Rapture. Places time has flat forgot." He scratched at the stubble on his chin, the motion a conscious or unconscious imitation of Emmett Haas ruffling his beard.

"You may have spent too much time here already," I said. "You sound like one of the Ordained."

"Shit," Willie said. "It ain't nothing like that." He grabbed his fishing rod and opened the Cavalier's door. But he didn't get out.

"Those coots believe in the reign of heaven. They think they're all gonna end up happy together in cotton candy land. What they're gonna get is the reign of chaos."

He repeated "reign of chaos," the words flat and rhythmless like the speech of a computer. Not for the first time, I felt he was reciting something he'd gotten down by rote.

"The world's going south, man. And it ain't coming back in a hurry. Maybe not for another thousand years. So I don't believe in no happy endings. I won't live long enough to see one. All I'm hoping for is to survive as long as I can. To ride out the approaching storm," he added, dropping back into the prepared copy.

"Is that what the guys you work with think?"

"Those dim bulbs? They only think about saving enough money to move up to Indianapolis. They don't know they're in the right place already, the place people from nowhere go to get lost.

"Of course, out west farther would be even better," Willie continued, pulling his knapsack onto his lap. "I don't mean the West Coast. That'll be hell with a tan. I mean Idaho or Montana. Someplace the fighting will never reach."

"Why not go there, then?"

"'Cause you need to know how to live off the land to survive in a real wilderness. You need to be a damn tingler. And I ain't one, not yet. But I'm working on it. This fall I'm going to learn how to hunt. I've got those lessons lined up already. In the meanwhile, I've got to get this damn fishing down."

He climbed out of the car and pulled his knapsack on with a grunt. "Thanks for the ride, man."

Twenty

WILLIE'S SHORTCUT carried me right into the center of Brookside. At any other time, I might have driven right through the place without noticing it. But I'd spent a couple of days in Rapture, so Brookside seemed like a regular metropolis. It had paved streets, a traffic light, two churches—both Baptist—and three fast-food restaurants. Those made me feel more religious than the churches.

I stopped at one called Hardee's for a very late lunch break. It took the drive-in operator and me several passes to work out an accent problem made worse by a whistling intercom. I knew the bacon cheeseburger I eventually acquired was a late lunch and not an early dinner because it had been cooked about the time Batsto's body had been discovered. There were other things about it that called Batsto to mind, but I was too hungry to dwell on them.

I was still chewing away at the last bit of bacon when I pulled into Dr. Stanger's lot. His full name appeared on a sign next to the front door: DR. THEODORE STANGER. His building was an old brick house or maybe not. The metal roof looked wrong for that, and there didn't seem to be enough windows. What windows there were didn't look right for a store, either, being tall and narrow.

Maybe it had always been a doctor's office, I thought, or once been a bank or the missing Third Baptist Church.

One of Dr. Stanger's patients was leaving as I climbed the front steps of the office. Actually, it was three of his patients on one pair of legs, a woman carrying two children. Despite her load, she held the door open for me. I wouldn't have gotten in otherwise, as the office was closed for the day.

The receptionist made that loud and clear as I stepped inside. She added, "And that door is locked," as though to suggest that I was technically guilty of breaking and entering. It was a rap I'd beaten once that day already, so I was undeterred.

"I'm not a patient," I said. "I'm here to see Dr. Stanger on an important matter."

The receptionist was a pyramidal young woman with a jutting jaw. The wiry hair on the top of her head had been brushed back, but it was still as close to vertical as it was to horizontal. There was a barrette pinned to the outermost layer of this hair, but it was strictly ornamental, like a coal button on the front of a snowman. She was seated behind a half wall that crowded a waiting area and an office into a single room.

Her age—she wasn't long out of high school—had given me the idea I could get past her on the strength of my unwiry but graying hair and a serious tone. But they grew up fast in Brookside. The young woman before me—Ms. Driser according to a nameplate on her desk—had done a particularly thorough job.

"Dr. Stanger sees salesmen on Tuesdays," she said. "Never on any other day. Never."

"I'm not a salesman, either. I'm here with an important message."

"Who from?"

"Dr. Krystal Bowden." I could have said the surgeon general or General Schwarzkopf for all the impression I made on her.

"What's the message?" she asked, picking up a yellow phone pad and a pen as though both were made of lead. It may have been her hands that were heavy. She wore a ring on every finger, thumbs included.

"It's confidential," I said. "For the doctor only."

That would have been my last line in the sketch but for a nurse who chose that moment to open a door behind the receptionist's desk. "Anyone else, Tawnya?" she asked.

Tawnya said no and I said yes at the same time. I hastily repeated the story about the message from Krystal, adding the word "epidemic" toward the end. It was the kind of inspiration of the moment I was always having to live down.

The nurse was probably Tawnya's mother. She had the same narrow eyes and wiry hair. But she lacked the receptionist's rough edges. They'd been worn away by decades of little surprises like me.

"Wait a minute," she said and disappeared through the door.

I backed away from the barricade, pretending to study a wall rack that contained some well-thumbed magazines. Never Gloat in Victory was a family motto. The nurse was back before I'd decided between *Sports Illustrated* and *People*. She guided me down a narrow hallway made narrower by stacks of cardboard file boxes, each one filled to overflowing with manila files. The clutter wasn't the result of some temporary reorganization, either. The boxes were dusty, and the pattern of wear in the hallway carpet showed they'd been a fixture for some time.

The nurse left me in a closet identified as EXAM ROOM TWO, saying, "The doctor will be right with you," as she surely had to the owner of every file in every box in the hallway archives.

The tiny room was paneled cheaply. Its principal feature was an examination table covered in white paper that came off a big roll fixed to the table's far end. Foreground interest was provided by a swivel chair covered in black vinyl and a matching stool. A chart on the wall nearest my nose listed the ten warning signs of depression. Halfway through the list, I was four for five, so I looked around for another distraction.

I found it in some faded color photographs hung above the examination table. At first I thought they must be pictures of Dr. Stanger's building, taken at different moments in its history. Several of the photos showed the brick building serving as a house, but the houses were different in each shot, having different shutters or no shutters, different front doors, different roofs. Even more disorienting was the landscaping. Huge trees in one picture gave way to bare fields in the next and then to the ornamental plantings of the suburbs.

About that time, my investigator instinct told me that the pictures were all of different houses that happened to be built to an identical pattern. But then, in a grouping at the far end of the wall, the little brick building ceased to be a house. It appeared as a series of businesses and even as a barn, bales of hay clearly visible through broken windows.

I was still puzzling it out when the door to the closet opened and Dr. Stanger shuffled in. He was at least sixty and built to wear his waistbands only inches below his shirt collars. Today the waistband belonged to shiny blue dress pants and the collar was on a white shirt with red stripes. A blue tie, clipped to the shirt, extended well below his belt. His hair was thinning, but what he had still reflected the regular spacing of his comb's teeth. His eyelids sagged and his pendulous lower lip drooped. His only sharp feature was his nose, but that was as sharp as a hawk's.

The walk from Exam Room One had winded him. He stood breathing through his mouth for a moment, his slender nose being inadequate for the task. After a few restorative gulps, he asked, "Recognize those pictures?"

"No," I said. "What are they?"

"Schoolhouses. Authentic Hoosier schoolhouses. One-room schoolhouses originally, although most of the ones you find today have been subdivided, like the rabbit warren we're standing in. Each schoolhouse was built to a specification laid down by the state legislature in Indianapolis."

He paused to swallow some more wind. "Those little buildings produced novelists, senators, doctors, lawyers. Too many damn lawyers. That is to say, they produced youngsters prepared to study to be all those things. Mostly they produced literate farm people, the glory of the nation.

"Now our local high school—the consolidated school they call it—is bigger than the college I attended, a big windowless thing like an atom bomb factory. And what it mostly turns out are functional illiterates."

"You think that's due to the architecture?"

"It's due to a thousand things," Stanger said, "but they're all interconnected." He wove his long fingers together, almost dropping the clipboard he carried beneath one spindly arm. "A million little decisions, little improvements, little concessions that have added up to our world. You can't point to any one thing, but some things, like those schoolhouses, are signposts of the journey.

"That's why I like them. One of the reasons. I used to spend my weekends driving around the state photographing them. I thought about putting them together—the pictures—in a book. Together with my observations on their import. A philosophical magnum opus. But I never did."

He sat down heavily on the stool, propelling it backward toward the door. The movement was well practiced, I realized. Unless the doctor crowded the door, there wasn't enough room for the patient to sit in the chair he was gesturing me toward. I wondered if the other patients felt as trapped by the arrangement as I did.

"You'd better start off by telling me who you are," Stanger said.

I did, barely getting out my name and that of Dr. Bowden before Stanger cut me off. "What's this epidemic?"

"Millennialism," I said, my chat with Willie still in my thoughts.

"Millennialism," Stanger repeated, gazing up at the ceiling like a man who'd been tossed an anagram or some other puzzle. "The belief in the millennium. Specifically, the belief in Christ's thousand-year reign on earth mentioned in Revelation. More generally, a belief in some great change—great happiness or great tribulation—connected with the end of a period of one thousand years. There's a question to chew on in your idle moments. Why does one person long for the end time while the next dreads it? Why for that matter do certain generations seem obsessed with the end of the world while others barely give it a thought?"

I said the first word of "I don't know."

"There's certainly no shortage of interest in the end time these days," Stanger continued. "It's practically endemic to Rapture, where Dr. Bowden lives. It's natural enough for people there to be thinking of Christ's Second Coming, since the town was founded to celebrate the event."

"Only He's coming by spaceship this time," I said, still free-associating.

Stanger laughed, his laugh being his gulpy breathing shifted into reverse. It coated his lower lip with saliva, which he wiped away with his handkerchief.

"Are you sure your message is from Dr. Bowden?" he asked. "Are you sure it isn't from Minnie Feasey?"

"Minnie?"

"That's what her husband Ora always called her. I was allowed to, too, after I'd treated her for about twenty years. I knew her long before she became a ufologist. That's a UFO specialist. It always tickles me that ufologist rhymes with urologist. Given what those space aliens are always examining, they're likely to be urologists. Interstellar urologists."

"Are you a ufologist?" I asked.

That question had the doctor wiping at his lower lip again. "Me? No. I'm a Mason. A person needs some stillness in his life, and that's plenty for me. But I used to enjoy Minnie's lectures. She was a patient of mine until Dr. Bowden moved in. So was Ora Feasey. We lost him a few years back. Heart attack. That's what made Minnie jump the rails, so to speak. That's my opinion. The two of them had just started their retirement when Ora had his attack. Which means that their whole life together—they were married forty years—had been aimed at a single mark. And they missed it. Minnie missed it. Ora just died. She ricocheted off in a new direction. She's been ricocheting ever since."

Stanger's wind was better when he was sitting down. Still, he had to break for air from time to time. He paused now, giving me the chance to get most of a question out.

"Do you know Prestina Shi—?"

"Another character," Stanger said. "Her hobbyhorse is herbs. She has the idea that the world was a healthier place a hundred years ago. You can tell her the average life expectancy was considerably shorter in those healthy times than it is today. She doesn't believe you. Has Shipe turned up?"

"No. That's why I came to Rapture. Dr. Bowden asked me to help her find Prestina. Could you tell me a little about her?"

"Did Dr. Bowden send you over here to ask me that? I don't believe it. She knows all about doctor-patient confidentiality. Besides, she probably knows Shipe as well as I do by now. Doesn't take long to read an open book."

I started to tell him the bad news about Krystal's own disappearance. As usual, he didn't let me finish. This time, though, his reason wasn't impatience.

"I know all about that. I just wanted to see if you were going to tell me yourself or lead me on. Deputy Dix called to tell me I'd be covering for Dr. Bowden indefinitely. He didn't mention you, though."

"He thinks I'm safely tucked away at the Double Nickel Motel."

"I got the impression there was more going on than Dix was willing to share. What else has happened?"

I told him about Clyde Batsto's murder. The news was enough to quiet the doctor until I'd made it through to a period.

"Why didn't Dix tell me all that himself?" he asked. "Does he really think he can keep it bottled up? If he does, he's even more of an outsider than I thought."

"Dix is an outsider?"

"Of course he is. Moved up from Evansville a few years back. No family with that history of allergies could survive very long around here. They'd be too busy blowing their noses to reproduce."

He dabbed his lip and asked, "Who do they think might have done in Clyde Batsto?"

"Dr. Bowden's name has come up."

"For the love of heaven why?"

I told him the item I'd been holding back, the drugs hidden in the herb shipments, convinced he'd find out soon enough. I then tried to tie that in to the larger issue of drug smuggling in Rapture, but that part of the story was old news to Stanger.

"What did I tell you about our schools going downhill? Here's a perfect example. To think of anyone connecting Dr. Bowden and drugs. Do you believe that nonsense?"

"No."

He reached over and put his cool, dry hand on mine. "Good man."

I realized then that I'd misread the doctor's relationship with Krystal. His few mentions of her—always formal and correct—and the references to the patients he'd lost to her had led me to think he resented her. Now I decided there might be a totally different emotion at work. To test my theory I asked, "Why don't you think she's involved?"

"Because I know her work. I know what she came here to do. It's what I came for myself, forty years ago. She means to make life better for the people of this godforsaken corner of the world. That's the direct opposite of what a drug dealer hopes to accomplish. The antithesis." This time, he wiped his nose as well as his lip.

"That brings us back to Prestina Shipe," I said.

"If you're thinking of Shipe as a suspect, you're even further off the beam than Dix. The Prestina Shipe I knew was a simple country woman. She'd as soon think of baking children in her oven as poisoning them with drugs."

Then, without any prompting from me, he started to talk himself into the idea. "It would be a twist anyway. One hell of a twist. It's dangerous to stereotype, to assume. Is it possible? Could such a person do such a terrible thing so late in life? Minnie Feasey did. She abandoned the religion she was born and raised to. Is setting aside your hope of salvation any less serious than selling drugs?"

"No," I said before I understood that the question was rhetorical. To deflect Stanger's renewed interest in me, I added, "Feasey had a traumatic experience to explain her course change. Did anything traumatic happen to Prestina?"

"Yes," Stanger said. "She got old. That's as traumatic an event as you could ask for. You'll find out someday. You'll wake up and realize that your dreams for your life haven't come true and aren't going to come true."

By that definition, I'd been old for twenty years. But Stanger was citing his own experience, not mine.

"I once dreamed of a Stanger Hospital. Would you believe it? Then, as the years passed, it became the Stanger Clinic." He looked around the little room with the bowed paneling. "Lately my dream has been that there'd be somebody around to take my place."

We both thought about the chances of that dream coming true.

While we sat there, I had another idea. "You said that Prestina has a naive faith in her herbs. Could she feel the same way about these drugs?"

"What do you mean?"

"Suppose someone convinced her that methamphetamine was the equivalent of a modern herb. That it was something beneficial that the government or the pharmaceutical companies were keeping away from people. Could she have been persuaded to help distribute them that way?"

"Hmm," Stanger said. "She is unworldly. But is anyone that unworldly? I wonder."

He wondered for a full sweep of the wall clock's second hand. Then he settled slowly back against the door. "No. It can't be Shipe. I'll never believe it. You'll have to look elsewhere. And you have to keep looking. Promise me that. You won't give up."

I told him I wouldn't.

"Good. And I'll keep in touch with the local grapevine. Maybe I'll hear something useful for a change. Where can I get hold of you tomorrow? The Double Nickel?"

"Try Deputy Dix's cellblock," I said. "I should be in custody myself by then."

Twenty-one

ON MY WAY OUT OF BROOKSIDE, I spotted a little green sign that said AIRPORT and pointed to the west, the direction the sun was taking. I made the turn and followed a road that itself followed a winding creek with sharply eroded banks of reddish clay. After a mile or two, the road crossed the water on an old iron bridge that had wooden planks for a bed. Some mottled cows were dining in a field next to the bridge. One or two of them looked up as the Cavalier thumped across it. Perhaps they were wondering if this was the day the whole affair would finally fall into the creek. That's what I was wondering, but it didn't happen.

Just beyond the bridge was Brookside Airport. I saw a rusted water tower first, an old-style one with four legs and a conical hat. It turned out to belong to a deserted factory across the road. The airport was too small to need anything larger than a water cooler.

I drove in past a low building that looked like a very long picnic shelter divided into stalls. That is, the building had a roof and walls running from the front to the back but no wall on the front or on the back. Each open-ended stall contained an airplane, more than one of them up to its belly in weeds. I had a feeling of déjà vu and finally tied it to a little airport on Long Island I'd visited once in an earlier life.

The main hangar at Brookside was barely large enough to rate the name, but it had been painted recently and it sported a bright orange windsock at the peak of its roof. There was a leanto-like shed attached to the side of the hangar nearest the gravel lot where I parked my car. The shed's door bore the legend BROOKSIDE AVIATION, and it was closed. The hangar's oversize garage door stood open, but there wasn't anything stirring inside or even anything that looked capable of stirring. The few planes on display there were partially disassembled. Two had given up their cowlings and one its engine. Another had lost its skin, revealing a complex and fragile skeleton.

The airport vigilance committee greeted me just outside the office door. It might have been a subcommittee, as it consisted of a small, silent dog. It was white with black spots, like the cows watching the old bridge—but probably not related to them. The cows each had four legs, after the pattern of the rusted water tower. The little dog had only three. It hobbled up and sniffed at the hand I held out to it and then at my shoes and the cuffs of my pants. Was there some lingering trace, I wondered, of Blue, the dog I'd comforted earlier that day? Or was this amputee sorting through the scents of all the stories I'd waded through since? If he could do that, he'd be worth his weight in T-bones.

I had one more story to hear before the sun set. I opened the office door in search of it, the little dog hopping in beside me. We found a man in gray coveralls and a black cap seated on the floor. Beside him were an open box, a few pieces of oddly shaped Styrofoam, and a half dozen objects in clear plastic packages. These included loops of cable, booklets, a remote control, and a VCR. The man in the coveralls was slitting the wrapping on the VCR, slitting it carefully as though he hoped to use the plastic for something else, perhaps to cover the naked airplane in the hanger.

"Who you got there, Trigear?" he asked, addressing the dog.

Trigear had traded in my mysteries for the scents of the empty box and didn't reply.

"Know anything about setting up one of these?" the man asked me. He wore his cap pushed well back, like a kid in a comic strip.

He was the only person I'd spoken to that day besides Willie who wasn't an authority figure, either by virtue of age or a badge. I reacted to the novelty by getting flip. "Sorry. I'm majoring in answering machines."

He snapped his penknife closed. "It's for my flight school. All the ground school stuff is done by tape these days. Are you interested in flying lessons? It's never too late to learn."

"That's the hope I cling to," I said. I pointed to a metal propeller that spanned the far wall of a nook that held a cluttered desk. The propeller's tips were bent back at crazy angles. "Aren't you afraid that souvenir will scare students away?"

"Just giving them a chance to learn from someone else's experience. That prop's from a Piper Arrow, a retractable gear plane. The pilot forgot to put his wheels down before he landed. They say there are only two kinds of pilots: those who have done that and those who will."

"What kind are you?" I asked, still sounding a little wiseassed to my somewhat detached self.

"I'm an even dumber variety," the man said as he stood. "The kind that owns an airport. My name is Clay Ford."

He was tall—six three or four—and rangy. His coveralls were tight through the shoulders and loose everywhere else, especially at the knees and elbows, where the material sagged under a coating of grease.

"My name is Owen Keane," I said. To satisfy my mood, I added, "I'm a ufologist."

"Come again?" Ford said, his regular features open and unsuspicious.

"Someone who studies UFOs."

"It was answering machines a minute ago," the pilot said, suggesting that his face was an unreliable indicator of his thoughts.

"I've spoken with a woman who reported seeing strange lights in the sky over Rapture. That's a town just south of here."

"I know," Ford said.

"Any chance you've seen something like that?"

"Might be. Care for some coffee?" He pointed toward a pot in the corner that was so discolored it was impossible to judge the level of its contents. At the same time, Ford moved toward the desk that stood beneath the damaged prop. "Help yourself," he said. "My hands are a little dirty."

I turned down the offer, noting that Ford's hands were a lot cleaner than his coffee pot. Still, he went through the motions of wiping them on a rag he found on the desk. Then he sniffed the rag, cursed mildly, tossed it aside, and opened a drawer of the desk. Out of it he extracted not a clean rag but a gun.

It was a big revolver with a long barrel, which he pointed at me.

"Hands up, please," he said.

I raised my hands.

"Behind your head would be better," Ford said. "And turn around."

The last thing I saw before I complied was Trigear making a hurried exit through a door near Ford's desk. When I was facing the door to the parking lot, Ford came over and patted me down. Then he told me to relax.

I turned around. My host was seated on the edge of his desk, pointing the gun at the floor. "What goes on?" I asked.

"You tell me," he said. "Start with who you really are."

"My name is still Keane. You can check my driver's license."

"How about your ufologist identification card? Have that handy?"

I thought for a wild moment that Ford was one of those abductees Feasey had told me about, one who had mistaken me for
a little green man, come to take him back for a checkup. But Ford
didn't look that rattled. In fact, he didn't look rattled at all.

A more likely explanation shouldered its way to the front of my
crowded head. Ford was one of the drug smugglers. I'd panicked
him by coming in and asking about the lights over Rapture. The
problem again was Ford's cool. He didn't look like a man who'd
been panicked. And he owned his own airport. He'd have no reason to be landing planes in Rapture.

All that reasoning went by in a blur, more of an impression
than an argument. My mind seemed more interested in an aca-
demic point: Does a person grow used to being held at gunpoint
after the phenomenon is experienced several times? I was trying
to account for how calm my voice sounded when I finally spoke.

"I'm not a UFO hunter," I said. "But I am interested in those
lights. I think they may be connected to a series of disappearances
in Rapture."

"Disappearances?"

I almost said kidnappings by way of clarification, but making a
federal case of it didn't seem like the right move somehow. "Two
women vanished from their homes. One early Tuesday and one
last night. I want to get them back safely. That's all."

I was giving Ford the chance to discuss the issue without mentioning drug smuggling. He didn't take me up on it.

"You want to find these women and you came here to talk
about lights in the sky. So you think the lights and the disappearances are connected. You're not a UFO nutball. So you must think
these women are missing because of the mystery shipments that
have been coming into this area by air. Are you a narc? I'd be in a
world of trouble if you were." He raised the gun slightly to indicate the source of his hypothetical trouble.

I'd been thinking that just the opposite was true, that an un-armed narc visiting Brookside Airport would be the one in the world of trouble. Ford's take on the situation gave me hope.

"I'm not a cop," I said. "I'm not a drug smuggler, either. I'm a friend of one of the missing women."

"I may owe you an apology," Ford said.

"Put that thing away and you can consider the apology accepted," I said. He didn't move. "Why did you think one of the drug smugglers would come here?"

"Because I've seen those lights you spoke about. Three weeks ago tomorrow. I'd been down to Louisville for the day, seeing a friend. I was flying back."

"After dark?"

"She's a really good friend," Ford said, showing his dimples for the first time. "Besides, night flying in this part of the country is beautiful. There isn't very much traffic, and if it isn't too late, the lights of the towns stand out like islands in a black sea. This was between nine and ten o'clock. I was east of here, tracking the two eight zero radial of the Nabb VOR."

I tapped his new VCR with my shoe. "Which videotape explains all of that?"

"Sorry. All I meant was I was navigating via a radio directional beacon. I was starting to think about beginning my descent when these lights came on out of nowhere. Two intense lights in the sky over Rapture. They were the landing lights of a plane. I never saw any navigation lights—the red and green wingtip lights and the rotating beacon all planes show after dark—just the landing lights. They were as bright as an airliner's, but set closer together."

"On the wings of a smaller plane?"

"I only know they weren't much higher than treetop level. Then they were gone. The plane might have landed, or the pilot might have spotted my lights and switched his off."

"In which case," I said, "he or she would have kept an eye on you, maybe even watched you land. So you've been waiting for someone to come nosing around, asking if you'd seen any lights."

Ford nodded. "I did for a while. Then I pretty much forgot about it. Until you came in. Guess I jumped to the wrong conclusion. Sorry again. Sorry I can't help you with those missing women, either."

He was tying my story to his with a neat bow. It was so neat it took me a second or two to realize that his end of the rope was short by about a yard.

"Why did you assume there was something illegal going on when you saw those lights?" I asked.

"There've been rumors floating around about DEA men working the county," Ford said. He was wearing his open, unsuspicious expression again. I didn't trust it.

"Those rumors didn't involve airplanes," I said. "What made you connect the two? Was it because the DEA's been out here, questioning you about strange planes?"

Ford hesitated and then said, "I guess." The hesitation reversed his answer's polarity.

"One of those missing women is seventy-two years old. The other one's the local doctor, Dr. Krystal Bowden."

"I've heard of her," the pilot said. "Good things."

He looked at the gun in his hand for a while. Then he said, "I heard a rumor that did involve an airplane. A very specific plane. A Helio Courier. That's a STOL ship they built back in the seventies."

"STOL?"

"Short takeoff and landing. The Helio has special wings with features like leading-edge slots and extralarge flaps, things designed to shorten your takeoff run and your rollout after landing. It has long landing gear struts, too. It was built for getting in and out of unprepared strips in the bush."

"You've seen one around here?"

"I may have seen the lights of one. If the rumor is right. I heard about it up at Greenwood Airport, just south of Indy. This was a couple of weeks before I saw the lights over Rapture. I was talking with a pilot . . ." Ford started to say the pilot's name and caught himself. "This guy and I worked as instructors together one summer while we were still in school. He'd heard a story from another pilot, a Greenwood guy who'd stopped off at Sullivan County Airport one night. That's a nice little field over by the Illinois line.

"This Greenwood pilot . . ."

"Make it easy on yourself," I said. "Call him Smith."

Ford showed me the dimples again. "Okay. This Smith was sitting in the Sullivan Airport's office, shooting the breeze, when a plane came in. A Helio Courier. You hardly ever see one, so Smith was curious. He got more curious when the Helio's pilot didn't ask to use the office phone to close his flight plan—to report to Flight Service that he'd landed. That made Smith figure the Helio wasn't on a flight plan, which is unusual at night.

"The plane had lost a magneto. That's a mechanical device that fires the spark plugs. They used them in cars years ago. Light planes still use them, two for each engine for redundancy. The Helio limped into Sullivan on one mag. The Helio is an unusual bird, but it has a fairly common engine. The local mechanic was able to come in and fix it that night. Smith offered to help and found out in a hurry he wasn't welcome. In fact, he claimed the Helio pilot threatened him when he got too close to the plane.

"Smith learned later from the mechanic that the Helio's interior had been stripped, maybe to save weight. The mechanic thought the plane might have been fitted with extra fuel tanks, too. And there was another modification: landing lights as big as your head."

"So what happened?"

"Nothing. When the engine was fixed, the pilot paid in cash and disappeared."

"Did the mechanic report it?" I asked, thinking it was a story that Fallon would pay to hear.

Ford shrugged.

"How about Smith?"

"People don't like to get involved."

"Is that why you didn't report the lights you saw to the DEA?"

"I don't know any DEA," Ford said a little sullenly. He got up, put his gun back in its drawer, and locked it.

"You haven't met the agents who've been checking out airports in this county?"

"If they checked this airport, they used a spy satellite. I haven't seen anybody around here. And Trigear and I sleep in the hangar."

He was angry. At himself, I thought, for being afraid to get involved. I was only half right, but that was progress for me.

"My father was a pilot, too," Ford said. "Out in California. Years ago he got involved with some hard cases. It had something to do with drugs. He never would tell me all the details. He wouldn't have told me about it at all, but I was always asking him how he came to walk with a limp. I thought he'd cracked up a plane. It turned out the hard cases had worked him over. After that, it came to me that my father more than walked with a limp. He lived with a limp. With his head bowed and his eyes on the pavement.

"Ever since I realized that, I've wanted to hit back at those guys for what they did to my father. To hit back at them or crumbs like them. When I finally got my chance, I turned out to be too worried about my own skin to do a damn thing."

"It's not too late," I said. I was thinking of taking him to see Fallon. But I made the mistake of asking another question. "Have you flown over Rapture in the daytime?"

"Of course. Lots of times."

"Is there a field there big enough to land a Helio Courier?"

Ford pushed his ball cap even farther back. "Dunno. This time of year most fields are still planted. I know how we can find out, though."

He tugged the cap down square. It gave him a gung ho look I didn't care for. I liked what he had to say next even less.

"There's still enough light left for a short hop. We can fly over there and check it out. Come on."

Twenty-two

"I'VE GOT WHAT WE NEED out on the ramp," Ford said. He collected a pair of sunglasses, handed me a bulky headset, and dug another out of the desk for himself. "Done much flying in light planes?"

"No." I would have gone on to say that I had to take Dramamine just to talk to a travel agent, but Ford was already out the door, the side door Trigear had used. It led to the hangar, which seemed vast and even orderly after the office. We didn't stay there long. Ford strode across the oil-stained concrete and out through the front door, talking as he went.

"I just gave this ship its annual inspection. I had it up for a test hop an hour ago, so we can cut short the preflight. The guy who owns it is a buddy of mine. He lets me use it whenever I get the itch."

Beyond the hangar was a patch of blacktop from which two very short gas pumps rose. Parked near them was a little yellow plane with a black lightning bolt painted down its side. I froze in my tracks when I saw it. It was the original of the little model that hung above Batsto's bed. I started to ask Ford if he'd known Batsto, but the idea of closing yet another circle frightened me more than the prospect of flight.

The plane sat with its tail on the ground and its nose high, its propeller tilted up at the cloudless sky. The prop caught my eye right away, because it was made of wood. My second cause for alarm was the cylinder heads protruding through holes in the cowling. The kicker was the realization that the cowling was the only metal skin on the entire plane. The wings and fuselage were covered in some kind of fabric.

"A beauty, isn't she?" Ford called to me. "Just the thing for going low and slow. It's a J-3 Piper Cub. A lot of people still call any light airplane a Piper Cub. This is the genuine article."

He started to untie a nylon rope that ran from a heavy staple in the blacktop up to a ring on the plane's wing strut. "Grab the tie down on the other side. I'll get the tail."

"Don't you have anything newer?"

"This is new as Cubs go," Ford replied on his way to untie the tail. "Almost as new as you can find. They started making them in 1939. During the war they built them for the army as the L-4. They were artillery spotters. This one dates from the next to the last year of postwar production: 1946."

He was up at the cowling by then. He lifted a section of it and pulled out a dipstick. "Plenty of oil."

"Good," I said. One of the few facts I'd collected about airplanes during my wanderings was that they didn't fly very well without oil.

"I topped off the gas before I parked it. We're ready to go. I'd leave that on if I were you."

I'd started to remove my sports coat. The thought of climbing into that little plane was making the cool evening seem very warm.

"It'll be kinda brisk up there," Ford explained.

"How's the ventilation in this thing?" I asked, thinking of the little nozzles on an airliner's ceiling that I routinely rotated to full blast as soon as I sat down.

"The only planes that beat it have open cockpits," Ford said. He opened the door, which was wide and bizarre, consisting of two trapezoid-shaped sections. The lower half was canvas covered and folded down against the side of the plane. The upper half, which was glass and looked like a cellar window drawn by Dr. Seuss, folded up against the wing.

"I'll get in first," Ford said. "It's a little bit of an acquired skill." The two tandem seats had rounded backs covered in the worn black vinyl I'd last seen in Stanger's examining room. I panicked all over again when I realized that Ford was getting into the backseat.

"You can have the front," I said politely if a little forcefully.

But the pilot was already in. "You have to sit back here when you solo this bird. It's a weight and balance thing. And you sit back here when you're teaching a student to fly it. Don't worry. It's got dual controls. What isn't dual I can reach.

"Use that little step there. It's stronger than it looks. Sit down first and lift your left leg over the joystick. Yeah, you've got to yank your leg in while you're lifting it. Watch the instrument panel. Right. Stick your foot in there to the left of the radio stack. There wasn't any room for radios in the panel—they didn't plan on them in 1946—so we had to hang them underneath. Sorry it's so cramped."

Cramped wasn't the word for it. My knees were almost up to my chin. I had to tuck my elbows in to avoid Ford's feet, which he'd slid up on either side of my seat. The situation got even worse when he told me I couldn't use the footrests I'd found underneath the dashboard.

"Those are the rudder pedals," Ford said. "I've got another set back here." He moved his feet back and forth, and I tucked my elbows in tighter. "Got your seat belt on? Good. Move your head to the left. Your other left."

He reached past my ear and started pulling knobs and pressing switches on the control panel, talking first to me and then to himself. "This ship wasn't delivered with an electrical system or a self-starter. Luckily, the current owner had both installed, or one of us would be out there swinging the prop by hand. Let's see. Mixture full rich. Electrical equipment off. Master switch on. Ignition switch to both mags."

He leaned out the still open door and shouted, "Clear prop!" To Trigear presumably. At the same time, the propeller began to turn. The engine caught a second later, and the prop became a wooden blur.

The engine noise seemed to have more rattling in it than was healthy. I scanned the simple panel and found an oil pressure gauge. It had a red, a yellow, and a green range. The little needle was in the yellow. I pointed that out to Ford. He gunned the engine, and the needle rose slowly into the green.

"Headset on," he shouted in my ear. While I struggled into the headset, Ford collected the wires that dangled from it and plugged them into a little black box near my left elbow. Then he reached down between my legs to flip some switches on the radio stack.

"I beg your pardon," I said, hearing the words come faintly through my headphones.

Ford came on next, sounding like an FM deejay. "Hear me okay? Move that boom mike a little closer to your mouth. The intercom is voice activated, as you've already discovered. Here we go."

I reached over to close the door. "Leave it," Ford said. "You wanted ventilation, right? And we'll get a better view of Rapture." He slid open a smaller window on the left side of the cabin for good measure. "Smell that grass?"

We had rolled off the tarmac and onto a grassy taxiway. My imagination fell in with Ford's suggestion. I decided I really could smell the grass as it was pressed down by the Cub's fat tires. It was a nice addition to the plane's other smells: gasoline, oil, hot metal, hot Owen Keane. I checked the oil gauge again, deciding I'd make it my special duty. The needle was still in the green portion of the dial.

The little plane stopped moving. Ford began talking to himself again or maybe reading from a checklist. "Seat belts fastened. Door and windows secured. Controls free and correct." The joystick whacked me on both knees. "Engine to eighteen hundred rpm. Oil in the green." He reached over my shoulder with his left arm. "Left mag okay. Right mag okay. Good news, Keane, we've got one more magneto working than that wounded Helio did."

"Swell," I said, my electronically reproduced voice sounding small and disembodied.

"Carburetor heat works," Ford continued. "Throttle back. Altimeter's still showing field elevation. Gyro compass agrees with magnetic compass. Ready to defy gravity?"

"Roger," I said. Ford banged me on the shoulder.

When he spoke again, he sounded less like a disc jockey than a public service announcer. "Brookside traffic, Piper seven zero six four niner is departing grass strip six, Brookside."

The little plane pivoted and waddled onto the runway, a long stretch of grass with a shallow ditch on either side. The engine rose to full voice, and we started to accelerate. Almost immediately, the tail rose off the ground. I realized I'd been leaning forward in my seat the whole time I'd been in the plane. Before I could force myself to settle back, we were off. The Cub turned a little to the left—weathercocking into the wind—but we continued to track straight down the line of the runway. Then the airport was gone, replaced by a glimpse of the old bridge and the cows and then mighty Brookside itself.

We weren't all that high, but the town had already acquired a certain unity, a cohesiveness it lacked at ground level. It even had beauty. The low sun was bathing it in an intense, Hollywood light and casting dramatic shadows that set off every ordinary little house, underscoring them, lifting them from their flat, square yards.

We banked to the left. "Next stop Rapture," Ford said. "No point in climbing any more if we're going spying. Brookside traffic, Piper seven zero six four niner departing the pattern to the south. Brookside."

As we continued to turn, the relatively flat land around Brookside gave way to rolling ground. Most of it was still farmland, but as first Fallon and then Ford had warned me, the cleared ground was almost all planted, mostly with corn, a lot of it turning brown. That made the cornfields stand out against the lush green landscape, but not as much as some other fields scattered about, which were a bright yellow.

"What is that down there?" I asked. "Mustard?"

"Right," Ford said, laughing. "They raise the hot dogs down in Texas. Isn't safe to have them too close to the mustard fields."

"So what is it really?"

"Soybeans. They get real pretty this time of year."

"They don't look very tall."

"They're not. Knee high."

"Could a plane land in a field of soybeans?"

"Once maybe. After that you could use it as a scarecrow. Any planted field is dicey because the ground's been plowed into furrows. Beans are worse than corn because they're viney. They grab hold of your gear and flip you over.

"There's Rapture up ahead. See those three wooded hills in a line? The town is on the middle hill. You should see this area in the fall. In another three weeks, there won't be a prettier spot in the country."

It was a contender for the title right now, I thought. The hills rose up from the surrounding farmland, a chain of volcanic islands in a green sea. The islands were also green, intensely so on their western, sunlit slopes. Here and there, the tops of individual trees had begun to turn, and the color change was more striking than anything I'd seen on the ground. There were daubs of gold and orange and blood red, but it was just a foretaste of the riot to come.

I found myself regretting that I wouldn't be around to see the whole landscape painted in the same colors. That reget led me to a discovery: for the first time in my life I was enjoying being in an airplane. The Cub was chugging through the glassy air like a boat on a millpond. The air rushing by was crisp—I'd drawn the lapels of my jacket together—but it wasn't reviving me. The air seemed to be intoxicating me, giving me a phony sense of peace and well-being. I felt as though the prop wash was removing the dust of my long day grain by grain. Rapture seemed a world away, even as it appeared beneath the tires of the plane.

The ground had risen to meet us. We were no more than a few hundred feet above the trees. Ford announced that he would do a three sixty, and we banked. I glimpsed Feasey's pink house and, down in its dark hollow, the coffin works. Someone was standing outside the building. Emmett Haas. I waved to him, but he didn't look up.

Then the plane bumped gently. "What was that?"

"We hit our own wake turbulence," Ford said. "That's the sign of a perfect three-hundred-sixty-degree turn. I don't see any likely landing fields for your smugglers, do you?"

I hadn't even been looking. I'd forgotten all about drugs and disappearances and even about my client. I scanned the horizon sleepily. Out beyond the nose was the third hill in the Rapture chain. The highest hill.

"There's something up ahead," I said.

"Damn," Ford said. "How did I miss that? It looks like the whole crown of the hill's been cleared. Let's take a look."

Ford had missed it—anyone might have—because the top of the hill was almost the same color as the trees that ringed it. The sun had descended to the perfect angle to set the damage off, revealing a shallow, oval crater, its floor a grass-covered field. A field on the highest ground anywhere near the town.

"Rapture Meadow," I said, feeling even dreamier. The high holy place of the Ordained of God. Haas had said it still existed, but seeing it there gave me a shock. I felt as though I'd stumbled across Noah's Ark or Shangri-la. "Is it big enough for a plane?"

"I think so. It must be eight hundred feet lengthwise. Let's line up for a landing and see how it looks. Don't worry," he said as he throttled back the engine. "We practice emergency landings like this all the time."

I wasn't worried, oddly. Finding Rapture Meadow had intensified my feeling that the entire flight was an experience set apart from my visit to Indiana, a discrete segment of time with priorities that were simple and understandable. Where I was now, Batsto hadn't died. Krystal and Shipe hadn't disappeared. None of them even existed. Nothing seemed to matter except coming to rest in the emerald field that was rising up beyond the Cub's long nose.

"Yeah," Ford said, breaking into my dream. "I could make it into that field. In a Helio Courier, I could even make it out again. We've gotten low enough for this experiment. Hold on now, Keane. We're going around."

I felt more than heard the little engine clatter back to life. I studied the meadow as we passed over it, looking for tire tracks and seeing only the pattern of a mower that cut a wide swath.

Then, as we passed the far end of the field, the Cub rose and dropped, as though we'd ridden over an invisible speed bump. My nerves came back on line with a jolt. "Was that more wake turbulence?"

"I don't know what that was," Ford said.

I glanced at my security blanket, the oil gauge. The needle was in the yellow and falling.

Ford had seen it, too. "Damn," he said. "A line must have broken; we're bleeding oil. It has to be the engine and not the gauge. Listen to it!"

I didn't have to listen. I could feel the engine shaking through the seat of my pants. The gauges on the panel had begun vibrating so much I couldn't read them.

Ford reached past me roughly. "Have to shut it down before it seizes." He yanked a fat knob at the bottom of the panel. The noise and vibration dropped away, and one blade of the wooden prop reappeared, pointing to two o'clock.

"The meadow," I said.

"No," Ford said, calm again now. "We're too low for a one eighty. We'd spin into the trees. We have to make it down to the flat and take our chances. See if you can switch the radio to the emergency frequency. One twenty-one point five. The knob's to the left of the display."

I found the knob but never managed to turn it. I was distracted by the sight of treetops just below our wheels as we swept down the hill.

"Forget it," Ford said, his head next to mine as he leaned forward. He flipped a switch on the panel and the radio stack went dead. "Lose the headset. Protect your head if you can. I'm going to try for that field to the left."

I spotted the break in the trees. The field was small and golden yellow. Soybeans. I whispered the word, but in the engineless plane, Ford heard me.

"Them or hardwood," he said.

I could see the furrows in the field. Ford lined us up with them as the belly of the plane kissed the top of the last tree. In that instant, our problem turned itself inside out. Instead of dropping too fast, we weren't dropping fast enough. We floated on and on as the trees lining the far side of the field rushed toward us.

"Don't stall it," Ford said, whispering now himself. "Don't stall it."

We touched down hard, and I remembered Ford's instruction to cover my head. I got one arm around it and braced the other against the instrument panel as we nosed over.

Twenty-three

I DON'T THINK I EVER LOST CONSCIOUSNESS. I shut my eyes, though. The first thing I saw when I opened them was printing. Or was it writing? Some of the characters were squared and bold, but others were faint and flowed like script. The nearest ones were so close to my eyes it hurt to focus on them. So I looked at the ones in the middle distance, which were hazier and appeared to be written on top of other characters. Many others. It was like reading a book with no paper, just layers and layers of type. Silver type in a black void. And I couldn't decipher a single letter. I wasn't alarmed by that. I'd figure it out, I knew, when my head cleared.

It cleared with that thought. I realized that I was lying slumped forward with my face resting against the instrument panel. My mysterious writing was only the scratches on the panel's ancient paint, hundreds of them, bold and faint, made by random finger-nails and tools. I'd read more into less in the past, I might have re-flected, if I'd been in a reflective mood.

I wasn't up to it just then. I'd been struck on the head, but I couldn't remember it happening. My right shoulder felt like a jammed finger, and my left arm, still under my head, ached as it had when I'd broken it years before. Good, I thought, I've broken it again. Krystal can set it for me this time and do it right.

Further planning of my future was interrupted by movement in the seat behind me. Above me, I mean. I'd deduced from my dependence on the instrument panel that the plane had come to rest on its nose.

"Keane," Ford said. "Are you okay? Can you get out? We should get out of here. There still could be a fire."

That observation swept away what cobwebs remained. I undid my seat belt and exited the plane feet first. Ford, suspended above me, hurried me along. He did that by urging me and—more effectively—by bleeding on me. I thought I'd have to help him down, but he was out of the Cub before I'd found my land legs. He led me a safe distance from the plane, where we could look each other over in the dying light.

Ford was bleeding from his nose. It was probably broken, but that was only my uneducated guess. I was more confident about what he'd broken it on, namely, the back of my head. I only had to touch a certain spot to flash back to the blow I'd felt as the plane came to rest.

Ford's bloody nose and the corresponding lump on my head were the worst of our injuries. The arm I thought I'd fractured again was only bruised. My right shoulder, though sore, worked fine, even after the solicitous Ford had yanked on it to unjam it.

"Thank God," he said after we'd finished tallying the bill. "I can't tell you how pissed I am at myself, Keane. I got us way too low on that last pass. I never should have risked it. I wrecked the plane and almost broke our necks. Damn," he concluded and giggled.

I felt a little like giggling myself, but hearing Ford do it cured me. It cured him, too. He wiped at his nose and asked, "Who is Lynn Baxter?"

"Who?"

"Just as we touched down, you said, 'Lynn Baxter.'"

That was news to me. Baxter was another of my lost clients. An especially lost one, as she'd been dead for forty years when I took up her murder case.

"She was a woman who died in an airplane crash," I said.

"She wouldn't happen to be the patron saint of airplane crashes, would she? Somebody was looking out for us. We wouldn't walk away from that landing again if we tried it ten more times."

Ford would be dead of old age before I'd try it one more time, but I didn't get the chance to tell him so. He'd filed me away under old business and gone to look over his real concern, the wrecked plane.

When I joined him, he was examining the plane's belly, sniffing it, feeling it with his fingertips and rubbing them together. "Here's our oil," he said. "I just changed the damn stuff, too."

He followed the river downward to what had been its source when the plane had been right side up: the metal engine cowling. There were two holes in the bottom of the cowling. One was the size of a silver dollar and regularly shaped. It was in the exact center of the cowling, at what would be its lowest point when the plane was resting on its wheels. A drain hole, I thought. The second hole was a little to the left of the first and a little closer to the Cub's buried nose. It sat in a shallow, irregular depression in the metal.

"What the hell?" Ford said, poking at the second hole. "What is this?"

He rooted around inside the cockpit and came out carrying a small, black flashlight. Its beam was surprisingly bright, but it didn't help Ford with his dialogue. "What the hell is this?" he said again.

He handed me the light and began working on the cowling's screws with a penknife. "Lean your weight against the fuselage, Keane. If you feel things start to shift, call out."

The plane didn't budge. Not even when Ford pried the bottom of the cowling back. "Shine the light in there," he said. "See that? It's the oil sump."

I saw a glistening black object the size and shape of a football. There was a hole in it that corresponded to the smaller one in the cowling.

Ford let the cowling clang shut and jumped to his feet. "Son of a bitch," he said. "We've been shot down!" He took a step back and kicked at the beans, tearing up whole plants and clods of earth. "That bump we felt, remember? Those sons of bitches shot us down!"

He turned on me then, which was logical enough. I'd brought the drug smuggling to his door. I'd played on his guilt over not reporting the mystery lights. I'd made him trot out the old feelings about his father, the game-legged pilot who had failed at some crucial moment in his own life. If I'd never been born, none of this would have happened. The plane would be tied down safely in Brookside. Ford and Trigear would be ordering their Friday night pizza right now.

I read all that in Ford's wild eyes and decided I was lucky he'd left his gun in his desk. I was the armed one at the moment. I shone the flashlight in Ford's face. He blinked and waved at the light.

"Turn it off. I'm okay. I just lost it for a minute. Nerves, I guess. There's a light through those trees over there. Must be a farm-house. I'll go phone for help. You watch the plane."

"Are you going to report this to the DEA?"

"I don't know. Those guys weren't kidding, Keane. Nobody could have been sure of hitting that engine. That bullet was fired at the plane, period. It could have killed either one of us."

"Both of us, if it had hit you," I said, but he wasn't listening. He'd gotten too close to the truth for his own comfort. Now he took a rhetorical step backward.

"Besides, it might have just been some kid screwing around. Probably was some kid. Hell, the state released some bald eagles down here last year to try to get them reestablished, and some idiots shot them. They'll shoot at anything. Kids."

He wasn't even looking at me by then. He waved away my offer of the flashlight and marched off toward the farmhouse. He limped now, I noted.

I waited until I could no longer hear Ford, which was some time after I lost sight of him. Then I started off in the opposite direction. I wasn't afraid that the drug smugglers would track us down and finish the job. They couldn't know how effective their single shot had been. And if they guessed, they'd never find the little plane in the dark. I was afraid of Deputy Dix, the man who'd warned me off the case. The man who'd lock me up if he got his hands on me again. The man who'd surely hear of the crash, even if Ford stayed in denial about the most likely cause. Dix would say he was putting me away for my own safety, and I'd be forced to agree with him.

Beyond the trees that edged the field, I found a gravel road that hadn't been visible from the air. It gave me the choice of going back up the hill or farther down into the valley. I chose to go up, despite the possibility of meeting someone with a rifle. Rapture was up there somewhere. Rapture and civilization.

I hadn't gone very far before I decided I was climbing a mountain. The lead in my shoes was another reaction to the crash, I knew, like Ford's rage and my throbbing arm. Another was acute hearing. I seemed to hear a million night sounds in the woods I passed. I would have started at each and every one of those million, but my fatigue protected me, making me fearless for once. Almost fearless. When I spotted a short figure by the side of the road, I did start, tired or not. Then I fired my all-purpose flashlight and death beam at it. The figure was a mailbox. More than that, it was a mailbox I knew. Dr. Krystal Bowden's.

Without any real plan, I started down Krystal's lane. I snapped off my light first. Dix might have been watching the place, which would have been awkward. I was hoping Agent Fallon had drawn guard duty. I was anxious to talk to him.

The moon was fat and orange and not much higher than the trees, but it cast enough light for me to see that anyone watching the trailer must have walked in like me. The only vehicle visible was one I hadn't expected to see: Krystal's Jeep. Dix and company must have put off vacuuming it for fiber evidence until Monday.

I circled the clearing, proving I was a child of the suburbs with every noisy step. At the end of the circuit, I was satisfied. Anyone hidden nearby would have grabbed me by then. Or made tracks. Even Blue III was gone. The only thing guarding the trailer was a ribbon of yellow police tape strung around the building at waist height. DO NOT CROSS, it read. I laughed at it. Literally. Out loud. The laughter sounded a lot like Ford's giggle, so I cut it off.

I checked the trailer's door. The screen door I'd sliced through that morning had been reinforced by the trailer's metal door, which was locked. I knocked for luck. It would be embarrassing to break in and find a lawman sleeping on the couch. No answer. I scouted the end of the trailer that held the spare bedroom. From the hood of the Jeep, I could reach the bedroom's sliding window. It was locked.

More scouting. Between two trees near the shed I found a pile of wood Krystal must have been saving to burn in her dream cabin's fireplace. I picked a likely log and climbed back up onto the Jeep. My first blow knocked the glass clean out of the frame. It fell on the bed without breaking. I laughed again at that. I tossed the log through the open window, because it struck me as a funny thing to do. Then I climbed in after it, stiff shoulder and all.

The boxes of herbs were gone. I wasn't interested in them anyway. What I wanted was in Krystal's kitchen. I used the phone that hung there to try Fallon's number at the Double Nickel. No one answered, not even a desk clerk. I looked around for a consolation prize in Krystal's pantry and refrigerator. I found bread and peanut butter and beer and ate a picnic dinner on the kitchen floor.

Then I made for Krystal's bedroom, dragging my bad shoulder along the hallway wall as I went. I lay down on the doctor's bed, feeling safe for the first time that day.

"Rapture never strikes twice in the same place," I said and fell asleep.

Twenty-four

FOR ONCE NO BAD DREAM WOKE ME. At least no dream I could remember. Instead of terror, I was roused by a mild case of disorientation. I thought I was back in Oldenburg, in the bed Brother Dennis had borrowed for me. It was Friday morning all over again. I had to drive to Rapture to meet Krystal, hand her some excuse, and then run for New Jersey. But I wouldn't find her, I knew, and the endless day of searching and questioning would begin again.

I looked around. I was in Rapture, not Oldenburg. In Krystal's trailer. In the very same spot on her bed where I'd come to rest. It was still dark, but the darkness had taken on a silvery edge. Either I'd slept through till winter and the first snow or the moon had risen. I got up to see which of the two possibilities was correct. It turned out to be the moon alternative, but I had to stare out the window for a few seconds to be certain. The moonlight was so bright it was hard to tell the effect from a heavy frost.

I sat down again on the bed, trying to shake the feeling that I was trapped in some repeating loop of the past. I told myself that my whole life was the repeating pattern. I'd let Krystal draw me into a mystery again, thinking that I could handle it. Instead, like an alcoholic who risks one short beer, I'd awakened in a strange bed and slept-in clothes, with a sore head.

I listened to my whole familiar lecture, agreeing with every point of my argument but knowing that my conclusion was wrong. The sense of familiarity I was wrestling with was more than just a general regret over falling off the sanity wagon again. It was a specific response to something that had happened in Rapture. But what?

I got up and walked into the kitchen, kicking over an empty beer can I'd left there. I found Ford's flashlight, unlocked the front door, and went out into the yard, my subconscious saying, "Warmer, you're getting warmer," or words to that effect.

I didn't need the flashlight at first. The moon's light was bright enough to read by. I took a few steps toward Krystal's lane and stopped. Not that way.

I circled the trailer, pausing by Blue's ring of packed earth to look up at the moon, small now and white. As white as Batsto's skin had been, I thought, when Fallon had uncovered his face. As pale as my own face had suddenly become, I was sure.

I followed my moon shadow toward the giant oak that marked the start of the dry creek bed and the end of the moon's realm. By the flashlight's yellow beam, I descended the stone steps of the bed until I reached Batsto's first resting place. "You're hot," the little voice was saying now. "You're burning up."

Batsto's empty grave was still empty, but that wasn't the relief I'd expected it to be. I knew the hole in the ground had drawn me from Krystal's bed. It was the source of the feeling that had shaken me by the shoulder, the feeling of playing the same scene once too often. I knew I'd stood by that grave before. Not that morning, but twenty years earlier. Not in this forest, but in another like it, in another God-forgotten corner of Indiana.

In that grave, I'd found another missing man, another Clyde Batsto. His name was Michael Crosley. Like Batsto, Crosley had died of a blow to the head from something very like a rifle butt. I'd identified the murderer and seen him sent to prison. He was Krystal's father, the man I'd come to Indiana to speak against. Curtis Morell.

I scrambled up the dry creek, slipping and sending stones down the hill, their clatter creating the illusion that Morell was a step behind me and gaining. My panic attack lasted until I reached the top and the moonlight. Then I accepted what I'd been repeating to myself. Morell wasn't chasing me. He couldn't be. He was safely locked up in Michigan City.

Or was he? I swung the flashlight beam around, but it wasn't bright enough to compete with the moon. Of course Morell was still locked up, I told myself. At least he had been on Wednesday, when I'd attended his parole hearing. Prestina Shipe had already disappeared by then, so he couldn't have been responsible. If Morell had escaped since the hearing, Brother Dennis would have heard. Morell couldn't be loose in the woods around Rapture. He couldn't have killed Clyde Batsto.

But I knew he had. All the light the moon could pump out wouldn't make that black insight fade away. I backed toward the trailer, scanning the woods as I went.

Once I was safely inside, I thought of trying Fallon's number again. But I could already hear the answer he'd give me. The crime had Morell's signature because it had been committed by Morell's daughter. She'd taken up her father's profession, why not his modus operandi as well? That would fit in perfectly with Krystal's warped sense of humor, Fallon's catchall explanation for every oddity about the case. She'd wanted me to read her father's signature on Batsto's corpse, the DEA man would say. She'd wanted to frighten me, or give me a chance to guess that she'd reopened the family business. The worst of it was I half believed those possibilities myself. I didn't want Fallon to convert me completely.

So I left the telephone alone. I used the last of the flashlight's juice to search the trailer. I'd already determined that Krystal's key ring was missing from the hook by the door. It was now in Dix's pocket, figuratively speaking. I was looking for a spare key to the Jeep, thinking I'd start in the trailer and then search the underside of the truck itself if I had to. Maybe after the sun was up and all bogeymen had gone to ground.

As it turned out, I didn't have to wait for the sun. I found the spare key in the bottom drawer of Krystal's dresser, taped to the back of a lease agreement. By that time, it was six o'clock, and I'd begun to worry about Dix dropping in or being somewhere nearby on patrol. So I didn't stop to clean myself up or to shave with one of Krystal's disposable razors. I smoothed the bed, pocketed my empty beer can, and set the pane of glass back in the spare bedroom window as best I could.

Those attempts to hide my tracks were more or less ridiculous given what I did next, which was to steal the Jeep. I was sure Dix would see it that way, as grand theft auto, though I considered it a loan. The truck had a standard transmission. I'd spent my youth shifting the gears of a certain Volkswagen Karmann-Ghia, but my youth was a long way behind me. Luckily, no one was around to laugh as I bucked the Jeep out of its parking space and stalled it twice on the dirt lane.

By the time I'd ascended to the top of the ridge, I'd gotten used to the clutch. I could have given Dix a run for his money if he'd been on patrol. He wasn't. I got my bearings and found Willie's shortcut to Brookside. Half an hour later, I was eating a greasy sausage on a greasier biscuit and looking for the little green road sign that pointed the way to the airport.

I'd already decided what I had to do that day and that I couldn't do it in Krystal's truck. Dix would have an all points bulletin out on the Jeep as soon as he knew it was gone. He'd even have a pretty good idea who had taken it. He'd know by now that I hadn't made it to the Double Nickel. He'd probably have heard from Ford about the plane crash. He might have figured that I was wandering around lost, more of a danger to myself than ever. None of that was a problem as long as Dix thought I was doing my wandering in the Jeep or on foot. But once the deputy found out I'd retrieved the Chevy—step one in my master plan—all units would be on the lookout for a faded red car with New Jersey plates. It came to me that I might solve the dilemma by jumbling Dix's two bulletins, his Jeep one and his Jersey one, together.

When I got to Brookside Airport, I pulled into the deserted factory across the road. No hint remained of what they'd made there; they'd cleaned up after themselves that well. I parked the Jeep in a narrow loading bay behind the main building, where it couldn't be seen from the road. Then I removed the truck's single Indiana plate using my pocket knife, thinking of Ford using his knife on the Cub's cowling while I waited for the plane to fall on us. The artwork on the plate was another reminder of the previous evening. It showed the black silhouette of a farm, backlit by the bloody afterglow of a sunset.

My Cavalier was parked where I'd left it in the airport's gravel lot. I approached it using my best parody of stealth, remembering Ford's remark about sleeping in the hangar with Trigear. He'd slept with the dog and his revolver both last night, I was sure. The pilot hadn't let the air out of my tires or otherwise secured the car. I was able to back it out onto the road without drawing a single bark.

I switched plates on a deserted stretch of road just south of Bedford, stowing the two Jersey ones in my suitcase. While I had it open, I drew out my last change of clothes and my shaving kit. I could have stopped in Bedford to change and shave, but the town was too close to Rapture for comfort. That bit of nerves paid off for me. When I finally reached the interstate, I found a gas station that rented showers to truckers. And to amateur detectives, although they didn't advertise that part of the service.

I used a phone booth out by the diesel pumps to call Brother Dennis. The monk sounded like he'd just gotten out of bed, but then he tended to sound that way. I had a story to knock the sand out of his eyes. He listened while I described Krystal's disappearance and Batsto's murder. Then he came up with the same answer I had, without the benefit of a nocturnal stroll in the woods.

"Morell," he said.

I was more relieved than irritated at having my punch line snatched away from me. "That's what I think, too."

"But, Okie, it can't be. He's still locked up. The hearing at the prison isn't till next week. If he'd gotten out somehow, I'd know about it. I still have friends at the prison from all the trips I made up there."

"I was hoping you did. I need a favor. I need you to get me in to see Morell. Today."

"That's not possible, Okie. You have to set those visits up in advance with the Department of Corrections. You couldn't get in to see him before next week. Maybe the week after."

"It has to be today. Whatever is going to happen in Rapture will happen tonight. After that, it'll be too late to help Krystal."

"But the prison rules—"

"Did you schedule your visits in advance?"

"Yes. I mean, at first I did. I had to. Then later, when they got to know me, I'd just call a friend I had up there. But that was for me, not you. I'm a religious, you're not. And they know me, they don't know you."

"How long will it take me to drive to Michigan City?"

"It'll take you—I don't know—four hours maybe."

"I'll call you back in three. You've got until then to talk your friend in Michigan City into it. If he has to know me to trust me, tell him the story of my life. That should leave you two and a half hours for wheedling. Tell him I'd from St. Aelred's if that helps. It's true in a way."

"Even if I could swing it, Okie, it isn't a good idea for you to see Morell. I told you, the man is evil. Irredeemably evil. It frightens me to say that. I feel like I'm blaspheming even to believe it could be true. But I do believe it."

"I'm not going up there to redeem him. I just want to talk to him."

"It isn't safe. Morell is as lost as a man in hell. As lost right now, alive and breathing, as any being in the pit. And he'd like nothing better than to drag someone down with him. I think he'd like you most of all."

A semi pulled slowly away from the pumps, its twin stacks sending out puffs of black smoke in rhythm with the growling of its engine. I pressed a hand against my free ear. "Me?"

"He hasn't forgotten you. He still hates you. I thought long and hard about that before I brought you back to Indiana for the hearing. I thought you'd be safe enough in Indy. But if Morell is somehow reaching out as far as Rapture . . ."

He caught himself then. In another second, he'd have convinced himself that Morell had horns and a pointy tail. He'd have convinced me, too, and I was frightened enough already.

"Do your best for me," I said. "I'll call back in three hours."

Twenty-five

I ONLY NEEDED to consult my auto club map once for the first three hours of my drive—the three hours I'd given Brother Dennis in which to work his miracle. There was only one road for all that driving, the road I'd been standing next to when I'd called the monk, I-65. The highway described a wavering diagonal line through the state's center, Indianapolis, to its northwest corner, the sprawl around Chicago, which was called Gary on the Indiana side of the fence.

Except for the hour it took me to pass through Indy and its never-ending suburbs and a glimpse of the outskirts of Lafayette, the drive was through farmland. South of Indy and for a little while north of it, the farms and the ground they occupied weren't unlike the ones near Brookside: small holdings on slightly rolling terrain with fringes of forest just thick enough to sustain the illusion that each farm might be the last. Around Lafayette, the land flattened and the farms flowed into one another. The isolated stands of trees stood out in the fields of corn like the peaks of drowned mountains.

Around noon I stopped at the town of Rensselaer to eat something and make my second call to Oldenburg. I ate first. I knew if I called first and Brother Dennis had come through for me I'd be too scared to swallow. I picked a nonfranchise restaurant named

Wag's where the waitress—who'd been in diapers when I'd last visited Indiana—called me Honey and generally treated me like a kid who'd left his school bus at the wrong stop. I ordered a Roast Beef Manhattan, as I was feeling more nostalgic than ever for the East Coast. It turned out to be a roast beef sandwich on white bread with stiff mashed potatoes and stiffer gravy piled on top. I ate a little of the Lower East Side and called it quits.

I made my phone call from a wall model mounted between Wag's restrooms. Brother Dennis picked up so quickly I knew he'd been sitting with a hand on his phone.

"Okie, where are you?"

"Rensselaer."

"Is that all the farther you've gotten?"

"I had to obey the speed limit. I'm using a borrowed license plate."

"What? Forget it. Don't tell me about it. You'll have to hurry. I told them you'd be in Michigan City by one o'clock."

"You got me in?"

"Yes. Now listen. I told them you were from St. Aelred's, like you suggested. Remember that. You're representing the seminary."

I smiled a much needed smile at the monk's concern. I'd been representing St. Aelred's for twenty years and in some very unusual ways. It wasn't likely that my stop in Michigan City would add much to the damage I'd already done.

"Are you sure you want to go through with this, Okie?"

"How do I get in?"

"Ask for a man named Benner when you get to the main gate. Robert Benner. There's one other thing, something that could still gum up the works."

"What?"

"Morell has to agree to see you. Bob is finding out right now if he will. They can't force Morell to see you if he doesn't want to."

"You know Morell," I said. "Do you think he'll pass up this chance?"

The monk's reply was unfortunately phrased. "Not on your life."

Indiana kept its most dangerous criminals at arm's length. The town of Michigan City was built right on Lake Michigan, not all that far from the state of the same name. I was late arriving because of traffic on I-94, the road I took east from Gary. I thought the prison might be on the lakeshore or maybe even out on the water, a rocky, midwestern Alcatraz. So I wandered to the little city's lakefront via blocks of older, run-down houses and businesses with nautical references in their names—Lighthouse Motors, the Blue Water Bakery, the Cove Diner—that were echoes of the Jersey shore. Specifically, the echoes were from the north Jersey shore, where the old urban sprawl runs all the way to the high-water mark.

I negotiated a tiny traffic circle and came to a public park that was set against the water's edge. I left the Chevy in a public lot next to a marina that had more slips than I'd ever seen in one place. The park—Washington Park—was an old one with a birdcage bandstand and crumbling stone walls along its paths. The same stone had been used to build benches with rounded backs that rose out of the ground like neolithic tombs. The benches were all occupied on this Saturday afternoon, and picnickers had staked out most of the grass. The open stretches were patrolled by pigeons and gulls and crows, the last a nice Indiana touch.

That left no room for me, so I walked along the edge of the marina, first west toward a huge power plant with a rusted smokestack and then back east toward the park. I justified the walk by trying to plan my approach to Morell, something I'd managed not to do through all my long drive. But my mind kept straying to the comings and goings in the marina and out to the crisp horizon where a dozen pairs of white sails were visible.

I might have hidden among the pleasure boaters all afternoon if something hadn't made me glance toward the Chevy. A policewoman was standing next to it, examining the windshield. I managed to cross the parking lot without appearing to run. Still, I drew her eye.

She was built like a grammar school linebacker, and her brown face hadn't a line or a wrinkle. It hadn't a trace of an expression, either, which might have explained why it was wearing so well. "This your car, sir?"

I admitted it and asked whether there was something wrong, saying Officer as every other word.

"I was just noticing your inspection sticker. It's from New Jersey. But you have an Indiana plate."

I couldn't see a patrol car, but I had no trouble spotting the boxy radio she wore on her gun belt. If she got curious enough to use it, I would be knocking off early.

"I'm from New Jersey," I said. "I just moved out here. I haven't had an Indiana inspection yet."

"We don't have vehicle inspection in Indiana, sir. Didn't the highly trained BMV staff tell you that when you registered your car?"

"No," I said, trying to smile enough for both of us. I was feeling like an illegal alien caught wading in the Rio Grande. I'd been feeling that way for days, and I was sick of it. I longed for some common ground where a Hoosier and a Garden Stater could meet as equals. Something the officer had said had given me a glimpse of that promised land, and I slid for it, headfirst.

"At least I don't remember them telling me. You know how those motor vehicle places are. By the time you get through the line, you're lucky to remember where you parked."

"I hear you," she said and smiled.

I took the smile as permission to change the subject. "How do I get to the prison?"

"Screw with me," she said, her smile disappearing in a blink. She held the deadpan for what seemed like an hour. Then she laughed, a surprisingly girlish, musical laugh. "Relax. That's our standard joke around here. Like, 'How do I get to Carnegie Hall?' "

"Practice," I said, laughing too.

"Right. We get asked about the prison every other day. It's on the western side of town, over by Indiana Dunes State Park. How'd you get way over here, somebody give you bad directions?"

"I'm just stalling," I said. My heart missed a beat when I realized I'd accidentally said what I was thinking, but there was no turning back. "I don't really want to go there."

"Visiting a relative or a friend?"

Either lie would have served, but I stayed with the truth. "An enemy. A guy I knew twenty years ago when I was out here going to school. He killed a friend of mine. Not a friend really. A classmate."

"What did he do to you?"

"I guess he tried to kill me, too."

"You're not sure?"

"I'm sure. I just don't like to say it out loud."

She settled back against the side of the Cavalier, placing her hand between the butt of her gun and the paint. "I wouldn't like to say that, either. So why go to see him?"

"I think he may have gotten another friend of mine into trouble. Just this week." I expected the cop to call me on that. Brother Dennis had, despite his almost superstitious faith in Morell's evil. She didn't speak, so I called myself. "It's a stupid idea, I guess. He's locked up tight."

"He's locked up, but there's nothing tight about it. Stuff gets into that prison you wouldn't believe. And stuff gets out. Namely released prisoners. They give the inmates who stay behind a way to reach out and touch the rest of the world." She balled up her right hand and smacked her open left.

"In return, the guys inside give the short-timers the benefit of their experience. For every con who comes out trying to go straight, there are five—maybe ten—who've picked up some new plan for screwing up. We call the prison Michigan City University sometimes. The good deal for us is the graduates don't hang around here. They like to get as far from their alma mater as possible."

"No reunions?"

She laughed her delicate laugh again. "No, just postgraduate work. The only good part about throwing all your criminals together so they can trade ideas is that their ideas suck or they wouldn't have gotten caught in the first place."

She stood up. "So are you going in there telling or asking? You look like an asker."

"I guess I am. I want to know what he's up to."

"My advice is don't ask him. These guys love to talk. Talking to each other doesn't do it for them. They need an outsider to really let loose. Sit on this guy like you're waiting on a pitch you know is coming. He'll end up telling you everything he's into. Try being too mean to talk."

She was smiling at that idea before I'd even made a joke of it. "How about being too scared to talk?" I asked.

"Go with it."

Twenty-six

I SET OUT for the prison without any more pacing or meditation, encouraged by the policewoman's parting smile and the fist she held aloft as I drove away. I headed west and found Indiana Dunes State Park, but not the prison. When I'd gone far enough to be sure I'd missed it, I drove inland for half a mile or so and then back east along a modest residential street. Through its trees, I caught a glimpse of something I mistook for a lighthouse or a mock-up of a lighthouse, the touristy, nautical flavor of the town still fresh in my mind. Then I topped a small rise and saw that my lighthouse was really a guard tower on one corner of the prison wall.

I'd arrived at the prison's backyard, an area of service buildings and garages surrounded by a red split-rail fence that wouldn't have kept in a determined cow. When I made the left at the property's southeast corner, I got a clear view of the prison's actual wall, which was redbrick with heavy buttresses. That is, the wall was brick up to a certain height, its original height, I guessed. Above the brick was an extra ten feet or so of modern concrete, to which the watchtowers were attached. I could see the peaked roofs of red buildings beyond the wall, one of which was a chapel, to judge by its round stained-glass window.

The prison's parking lot was across a narrow road from the main gate. Here the property was bordered by a black iron fence that ran between concrete posts whose white paint looked like the latest of a thousand coats. On the grassy land between the fence and the prison wall stood a pair of old frame houses in immaculate condition. A speedboat was parked in the driveway of one of the houses. The other had a glider swing in its yard. The warden and his deputy had lived in the houses once upon a time, I thought. Who did now? Probably the guys who mowed the prison grass.

A sign at the main gate gave the institution's formal name, THE INDIANA STATE PRISON. Beyond it was a tollbooth-like station complete with a railroad crossing arm. I walked up to the window and asked for Robert Benner. The guard directed me to a little limestone and brick administration building whose modern, practical lines seemed out of place on the prison grounds. Benner's cubicle, where I eventually arrived, was also modern and severe, but it had been brightened up with Polaroids of children and fish.

"You're late, Mr. Keane," Benner said when I was delivered to him.

In my nervousness, I fell back on detective talk—my tin-eared imitation of my paperback heroes—always a bad sign. "What's the problem? Did Morell have a hot date?"

Benner glanced up and then leaned back in his chair. He was as gray as the decor, bearded, tanned. His white shirt had short sleeves. I noted a faded tattoo on his forearm, the Marine Corps insignia. A link to Brother Dennis? A link to the friendly cop back at Washington Park with the military cadence in her speech? Yet another hint of a vast network of links that tied together everyone but me?

"No," Benner said. "I had the date. With a fish. Your visit's kept me at my desk an extra hour or two today."

"Sorry."

"It didn't kill me. I was catching up on some paperwork this morning when Dennis's phone call came in. Lucky for you I was."

"Lucky," I repeated, because the rhythm of our exchange seemed to call for it.

"How is Dennis?"

I didn't answer. I'd gotten distracted by a newspaper clipping pinned to the wall behind Benner's head. Its headline read: BENNER GIRLS IGNITE YARDVILLE BANK. I misinterpreted that, understandably, given my current surroundings. I had to read the story's lead before I understood that it wasn't describing a crime. The Yardville Bank was a soccer team and the Benner girls its stars.

Meanwhile, Benner was repeating his question. "He's fine," I said. "Prospering."

"Glad to hear it. How long have you known him?"

"Twenty years," I said, still in name, rank, and serial number mode.

"You're from St. Aelred's?"

"That's where I met Brother Dennis. I work on my own now."

"Social work?"

"I like to think so."

Benner could have done without the lip. I could have, too, but there was no stopping it now.

"Dennis thinks a lot of you," Benner said. "That's better than a letter from the governor as far as I'm concerned, which is your second bit of luck. Dennis's word is taking the place of the background check we usually do on visitors. The rest is up to Mr. Morell. I'm happy to report that he's agreed to add you to his visitation list."

There was a dramatic pause. Then I asked, "Does he see many people?"

"No. Not since Brother Dennis stopped coming in 1989."

"Does he get many phone calls?"

"We don't allow incoming phone calls, Mr. Keane. This isn't a work release program. The prisoners are permitted to make a certain number of collect calls out. We keep a log of those."

"So you know which numbers Morell has called?"

"We would if he'd called any. He never uses the phone. Never writes a letter."

"How about computers?"

"There are computers in the library, but they're not connected to the outside world. What are you after?"

"A way Morell might be connected to the outside world." Something that didn't involve telepathy or ectoplasmic projection or anything else that went bump in the night.

"If you're talking about some illicit communications, something Morell doesn't want us to know about, he could be using an intermediary, another inmate who phones regularly or sees visitors who could pass messages in and out. That service goes on all the time, usually because an inmate has had some trouble and lost his privileges."

"What kind of inmate is Morell?"

"A quiet one. Especially as he's gotten closer to his parole hearing. I'd be lying if I said I really knew Morell. We have over eighteen hundred guests here on any given day. But I've done some research while I've been waiting for you. Morell's pretty much behaved himself since he moved up here from Wabash Valley. This place brings that out in some guys. They learn to behave, most of them."

"They learn other things, too. I've heard that the prison is sometimes called Michigan City University."

"So have I," Benner said with a shrug. "Prisons have been vocational centers for criminals since the first one opened. Are you thinking Morell is training or being trained?"

"Both. Could he have made a connection in here, somebody with a drug supply who was looking for a regional distributor?"

"Yeah, Morell could have made any number of connections in the years he's been in. With the big suppliers and the local buyers both. There probably isn't a better place to do that than a prison, not until the druggies start holding national conventions. Is that what you're here to ask Morell about?"

"I'm not going to ask. I'm going to sit there and wait for his fastball."

Benner shrugged again. "If he throws a brushback, don't forget to duck."

I was passed through a metal detector and patted down for good measure. Then Benner led me along a windowless corridor and through several checkpoints manned by guards. The last locked door opened into a room that resembled a college dorm lounge. It had a row of vending machines, pairings of worn easy chairs, and several tables, each the right size and with the right number of seats for a game of bridge.

One of the tables was occupied by a man in denim overalls and a crying woman. After I'd made sense of that tableau, I felt a little like crying myself.

"Is that a prisoner?" I whispered to Benner.

"Yeah. What's the matter? You weren't expecting a private room, were you?"

"I was expecting a chain link fence with chairs on either side."

"Like in the old Jimmy Cagney movies? We use Plexiglas nowadays, not wire fencing. But that room is reserved for noncontact visits, for inmates who are under some disciplinary restriction. I told you, Morell's been behaving himself for years. He rates contact visits."

A uniformed guard was stationed with his back to the light of a barred window. "But the guard stays, right?"

"He's called a correctional officer, Mr. Keane. Not a guard. Especially not a screw. Yes, he stays." Benner was enjoying the spectacle of my melting persona. "Pick a chair and pull yourself together. Morell will be here in a minute."

Twenty-seven

THE CHAIR I PICKED WAS IN THE PAIRING closest to the correctional officer overseeing the room. It was my last attempt to control the interview and a waste of my time. When Morell came in, escorted by another officer, he glanced my way and then walked to the pair of chairs farthest from the guard.

Morell was bigger than I remembered, more bearlike in his build and his shuffling walk. He'd lost a lot of hair, and the beard he'd grown to replace it was almost as gray as Benner's.

I kept my seat for a time, thinking his curiosity would draw him over. He never even looked my way. So I stood up and crossed to him.

He was wearing glasses these days, thick ones in unstylish frames. They were bifocals, I noted as I sat down. It made me feel even more vulnerable to realize that I wouldn't have recognized Morell if I'd passed him on the street.

He knew me, though. "Owen Keane," he said, in the low, flat voice I remembered better than his face. "Owen Keane." He smiled with genuine pleasure, showing me some well-cared-for teeth. Then he sat back and waited.

I would have been babbling at full speed by then, if it hadn't been for the policewoman's advice. Even armed with that, I almost lost the silence contest. I was considering a question about Morell's upcoming parole hearing when he reached over to poke at an ashtray on the coffee table that separated us.

"Smoke if you want. Oh that's right. You quit, didn't you? Around the time you went to work in that law firm. You didn't last long there, did you? Quitting that job was a bad move, Owen. Look how trendy law firm detectives have become. But you're nothing if not out of step."

He was really grinning now, feasting on my reaction like a man breaking a long fast. "That's right, Owen. I've kept tabs on you. I've had you watched. I've followed you through every sorry stop in your sorry career. Like that drive-through psychobabble place where you were a gofer. Hand to Hand. That was another short stay, like the law firm. Ohlman, Ohlman, and Pulsifer. When you say that name, you can almost smell the dust.

"You lasted longer in those factory jobs you had. And that one in the casino where you tended bar. I got a kick out of picturing you doing that. But you never stick anywhere, do you? Do you get restless, or do your bosses get nervous when they realize they've hired a nut?"

He didn't wait for an answer. He didn't want me to pull myself off the ropes. "You know what I think it is, Owen? The problem, I mean. It isn't that you were booted out of that seminary. That was a positive thing. It saved you from becoming a living relic from the Middle Ages. The problem was that Mary Fitzgerald chick—sorry, I mean Mary Ohlman—dying in that automobile accident. That's what really fucked you over.

"That's my theory. If she'd lived, you would have gotten things back together. Outgrown all this bullshit. You still would have had hope, you know? Hope that you could have undone all the mistakes you'd made. Even after Mary married and had that kid—Amanda, right?—you could have dreamed about getting back together. As I remember her, Mary was worth dreaming about."

Morell got cocky then and made a mistake. "How you fixed for change, Owen? How about standing me to a soda and a candy bar. A Milky Way. And make the soda a Pepsi, not a Coke."

I was desperate for a breather, so I got up and walked to the machines, repeating to myself that Morell couldn't possibly have had me watched all those years, no matter how accurate his information was. There had to be another explanation.

It came to me when I was standing at the soda machine, a Milky Way in my hand. Even in my dazed state, Morell's choice of snacks made my old fillings ache. It occurred to me that I already knew of Morell's sweet tooth. Someone had told me about it. Brother Dennis. He'd brought Morell candy when he'd visited him. And news of the outside world. The news of me and Mary that I'd passed on in my letters. That's what the monk had really meant when he'd said he'd betrayed me by visiting Morell. He'd innocently fed Morell's interest in me. Now the inmate was parroting back what the monk had told him to throw me off balance. That was why he hadn't mentioned anything I'd done after 1989, the year Brother Dennis stopped coming.

I didn't get the chance to challenge Morell on it. He laughed at me as soon as I sat back down. "Figured out my little joke yet? Sure you have. You always were easy to scare, Owen. Easy to scare but hard to shake.

"Damn, I've wanted to talk to you for one hell of a long time. I've wanted to get your take on this world of yours. A lot has happened in the last twenty years. Do you watch MTV? I can't get it here. I've got a television, a Sony, but I don't have cable. What side did you take on the 'Cop Killer' debate? Was Time Warner right to defend that song on First Amendment grounds? Or were they just going for the bucks? Didn't the whole thing make you think of Stalin's old saw about a capitalist being the guy who's happy to sell you the rope you're going to use to hang him? Was there a video for 'Cop Killer'? There had to be. I'd really love to see that.

I've listened to 'Cop Killer' on my radio a hundred times, trying to figure out what it says about the world out there. And that other song, what's it called? The one about nailing a woman to a table, and not by her hands and feet, either, in the accepted Christian tradition. You've heard that one, right?"

"No," I said.

"No?" Morell was appalled. "This is your culture, Owen. Aren't you in on it? Have you got your head hidden in some old book? Are you trying to figure out Schopenhauer while the house burns down around you?

"Or maybe you just don't like music. I can't talk movies knowledgeably. I read the reviews, and they sound amazing, but the ones I see on television have been cut to shit. What do you think it means, though, Owen, that all this Hollywood technical genius goes into more and more realistic portrayals of people being eviscerated? What does it say about the audiences and their deadened sensibilities when you have to blow intestines all over the place to get their attention?"

"Maybe there isn't that much visual impact in a man being hit on the head with a rifle butt," I said.

"Touché, Owen. Too-fucking-ché. But let me tell you, there can be a ton of visual impact in a skull being cracked by a rifle butt, if it's filmed correctly. There has to be. It's the most important moment in the life of the man whose head gets busted. Maybe for the guy with the rifle, too. You could show it a hundred times and not use it up. Maybe a thousand times."

He'd visualized it that many times himself, he was saying, and it hadn't lost its pull. He watched it again now, as he chewed away on his candy bar.

Then he shook his head. "So you're not a film critic either. Okay. What about fine art? What about Robert Mapplethorpe, the photographer? Or that other one, Andres Serrano? There's an artist you've got to have an opinion on. He's the one who did 'Piss Christ.' You've seen that, haven't you? The photo of a crucifix in urine. What does a serious discussion of that as art say about a society? That it's reached some broad sunlit upland of tolerance? Or that the fucking bottom's fallen out?

"Answer me, Owen."

"I don't know."

"You don't know? You don't even have an opinion? You're letting me down. You're not the Owen Keane I locked horns with. He was willing to take a shot to the head for a belief system, even though he'd seen through it himself. I mean, I know you ended up running away from St. Aelred's, but you never really gave up the fight. Or have you? Was I right when I joked about this hit-and-run life of yours being a reaction to sweet Mary getting offed? Is it only that and not some crazy stand?"

He tried to wait out my secret. Luckily, I hadn't one to betray.

"I've got a theory of my own, Owen. About what all this bloody, ugly, brutal art means. There's this cliché in detective fiction and movies. You've run across this one, I know. The murder victim is lying there bleeding to death. And he dips a finger in his own blood and writes a cryptic clue. You've read that one a hundred times, right? Or seen it on television.

"That's what I think all this crap your dying society is churning out amounts to. It's a message written in the culture's own blood. A cryptic note for whoever comes after you to find and figure out."

Morell really had been waiting a long time to share his insight with someone. After he'd gotten it out, he settled back in his chair, spent and happy. He held his empty soda can up by his ear and flicked at its tab while he considered me.

"Our time's almost up, and you've barely said a word, Owen. If you're not going to talk to me, why'd you bother coming?"

So much for my waiting game. I'd forgotten that Morell would have something to say about the length of my visit. I watched him signal to the correctional officer, watched the officer lift the telephone at his elbow.

In desperation I switched to a half-thought-out Plan B. "I'm here because of your daughter, Krystal. I think she's in danger."

"Danger?" Morell repeated, placing a hand over his heart. "Are you trying to finesse me, Owen? I love it. Like I don't know that Krystal is in trouble. Like you don't know that I know. Only she's in more danger than you ever dreamed."

He leaned across the coffee table and dropped his voice to a whisper. "Dr. Bowden will be lucky if she gets off with serving twenty years in the women's prison in Indianapolis. She's a drug smuggler and a murderer."

"No she isn't."

"Well no, not really. But who's going to believe her? That's if she even lives long enough to tell somebody her side of the story. She's between a rock and a hard place if any ungrateful, back-stabbing daughter ever was. And you're the only one who can save her, Owen."

"How?"

"You have to go back to Rapture and find her. Tonight. To-morrow will be too late, as the old song says. It's now or never. And you can't go to the police. No one outside Rapture will believe you. Not in time. And there's no one inside Rapture you can trust. No one. Believe me on this. You've got no way of telling who my people are.

"So it's got to be you, Owen. You can be the hero again. Or you can run away, like you ran away from St. Aelred's in '73."

The correctional officer who had delivered Morell came back into the room. Morell stood up and nodded to him. Then he leaned down and whispered in my ear. I forced myself to remain absolutely still, exactly as I would have done if some dangerous animal had been breathing on my neck.

"If I were you, I'd run," Morell said. "I'd go back to the silly life you've been living all these years. Because if you go to Rapture, you'll get what Clyde Batsto got. Your grave has already been dug. It's been waiting for you for twenty years."

Twenty-eight

I MANAGED TO GET OUT OF THE PRISON without answering any of Benner's questions. Morell and I agreed on that much. There was no time to involve anyone else. Before I could convince all the people I'd have to convince, it would be too late. Even if they believed my story at the first telling. And I couldn't remember the last time that had happened.

It was after three when I drove through the prison gates. I couldn't be back in Rapture much before eight. It would be dark by seven, but that was okay. Ford had seen the lights in the sky between nine and ten o'clock. I could make that deadline if I kept moving. If I really concentrated, I might even arrive with a plan.

As a first step toward that happy goal, I reviewed what I knew or thought I knew about the setup in Rapture. Curtis Morell was behind the drug distribution operation based there. Morell had somehow managed that feat from inside the Indiana State Prison. Maybe he'd dreamed up the scheme after coming into contact with representatives of the drug suppliers and hearing about their problems. Or maybe he'd wormed his way into an existing network. Morell was working through one or more confederates, at least one of whom was surely a graduate of Michigan City University. My money was on Willie, the apprentice woodsman. In

Morell's vision of social decay, I thought I'd found the original of Willie's secondhand philosophy. The methamphetamine came in by plane from the south, was unloaded in Rapture Meadow, and then shipped out in selected consignments of Dr. Prestina's Miracle Herbs.

I'd sorted out that much by the time I stopped for gas in Merrillville. The adenoidal clerk who took my money asked if I had a big night planned. I didn't answer him. Trust no one, Morell had said.

Back on the road, I addressed the question of Rapture. Why had Morell picked that town? Because his daughter was there, the daughter who had testified against him at his trial. The daughter who had gone on to make a success of her life. Had revenge against Krystal been the seed of Morell's whole plan? Or was it just a fringe benefit he'd toyed with? I couldn't say.

That hanging question left me uneasy. Around Rensselaer I experienced a dark night of the soul regarding my client. Suppose Fallon was right, I thought, about Krystal taking up where her father had left off. Could she be another of his secret partners in Rapture? She'd told me that the mail-order herb business—the key to Morell's scheme—had been her idea. But Morell had agreed with me that his daughter was in danger. Why? Maybe to finesse me, while I was trying to finesse him. Maybe to get me back to Rapture, where his daughter had lured me earlier. Where my open grave was waiting.

I actually slowed down while I kicked that idea around and it kicked me back. The semis rode my bumper or thundered past me, their tangible, familiar threat comforting compared with the ghost story I was weaving. The vision of a moonlit, empty grave waiting in the woods was so strong I would have wrecked the car staring at it if I hadn't happened to be on a straight stretch of road. I felt myself slipping back into the paranoid vertigo I'd felt when I'd let Morell convince me—against all common sense—that he'd been watching me for twenty years.

I rolled down my window and stuck my head out into the bugs and the diesel exhaust. Morell had been right, I thought. I did scare easily. I knew then that scaring me had been the whole point of his parting shot about my waiting grave. He'd wanted to scare me away. He didn't have an elaborate trap waiting for me anymore than he'd had me watched in New Jersey. He couldn't have known I'd come back to Indiana to be trapped. I hadn't known myself until I'd actually set out.

The last thing Morell wanted was me back in Rapture. All his encouragement about my saving Krystal had just been bluster. He didn't want me down there fouling things up for him, a variable he couldn't control. Which meant that Krystal hadn't invited me to Rapture in the first place at Morell's bidding. I'd been right about her all along, and Fallon had been wrong. She had somehow gotten close enough to the truth to be a threat to her father. As Clyde Batsto had. So they'd been removed.

What about Prestina Shipe? Was she also an innocent victim, as Dr. Stanger had insisted? I couldn't accept it. I needed her as a prop for my house of cards. Someone had to be tampering with the herb shipments and sending them to the right addresses. If not Krystal, then Prestina. Somehow Morell had corrupted her, despite her age and innocence. Perhaps through them.

Why then had Shipe disappeared? Had Morell staged that to throw Krystal or Fallon off his track? And why had Morell caused the drugs to be planted in Krystal's trailer? To frame her, of course, but why do it before the last shipment was safely delivered? Fallon believed there wouldn't be another shipment, that the whole operation had moved to another town in another state. I was suddenly sure that the DEA man was wrong about that, too. There had to be more methamphetamine on the way. Morell would have had no reason to scare me away from Rapture if the operation had packed up and moved on.

That was as far as I got after hours of running in mental circles. I told myself that the rest of my answers were waiting in Rapture. All I had to do was get there. South of Lafayette I turned on the radio and searched the dial for some replacement head filler. I finally settled for a religious station whose announcer sounded closer than my backseat. His voice had a folksy rural twang that set me on my guard. So did his subject matter: the Last Days. As Stanger had said, there was a lot of current interest in that topic. I remembered a question Stanger had put to me, or rather, a question he'd tossed into the ether: Why does one person dread the end time while another longs for it? It was a restatement of what was for me the basic question, the one that came on sleepless nights and in broad daylight on empty streets. Maybe its answer was hidden in Rapture, too. Stranger things had happened.

I stopped for coffee in a little spot north of Indy called Lebanon, sipping the stuff constantly as I drove and nodding as I sipped. By the time I reached Indianapolis, I'd hit the rumble strips on the shoulder half a dozen times. The traffic around the capital woke me up a little, the traffic and the signs for I-70 East, the escape route I'd been longing for all week. I didn't take the eastbound road when it finally came, and that seemed as fateful a decision as leaving St. Aelred's had been.

Just before I reached the exit for Highway 50 and Bedford, I stopped at the truck plaza I'd visited earlier that day. I used the same phone booth I'd used that morning to call the same man, admiring how well that circularity fit into my whole visit to Indiana. My whole life.

Brother Dennis was mad at me for not calling him sooner. His mood didn't improve when I told him how my interview with Morell had gone and what I was up to now. The monk was reduced to repeating "Okie" over and over again like an disconsolate mourner. He quieted down when I told him I needed his help. I asked him to stay by the phone, and if he hadn't heard from me by midnight, to send the state police to Rapture Meadow.

The curves and hills of Highway 50 brought me back to full wakefulness. Or maybe a familiar knot in my stomach did. I thought about stopping in Brookside to enlist Clay Ford and his revolver. I didn't stop. There was a good chance that Morell's warning to trust no one was just another bluff intended to hamstring me, to keep me permanently outnumbered, but I had taken the warning to heart. I'd decided miles back that my best chance to help Krystal was to slip into Rapture unobserved. And my best chance to do that was to do it alone.

I took the shortcut from Brookside to the ridge road, the backdoor route that avoided Rapture itself. I gained the ridge and then descended immediately, heading for Krystal's trailer, watching for other headlights but not seeing any. I planned to wait at the doctor's trailer for an hour or so, assuming that Dix hadn't found the broken window and boarded it over. I'd made better time than I'd expected. It was seven-thirty when I spotted Krystal's sentry mailbox.

I didn't turn into Krystal's driveway. I drove past it and parked the Chevy in an access road for a field of corn. Then I followed the drive on foot again, carrying my own flashlight this time in place of Ford's, but not using it. The moon was low and orange and almost useless, but something told me to make do with its light. That same bout of intuition kept me standing in the trees at the edge of Krystal's clearing for a long time after I'd decided that the coast was clear.

I was still standing there when a light came on in the woods to my left. It was the dome light of a car that had been backed into the trees. I caught a second's glimpse of Deputy Dix climbing out of his cruiser, and then the light was gone. I heard him walk a few steps into the woods. Then I heard him creating a little of the kind of art the photographer Serrano specialized in. By the time the dome light came on again, I was halfway down the drive.

Twenty-nine

DIX DID ME A FAVOR BY CHASING ME away from Krystal's trailer. If I'd gotten inside and sat down, I might have fallen asleep and missed all the night's excitement. Even if my nerves had kept me awake, I would have been late for the party. I'd underestimated the time it would take me to climb to the top of the ridge on foot. And I hadn't factored getting lost into the equation.

I had a vague sense of the direction I should take. I thought the ridge road would lead me to Rapture Meadow or at least to a side road or track that would take me there. The way might even be marked for the benefit of Rapture's dwindling tourist trade, but I wasn't counting on that. I knew from Emmett Haas's description and my own observations that the meadow was the highest point in the area, so the correct road would be the one that went up. I knew there had to be a road or at least a path of some kind because the Ordained had kept livestock there. If I needed a more recent proof, I had the drug smugglers. They were getting there somehow, picking up their shipments, and getting away.

My reasoning was airtight, but reality wasn't having any of it. As I followed the ridge road, it leveled off, turned from pavement to gravel to grassy dirt, then jogged to the left, to the south, toward the scattered lights of the valley. I backtracked, using the flashlight to check for turnoffs I'd missed. There were none. That left me with a choice: stick with the road, trusting that it would eventually climb again, or strike off through the woods.

I stood there imagining Morell behind every tree, remembering how much I disliked a forest at night, remembering why. It was almost nine by the luminous dial on my watch, and that decided the issue for me. I stepped into the woods, telling myself I had only to track the high ground to find the meadow.

I found that I had to use the flashlight constantly just to stay on my feet. The ground rose, but not steadily. There were gullies to cross, ribs of bare stone to climb, and even a genuine cliff. It wasn't much of a cliff, maybe only a ten-foot drop to another limestone creek bed. This creek had gurgling water in it, which tipped me to the danger. I stood on the edge for a time, sucking in the humid air and sweating out the moisture. At one with my ecosystem, if any gumshoe ever had been.

The creek turned me to the left and eventually led me to a tended path. It was only two or three feet wide, but it looked better to me than an eastbound highway. The path was paved with wood chips, and it crossed the creek on a bridge made of two felled trees planked over. The trees hadn't been matched very well for size or straightness, which meant that each board of the planking tilted at a different angle. Below, the gurgling creek was just as inviting and just as remote as it had been from the top of the little cliff. I paused at the very center of the span to listen to the water. When I did, I heard the plane.

I laughed out loud. Or rather I imitated the creek below me, giggling as Ford had done the evening before when he'd realized how close we'd come to dying in the borrowed Cub. Ford had asked me about the name I'd called out as we'd hit—Lynn Baxter—an amazing job of recall on my part, as I hadn't thought of her in years. On the other hand, I'd often thought of the plane in which she'd died way back in 1941, a clipped-wing Monocoupe nicknamed the phaeton. It had become a symbol for me of the demon I chased, and who sometimes chased me back, the principal feature of a nightmare that had haunted me for years before finally burning itself out.

And now I'd managed to recreate the nightmare in real life. It was another vicious circle for Brother Dennis's collection. That is, it would be if the nightmare plane really was—as I'd always believed—Lynn Baxter's *Phaeton*. Standing there on that crazy bridge, I saw another possibility. The plane in my dream might always have been a Helio Courier loaded with drugs. The dream wasn't then a replaying of an old investigation that had derailed my life. It was a prophetic glimpse of this very night, a warning.

I might have stood there all night scaring myself if I hadn't seen the lights in the sky. There were two of them, huge and diffuse in the hazy air, and they were close. The meadow had to be just ahead of me, maybe no more than another hundred yards. I took off at a run, shining the flashlight well down the path, taking the risk because I was certain that anyone near the meadow would be looking up toward the plane.

When I reached the edge of the trees, the plane was lined up to land. The lights were intense now, the twin beams transforming the meadow that had looked so flat from the air into a range of hills and valleys done in miniature. The plane's engine noise was fainter than it had been when I was standing on the bridge. The twin lights fell down like racing meteors, so quickly that I caught my noisy breath, feeling again my own plunge into the soybean field.

Then the lights checked their descent and rushed toward a point a little to my left. The engine was so muted now that I actually heard the thump of the tires as they hit. At that instant, the lights began bouncing wildly, sending a mad light show of dancing shadows deep into the forest. I watched the lights approach the trees to the left of my hiding place. They pivoted away from those trees—and from me—at the last second. As they turned, the lights briefly exposed a figure hidden like me in the fringe of the woods: Marietta Feasey.

The pilot must not have seen her, because the plane kept turning until it was pointed back the way it had come. It taxied off, slow now and awkward. Its departure exonerated Feasey, as far as I was concerned, made her another uninvited guest and not an unlikely member of Morell's ground crew. I stepped into the meadow and ran across to the spot where she had been, calling "Marietta" softly as I neared the trees so I wouldn't scare her.

She scared me instead by snapping on an electric lantern and shouting, "Who is it?"

"Neil Armstrong. I mean, Owen Keane. Turn off that light; they'll see us."

"Who will?" she asked, but she switched off her light. Before I could answer, she added, "It's just a plane, Mr. Keane. Not a space vehicle at all. Just an airplane. I don't know why on earth it landed here."

"It's bringing in drugs," I said.

"The drugs those young men are searching the county for? I talked to one of them. What was his name?"

"Fallon. Are those binoculars? May I borrow them?"

The plane taxied about halfway up the meadow and then turned its lights onto the woods on our side of the open ground. Answering lights came out of the trees, automobile lights, I guessed. They were weak and yellow compared with the plane's, but they gave me my first good look at the Courier. It had the same basic configuration as the unlucky Cub, but it was much larger and it sat higher off the ground. It was covered in silver metal that gleamed dully where the light hit it. There were three windows in place of the Cub's one, no wing struts that I could see, and a tall, squared-off tail that reminded me of a kid's balsa wood glider. I could read the first three figures of the plane's registration number: N34.

A man came out of the woods, walking directly up the corridor of light. It was Willie, the coffin works survivalist. He stepped well around the plane's propeller, which was still turning, and opened a large door on the side of the fuselage. I couldn't see inside. Willie then backed away from the plane and waved toward the woods.

A pickup truck pulled slowly from the concealing trees. It was a truck I hadn't seen around town, a dull red junker old enough to have a rounded hood and protruding headlights. The driver pulled it around the Courier's overhanging wing and then backed it up to the open hatch. Then he got out and walked around the front of the truck, passing through both headlights. I recognized the tall khaki figure of Steve Fallon of the Drug Enforcement Administration.

I think there was actually a second or two when I expected Fallon to flash Willie a badge and cuff him. That was followed by a much longer period during which I willed Fallon to do it, to step back and save himself. While I was wasting my time with this, Fallon and Willie worked in the red glow of the truck's taillights, unloading small boxes from the plane.

They were almost finished when I remembered my fellow watcher. I offered the glasses to Feasey. She shook her head. My eyes had recovered from the dazzling effects of the landing lights, and I could make out Feasey leaning against the trunk of a tree, a little figure dressed—like Fallon—for an expedition, right down to her gardening gloves.

"All my hopes," she whispered over and over again.

I patted her arm. That didn't break the spell, so I said, "It's all right, Minnie."

She looked up at me then. "I was hoping the future would be

here tonight," she said. "Praying for it to be, for the chance to live to see it. Instead, I lived to see the death of the future. The death of hope."

"How did you get up here? Do you have a car?"

"A car? No. I walked. The path leads up from town."

For those who knew how to get on it in the first place. "Can you get back by yourself?"

"Of course." She pushed herself away from the tree. "What are you going to do?"

"I don't know. But I need you to go for help. Anybody but Fallon and his men. Fallon is one of the smugglers. I don't know whether Deputy Dix is involved. Better try Emmett Haas."

"Emmett Haas," she repeated in a disgusted voice, as though I'd asked her to bring back Smokey the Bear. "What we need are the state police. I'll get them up here. Keep those glasses. You may need them."

She turned and marched away. I leaned against her tree for a time, wondering whether she'd even find the path. Then I headed for the plane. I made my way along the edge of the clearing, knowing it would be faster than stumbling through the woods. It would be quieter, too, but noise wasn't really an issue. The plane's idling engine was covering all the noise I could make as I trotted along in a crouch, Feasey's heavy binoculars banging my chest once for every step. The only real danger came from the truck's headlights, which were pointed in my general direction.

Suddenly those lights swung directly toward me. Someone had gotten behind the wheel without my noticing. I dove onto the ground, pressing myself and the binoculars into a depression whose grass was wetter than my shirt. The beams passed over me, almost solid things in the thick air. When I looked up, I saw Fallon standing in the plane's lights, waving to the pilot. The Courier's engine roared in reply. The plane pivoted away from me and began taxiing toward the far end of the meadow. The old red truck had stopped by the edge of the woods, its taillights toward me.

I stood up and ran for the truck, trying to close the gap before the plane turned to take off. Fortunately, it signaled its turn in dramatic fashion, lighting the ring of trees like a moving sunrise as it swung around. I stepped back into the woods just as the twin searchlights lit the meadow from end to end.

I stayed there, pressed against a tree that vibrated with the sound of the plane's straining engine, stayed there until the meadow went dark. That happened before the plane actually passed me. When I turned I saw that the Courier was already fifty feet in the air, its lights trained up into the hazy night.

Thirty

ONCE THE COURIER had cleared the field, it was quiet enough for me to hear the truck's door open. I was out of my hiding place and running before it slammed shut again. The truck was only fifty yards away now, but turning into the forest as I ran. I'd left Feasey's binoculars hanging on a branch, and that improved my speed over the ground. Even so, I was sure the truck would be gone before I reached the road.

It did disappear briefly, courtesy of the undergrowth in the forest, but when I reached the dirt track the truck had taken, it was still so close I crouched again instinctively.

I needn't have bothered. The pickup kept moving, if only barely. I could hear its springs groaning as the two taillights went up and down on an invisible seesaw. I understood that action when I took a few steps along the road and stumbled into deep ruts divided by random outcroppings of rock.

I'd had a vague notion that I would board the truck, riding on the rear bumper or maybe even crawling into the open back. I had the chance now to give that movie-inspired impulse more thought. The boxes they'd loaded into the bed weren't stacked high enough to completely block the rear window of the cab. I could see the outlines of Willie and Fallon's heads against the misty glow of the headlights. That eliminated the possibility of passing unnoticed in the truck itself. I ruled out the back bumper option because—as far as I could tell in the darkness—there was no bumper, only the brackets where one had once hung.

For the moment, none of that was a problem. The truck was moving so slowly that I could have overtaken it at a brisk walk. I dropped back out of rearview mirror range, caught my breath, and wondered at Fallon being involved. Fallon, the wounded lover. And my ally against the stolid Deputy Dix. He'd really suckered me with that. Why had Fallon been so interested in keeping me in the game? Because Morell had told him to? That was the reason, I was sure, behind Fallon's overtures to Krystal. It was Morell's way of keeping tabs on his daughter.

Of course, it was just as likely that Fallon had simply been attracted to Krystal, but I never really considered that. Or the possibility that she'd been genuinely interested in him. He wasn't good enough for her, and that was that. I disallowed their whole relationship, retroactively. Whether I did that because I was being protective or feeling jealous, I'd have to work out later.

The pickup was rounding a descending curve. It occurred to me that I hadn't stumbled or tripped in some time. The road was smoother now, with more grass than rocks. I waited for the truck to accelerate, forcing my hand, but it continued to creep along at little better than idling speed. As we continued through the curve, I caught a glimpse of a building in the truck's sweeping headlights. It looked like a white garage, but I couldn't see the house that went with it.

The truck pulled up in front of the building and stopped. I left the center of the road and hugged the trees as I approached the clearing in which the building sat. I got close enough to see that the little white structure was not a garage. It was the size of a country church, but there was no steeple. Then I remembered that Emmett Haas had mentioned a meeting house when he was listing the property he maintained for the Ordained of God.

Haas's hired man, Willie, must have declared himself a member of the sect. He opened the building's double front doors and stepped inside. A moment later the windows came to life. The way the light spread almost organically from one narrow window to the next told me the light was not electric. There was enough of it, though, for me to make out the ghosts of two buildings behind the meeting house. One was tall and narrow, like a white windowless phone booth. It was an outhouse, another artifact preserved in the Rapture time capsule. The second structure was the size of Krystal's backyard shed.

Willie and Fallon had begun to unload the truck. I stepped into the woods and worked my way toward the back of the meeting house. The truck was still running, but its gentle ticking didn't provide the cover the Helio's rumble had. Luckily, I had Willie on my side. He was running through some monologue I couldn't make out—maybe on the beauty of Montana or the advantages of freeze-dried food. He was still at it when I was safely out of sight of the truck. I crossed the open ground and looked in at the window farthest from the door.

The window had antique glass, as wavy and full of bubbles as the ice from a puddle. I could just make out that the interior was a single room, empty except for the cardboard cases that Fallon and Willie had stacked in one corner. Willie was still stacking. Fallon was examining the contents of one of the cases by the light of a lantern. I saw all that and ducked again between breaths.

Then I moved toward the larger outbuilding, detouring around the feeble rectangles of light cast by the meeting house windows. The shed had no windows. Its single door was secured by a heavy wooden bar resting in twisted iron brackets. I lifted the bar out. While I was setting it down, the door swung toward me all by itself.

Something stirred in the black interior. I fumbled for my flashlight. Its tired beam showed me two women, bound and gagged and huddled together on a bench against the back wall of the shed. One was Dr. Krystal Bowden. I knew the other only from a photograph: Prestina Shipe.

I stepped up into the shed and closed the door behind me. It swung open again as soon as I let it go. Krystal's gag was a dust mask, the kind I'd seen at the coffin works, its elastic band tied in a knot to take out most of the slack. When I pulled the mask down off her face, I saw that it was stuffed with cloth.

Krystal looked like her old, old self, the lonely little girl who played in the dirt. Her face was covered with it, and her hair was tangled. She said, "Owen," and then, "Where the hell have you been?"

The atmosphere didn't get much friendlier after that. I started to pull at the knots that bound her. Before I'd done more than register how cold and damp the skin of her arms was, she said, "Get Prestina's gag off first. She's suffocating."

I turned my flashlight on the other woman. She was Feasey's age and size, but she wore no glasses and her skin lacked the faintest trace of Feasey's tan. Her eyes were closed. Their lids fluttered when I pulled down her mask, but never opened fully.

"Good," Krystal said. "Now get me out of these ropes." While I worked she summed up the case for me, as though I'd been on a long coffee break. "Steve's the smuggler. He's working with my father, he and that Willie guy. They're holding Clyde Batsto, too. I don't know where."

I did, but it seemed like a poor time to fill her in.

"Wait till Emmett hears what they've done to his meeting house," she said. "And his meadow."

It was my turn to grumble. "Keep your voice down. They're in the meeting house right now. Fallon and Willie. They just accepted another delivery."

I'd given up on the knots and gone to my pocket knife, cutting Krystal's ropes one by one. It was slow work, made slower by the flashbacks I was having to a night twenty years dead when Krystal had performed the same service for me.

She let me know she was thinking of that night too by quoting the little girl who had saved my life. "You sure don't keep that knife very sharp, mister."

"It's had a rough couple of decades," I said.

Then she was free and holding Shipe's head while I sawed away at the single rope that held the old woman.

"She's in a bad way, Owen. She's been out here almost a week. And it was cold last night. It really drained her. They haven't given us much to eat or drink."

"I'm fine," Shipe said, taking me by surprise.

Krystal was holding the flashlight. By its light, I saw Shipe's eyes, small and red-rimmed and flickering. Her hair was tied in its trademark bun. So many strands had escaped, though, that the bun had a wild look, like an onion left in the larder too long.

"She's free," I said. "We have to get out of here now."

It was an agonizingly slow escape, with Shipe pausing forever between steps.

"It's no good," Krystal said when we'd gotten as far as the shed's doorway. "Prestina's too weak. We'll never make it."

"Leave me," Shipe said. Krystal shushed her gently.

"There's their truck," I said. "They left it running. We could try for that."

"No," Krystal said. "*You* have to try for it. Help me get Prestina into the woods. I'll stay with her. You take the truck and go for help. They won't even look for us. They'll think we all got away."

The plan had it all over standing in the open doorway of the shed. We carried Shipe around behind the outbuilding and a few feet into the forest.

"This is far enough," Krystal said. "Go, Owen. If they check the shed before you steal the truck, this won't work." Her big hand squeezed a little life into mine.

"Good luck," I said and left them.

I circled the meeting house at the edge of the clearing, afraid of bumping into Fallon and Willie on their way to the shed. As I neared the road, the light inside the meeting house went out. I heard the front door being shut and the truck door opening.

"Damn," I said and froze.

Then I heard Fallon yelling from behind the meeting house: "Willie! They've gotten loose! Get back here! Bring a light!"

Willie came around my side of the building but never looked my way. I was sprinting flat out by then. Willie had left the truck running and the driver's side door open for me. I slammed the door as hard as I could, imagining Fallon within a few steps of where the women were hiding.

The refresher course on clutch work I'd done in Krystal's Jeep held me in good stead. I managed to get the truck into gear and rolling without stalling it out. I heard Willie right behind me, swearing, closer than he should have been.

I floored the accelerator and, in a moment of inspiration, yelled, "Keep your heads down!"

It turned out to be good advice. I heard a sound like a thick branch snapping just as the rear window of the cab shattered.

Thirty-one

THE ROAD KEPT CURVING. That and finding third gear saved me. I heard two more shots, but the worst things I felt were the bits of glass that had fallen down my shirt. The road leveled, turned again to the left, and topped a rise. The pavement went from packed earth to gravel, and I knew where I was: on the ridge road at the point where I'd lost faith and struck off into the woods. I had a straight shot now into the center of Rapture.

I checked the rearview for lights every few seconds. I didn't see any, but I didn't relax, either. The variables made any mental scrambling after the odds a waste of my time. I had no idea where Fallon's truck was hidden or whether he had a radio or some other means of calling in help. His two strong-arm men could have been as close as the Double Nickel. Closer. And there was Deputy Dix. He'd been watching Krystal's trailer earlier, watching for me, I was certain. He could be there still, or he could be any-where up ahead, lying in wait.

When I wasn't checking the mirror, I scanned the road and the edge of the forest for Feasey. I never saw her or any sign of her footpath, which had to parallel the road and probably predated it. The thought of Feasey wandering from tree to tree made me feel lost myself. Then I thought of Krystal and Shipe and felt worse.

Krystal. I'd found her and given her up again, so quickly that I could have believed I'd dreamed it all if I hadn't had the stolen truck along for proof.

I was tempted by the turnoff for Brookside, but I drove on past it. The nearest phone was in Rapture, which made going there worth the risk. The town appeared before I'd stopped second-guessing myself. It was far from a blaze of lights, but that was normal enough. I turned down Feasey's street. Her pink house was dark. Below it, there were lights on in the coffin works.

I hid the truck between two deserted houses and approached the works on foot. On sore feet and stiff legs, after all the running I'd done at the meadow. Through the closed railroad-shed doors on the front of the building came the hum of machinery. I pulled on one of the big doors and found that it swung as easily as the little one on the meeting house shed had. I was careful to open it just enough to slip inside. I pulled it shut behind me.

Emmett Haas was working alone on the other side of the room. He had one of the big, tub-shaped coffins lying on its side on a worktable. Next to the table, a belt sander was playing a rhythm line that had to be as familiar to Haas as his own heartbeat—assuming he could still hear the sander after a lifetime of working near the saws. He didn't hear me as I crossed the sawdust-covered floor.

He was working on the coffin's wooden lining, as he had been when I'd last seen him. As I watched, he held a piece of sassafras against the turning belt, sending more of the wood's fragrance into the shed's humid air. He then fitted the piece in a gap in the floor of the coffin and nodded to himself.

I stopped at the neighboring worktable, intending to call out to him before I got any closer. I didn't call out. I'd caught sight of something on the table next to the coffin: an open fifth of vodka. If it had been scotch, I might have asked Haas for a drink before

I'd thought about it. As it was, I stood there wondering why the bottle spoiled the whole happy picture.

While I wondered, Haas took up a long knife that had the fat handle of a screwdriver. He used it to pop out the piece of sassafras he'd just placed in the coffin. Then he popped out the next piece and the next, until he'd removed the entire bottom lining. Beneath it was a cavity almost the full size of the coffin's base and lined in clear plastic. A corner of the plastic sheeting hung loose. Haas secured it with a staple gun. The sharp crack of the gun woke me up. I took a step back toward the front door, and Haas spotted me.

He dropped the staple gun and swung around without straightening his back. His posture and the way he held his open hands up made him look like a wrestler poised for a bout. His eyes were raw, as Shipe's had been. They leaped around the room, looking everywhere but at me. His face was blood red, as usual, and he had the usual sprinkling of sawdust in his fringe of a beard. Even so, I felt like I was seeing him for the first time.

We stood there for a long time, me trying to place Haas and Haas searching the shadows for someone or something. I was waiting for him to say that I'd startled him. He might have been expecting me to stammer out something innocent-sounding about how late he was working. We were both too tired to actually go through the dance. After a day or two had passed, I took another step toward the door. Haas stopped me by pulling a gun from the pocket of his apron.

It was smaller than the last gun I'd faced, a small, silver automatic. That made it wrong somehow, as the bottle of vodka was wrong. Even a flintlock would have been out of keeping with the setting, out of place in the hand of the last patriarch of an unworldly sect. But this shiny prop from some spy movie was an especially off note. It was too modern and too urban, like the drugs destined to ride in the coffin's secret compartment.

I had answers now for some of the questions that had bothered me on the ride down from Michigan City. I knew now how Shipe and Krystal could both be innocent. It was because the scheme had never depended on an insider in the mail-order herb business. The drugs in the herb boxes in Krystal's trailer had been a decoy, intended to frame Krystal and take the spotlight off the upcoming delivery. Morell had given up nothing with that move, apart from a few samples. His real distribution method had always been the coffins with their linings of aromatic wood. Was that a real Ordained touch, I wondered, or an innovation intended to fool drug-sniffing dogs? I would have discussed the point with Haas, but we were already past small talk. So I skipped to the larger question.

"Why?"

"Why not?" he asked back, stating the dilemma succinctly. Why not succumb to the temptation Morell—through Willie—had waved under his nose? What was to stop him? What law or belief or superstitious fear?

"I have lived my whole life here, Owen," Haas said, focusing on me for the first time. "I do not want to die here and end up buried in a coffin I made for myself. My whole life has been a coffin I made for myself. I want to spend a little time outside it. I want to be buried where no one knows me, where no one will put up a stone for tourists to laugh at. 'Here lies Emmett Haas, last of the crazy Ordained of God.'"

"But you've waited so long," I said.

"And for what? For nothing, Owen. Nothing has come to me. Nothing will come. God isn't going to appear one morning while I'm mowing the meadow and take me into heaven.

"*This* was my chance." He gestured to the coffin with his pistol. "My only chance. It is the one thing that has come to me through all the years of waiting and watching others go off to make some good thing of their lives."

"You can't think this is making some good thing of your life."

He hunched his back a little more. "This town was dying, Owen. The coffin works was dying. We had no money. *I* had no money. No pension. No future. What I told you before about selling our work to collectors and museums, that was only a story we made up to explain why suddenly, after years of struggling, we had orders again. Lots of orders."

"The orders were for drugs, Emmett. You have no idea what damage they're doing to the world outside of Rapture."

"What makes you think I would care if I did know? What did the outside world ever do for the Ordained except laugh at us? Or for Rapture except lure away its best people, its heart's blood? I spit on the outside world. If one more coffin filled with drugs would end the outside world tomorrow, I would build that coffin with my own hands. That would be one I would love to build."

"Build one for Rapture first. What you've done here has finished this town. It's finished the Ordained."

"The Ordained were already finished, Owen."

"Not while you and the others are still alive."

Haas shook his head. "The Ordained were finished long ago. Recognizing that was the great revelation of my life. I long have feared that the sect would end with my death. Then one dark night, a voice whispered to me that the end had come before my birth."

"I don't understand."

"You do not? It is the secret of the Ordained's remarkable faith. The secret they did not pass on. The secret is they had no faith. After the Great Disappointment, nothing. No faith in the coming of God's kingdom. No faith in God. Only the empty husk of faith. They named their steam engine Faith"—he gestured with the gun to the turning shafts above our heads—"because it was all they had. It was a joke, like this whole factory. That is why they built coffins here. Because it made them laugh to do it. Laugh inside, where no one could see. No one who was not Ordained. It was so obvious to them. They surely thought the Ordained who came after them would understand and share their joke. But we did not. I did not. Not until their joke had used up my entire life."

Without turning from me, he groped on the table behind him for the vodka bottle. He grabbed it, but didn't take a drink. His angry eyes were scanning the big room again—not looking for someone, it seemed to me now, *seeing* someone everywhere he looked. I glanced around myself and saw old machinery and shadows.

"You may be right about the Ordained, Emmett. I don't know. But it doesn't justify what you've done here. The ones who went before you wouldn't have thought so. You don't really think so yourself. You know what you're doing is wrong. You're the one who sent me to talk with Marietta Feasey. You knew she'd seen the lights of the smugglers' plane. She told you, or Fallon did, after he put out that fire. He went through the motions of talking with Feasey and then laughed her story off. You brought it back to life by sending me to see her. You were trying to turn yourself in."

All my talking had given Haas a thirst. He took a long drink from the bottle, his tired eyes never once coming to rest. He said, "I was not."

"Why did you help me?" I had to work to sort my last visit to the factory from all that had happened since. "I'd come to break the news about Krystal's disappearance. That knocked you backward. Fallon didn't warn you he was going to do that, did he? You didn't think those drugs of yours would hurt anyone in Rapture."

Haas took another drink.

"How about Prestina Shipe? How could you let Fallon keep her in an unheated shed like some animal? She's one of your own people."

"Prestina was too curious. She heard of the lights in the sky from Marietta. Marietta has an obsession to cloud her thinking. Prestina does not. She spoke to her neighbor, Clyde Batsto, about the lights. She questioned Clyde about different types of airplanes. Clyde loved airplanes and flying from his boyhood. I lied to you about not knowing that. He gave Prestina one piece of the answer. Fallon gave her the other piece, through the doctor. I warned Fallon against becoming too friendly with the doctor. I knew no good would come from that. She told Prestina about the drugs Fallon and his men were here to find. Prestina eventually connected them with the plane."

"That's why Prestina was so anxious to talk to Krystal last Sunday night," I said. I was giving up my own chance and Krystal's and Shipe's by standing there talking to Haas. I didn't believe he'd shoot me. He hadn't even put his finger on the trigger. I should have been finding help elsewhere. But I couldn't tear myself away from the answers.

"Yes," Haas said. "Prestina intended to tell the doctor what she had worked out. It was bad luck for her that she told me first."

"So you kidnapped her."

"No. Willie did. But she is being well cared for. When we are ready to leave, she will be released."

"She's going to be released the same way Clyde Batsto was."

Haas shouted his answer, but not at me. He called it out to the empty workstations around us. "No! That was a mistake. An accident. Once Prestina went missing, Clyde became suspicious. And he was frightened by then, too, afraid that Fallon was going to falsely accuse him of the smuggling."

"He was right."

"So we took Clyde, too. We had to."

"Whose idea was it to disguise the kidnappings as fake raptures?"

"No one thought of that when Prestina was taken. Willie just happened to surprise her at her breakfast. The doctor raised the specter of the rapture. That amused Fallon. So when he went to Clyde's farm to pretend to interview him, he set the shower running and spread Clyde's things about. Willie had already seen to Clyde."

"Killed him, you mean."

"I told you, that was an accident. Clyde tried to get away." Haas raised his voice again, addressing the whole room. "Willie hit him too hard."

"Are you sure Willie wasn't following orders when he hit Batsto? Look at me, Emmett. Who are you really working for?"

Haas singled me out with an effort. "I thought at first it was Willie. He came to me months ago, when I was struggling to keep the works open. He told me he had a way for me to save this place. He gave me the money to get it really going again. To hire more men. He showed me the drugs—just a little bag—and told me what we had to do with them. He talked very importantly about the people he had met in prison. He bragged about his plan when he was in drink. But I always thought there was someone else behind it all. Willie is so simple, and the plan is not simple."

I was doing a good job of not staring at the automatic. It became harder to do as Haas began to lower the gun, slowly.

"When Willie introduced me to Fallon," Haas was saying, "then I knew I had been right. I knew at last I had met the planner, the thinker."

"If Fallon is such a genius, why did he get so close to Krystal? Prestina might never have heard what was going on around here if Fallon had left Krystal alone."

Haas drank again. He wasn't just marking time, either; the bottle was down by a third. "I told you, I warned him. I said leave the doctor alone. He did it anyway."

"Maybe he had no choice."

"What?"

"You didn't answer me just now when I asked if you knew ahead of time that Krystal was going to be kidnapped."

"I did not know. You were right; it almost killed me when you told me. She has done so much for us."

"I'm sure Fallon told you he did it because Krystal was getting too close to the truth. What did he say about the drugs he'd planted in her trailer?"

"He said he did it to buy us time. Those were his words: 'Buy us time.' " Haas almost smacked his lips as he said it, as thought the phrase held a special attraction for him. "The doctor will be able to clear herself easily, once we are through here and gone."

"You don't believe that. You're not even sure she'll be released. You wouldn't have sent me to Feasey if you were sure no harm would come to Krystal."

"I had a moment of doubt when you told me she had been taken. I admit it. The shock caused that. When I had time to think, I knew that everything would be fine. Fallon will not harm the doctor. He has feelings for her. That is why he approached her even though it was dangerous. Even though I warned him not to. You said it: he had no choice."

"I wasn't talking about romance. Fallon was following orders when he approached Krystal, just like Willie was when he killed Batsto and buried him near Krystal's trailer—like Willie was when he came to Rapture in the first place."

"Who sent Willie here if not Fallon?"

"The man who came up with the whole plan. He's sitting in a cell in the Indiana State Prison right now. His name is Curtis Morell. He's Krystal's father."

Haas licked his lips. The gun was pointing at the sawdust. I had all the answers I was going to get. It was time to try for the door, I knew, but I couldn't leave my audience hanging.

"Do you remember telling me that Krystal had come to Rapture because of some ghosts from her past? You called them knots she had to untangle."

Haas nodded.

"Those ghosts followed her here. Krystal's father went to prison for dealing in drugs and for murder. Krystal helped put him there. Now you're helping her father get his revenge. He sent Willie to Rapture in the first place because Krystal was here. Your operation was perfect for them, so they took you over. But if the coffin works hadn't been here, they would have found something else nearby.

"This has never been about giving you your chance. It may not even be about selling drugs to the world you hate so much. The goal may always have been hurting Krystal. You can help me stop that, Emmett. It's not too late."

But it was too late. A car was coming down the hill at high speed. Willie and Fallon. If Haas heard the car, he gave no sign. He was licking his lips again and staring at nothing I could see. I circled a drill press, heading for the only other way out, the door that led to the engine room. Haas let me get as far as the belt sander next to him before he dropped his bottle and turned to face me. As he did, he raised the gun. His finger was on the trigger now. I kept moving, and Haas shuffled along with me, the old machines passing between us as we followed our parallel aisles.

"You stay, Owen. Stay! We will talk to them. We will find out the truth."

Outside, the car slid to a stop in the gravel courtyard. We were only a few steps by then from the back wall. Haas raised the pistol to the level of his wild eyes.

"They'll kill us both, Emmett. They may always have meant to leave you dead. They'll do it for certain if you get between Morell and Krystal. Come with me."

I held out my hand to him. He let the gun drop to his side. I could have stepped up and taken it if a banging hadn't sounded on the front door. Neither one of us had expected that, or the voice that came with it, yelling "State police!"

Haas reacted faster than I did. He swung around and stumbled toward the back wall. I moved to cut him off, but I picked the wrong door, the door I'd been trying for myself, the door to the open-ended engine shed. Haas made for his office. He got there ahead of me and locked himself in.

I pounded on the door, calling his name and bracing myself for the sound of a shot.

Thirty-two

THE SHOT NEVER CAME. Instead, policemen did, state troopers who hustled me away from the office door when I told them—calmly and rationally—that Haas was behind it with a gun. Or maybe I yelled it at them and waved my arms. I was afraid some provoking action would follow, some door breaking or tear gas firing, but neither thing happened. There wasn't even much in the way of coaxing. None of the troopers, it turned out, was certified in something they called armed conflict negotiation. Neither were the county deputies who had begun to straggle in. So they radioed for an expert and settled down for a siege.

Deputy Dix was among the representatives of the county gathered in the coffin works courtyard. Being Dix, he didn't seem to be in charge of anything, not even the deputy contingent, not even here, on his own beat. But it wasn't bothering him tonight. He even seemed happy to see me. The feeling was mutual, as the state police had put me on permanent hold after they'd heard about Haas and his gun.

"Keane, still with us, huh? That monk friend of yours did a hell of a job organizing the cavalry. I expect FBI helicopters any time now."

I looked at my watch. We were still a quarter hour shy of the midnight deadline I'd given Brother Dennis.

Dix laughed softly. "I guess he started phoning police agencies as soon as he hung up from talking with you."

"We have to get up to the old meeting house," I said. "Dr. Bowden and Prestina Shipe are hiding in the woods up there. The drug shipment is stashed inside the meeting house. Fallon and—"

Dix put a weightless hand on my shoulder. "They're okay, the doctor and Shipe. We sent men up to the meadow first thing. The doctor flagged down a cruiser. She and Shipe are on their way to the county hospital right now. A second car picked up Fallon, walking along the road like the tenderfoot he is."

The deputy paused to sneeze several times. Even that didn't get him down. "Willie ran into the woods, but we'll find him. He's the one that shot that plane you were in yesterday, ten to one. I didn't get the report on that until this afternoon. I knew then that something was going down tonight, whatever Fallon was saying to the contrary."

"But how did you know to come here? I didn't tell Brother Dennis that Haas was one of the smugglers. I didn't know myself."

"That Marietta Feasey woman suggested it. She called the state police post from a house on the Brookside road, and they radioed to us. How the old bat knew that Haas was involved beats the hell out of me."

I didn't understand that mystery, either. But it reminded me of an apology I had to make. "I thought you might be one of the smugglers yourself," I said. "I'm sorry."

"Don't be. I felt the same way about you. Especially after you took a walk on me yesterday. I've spent most of the last twenty-four hours looking for you."

"You almost got me tonight, at the doctor's trailer."

"You were there, huh? Serves me right for underestimating you city boys. I was at the trailer when the call came in to meet the state police at the substation. I almost didn't answer it. I thought it was another false alarm. I'd figured out that Fallon's anonymous source was using the phony tips to run us around. The idea was to get us so worn out we wouldn't know the real operation if we tripped over it. I didn't figure Fallon was the boy crying wolf, though."

"You must have had some inkling of it, the way you two got along."

Dix repeated "inkling" a few times, like he was memorizing it for future use. Then he said, "Heck, Keane, I don't have any sixth sense. During allergy season, I don't even have the regulation five. I just plain didn't like the guy. I didn't have any idea he was Mr. Big."

"He isn't." I reminded Dix of the background I'd already given him on Krystal and her father. Then I moved on to the trip I'd made to Michigan City and what I'd learned there.

"Damn," Dix said before he could edit himself. "It sounds like Mr. Morell's blown his chance for parole big time. So Willie was someone Morell met inside?"

"I think so. Emmett told me just now that Willie had been in prison."

"How did Morell get to Fallon?"

"I don't know. He might have heard something about Fallon's ethics through the prison grapevine. Or Morell might just have bought Fallon the way he did Emmett. Through Willie. You told me yourself that Fallon was on the way out at the DEA. He needed a big score to save his job. Maybe he decided the job was past saving."

Dix stretched contentedly. "We'll find out soon enough. Fallon's probably plea bargaining right now. Willie made a big mistake, giving that guy the chance to tell the first story."

"What about Fallon's men?"

"No sign of them so far. My guess is they're not involved. Fallon sent them back up to Indy yesterday, after he'd officially declared that we'd frightened off the smugglers. I thought he'd gone up there with them, but he hadn't."

The negotiator arrived by station wagon, and I was suddenly in demand again. He was a heavyset man named Bryce, who wore his reddish hair in the most audacious comb-over I'd seen in Indiana. I didn't stare at his hairline, though. His left shirtsleeve was empty and pinned up at the end. My eyes kept straying to the sleeve as we talked, but Bryce never called me on it.

He questioned me extensively about Haas's state of mind, while Dix stood by and sniffled. The deputy had used me as his entrée to the inner circle. Or maybe he was afraid I'd run off again if he left my side. The rest of the huddle consisted of the ranking state policeman and one of his troopers, the one who had dragged me away from the office door. When I gave Bryce a short history of the Ordained, the trooper started to laugh. Dix pretended to lose his balance, shoving the trooper sideways a foot or two and shutting him up.

"Sorry, pard," Dix said.

Once Bryce finished with me, I lost my cachet. The coffin works grounds were cleared of unnecessary personnel, a list I headed. I was pacing the road between the works and Feasey's house when Dix found me. I'd been thinking in my idle way of Willie and his rifle, imagining him stalking me in the shadows, giving up his chance to get away for one more shot at his master's archenemy. I wasn't frightening myself, which told me that either I didn't consider the possibility likely or I was too tired to care. I transferred my speculations to Dix as he climbed the gravel road toward me. I told myself that in a movie or a book the final twist would be a character like Dix—suspected and then cleared—revealing himself to be a henchman after all. Maybe by pulling a knife or a gun on the hero in an isolated spot. Dix pulled a disturbing idea instead.

First though, he complained about the state police. "You'd think they were disarming a gosh darn bomb down there," he said.

I deduced from that remark that he'd been kicked out, too. "That's the way they see it," I said. "Thanks for sticking up for the Ordained with that trooper. I didn't think you were a fan."

"I'm not. Guess I don't like to hear an outsider laughing at them."

It made me smile to hear Dix call someone else an outsider. I remembered that Dr. Stanger had classified Dix the same way. Everything was relative after all, it seemed. There was probably somebody around who didn't trust Stanger because he'd only lived in the neighborhood for forty years. It was the last smile I got from Dix.

"That dumb greenhorn," he said. "I should have popped him. It's like laughing at a funeral, which is what this all amounts to. This finishes off the Ordained, whether or not the one-armed guy can talk Haas into coming out."

I'd said the same thing to Haas, but the reality hadn't hit home in the excitement of the moment. It hit home now.

"One hundred and fifty years of waiting ends tonight," the deputy said. "It may have started as a farce, but it's ending as a tragedy."

"It didn't start as a farce," I said. "It started as a hope." And ended as the death of hope, that's what Marietta Feasey had said.

She'd gotten home somehow without my noticing. There was a light on in her little pink house. Dix spotted it when our pacing took us up to the top of the hill.

"How the heck did she know about Haas?" he asked. "Did she figure it out like Shipe? Did every septuagenarian in the county know what was going on? Did Feasey really know or did she just have one of your inklings?"

We only had to knock on her door and ask her to find out, but we turned and started back down the hill. I was still thinking back on Feasey's reaction up in the meadow at the moment she'd recognized the plane for what it was. The death of the future. She'd been completely devastated. It had been the Great Disappointment all over again. She hadn't known the truth about the lights in the sky, I was sure of that. So how had she known about Haas?

I thought back on our conversation in her high-tech television room, of her disdainful, dismissive references to "Old Emmett." I ended up replaying the whole conversation as Dix and I paced, including Feasey's parting promise to me that the abductees would be returned. She'd warned me then that they wouldn't be the same when they came back. I remembered how that idea had saddened and even frightened her, and I realized, belatedly, that she hadn't gotten the insight from any book on UFOs. She'd observed the phenomenon firsthand in Emmett Haas. She'd seen the change in him caused by his fall from grace, and she'd fitted it into her own cosmology. After she'd left me in the meadow, she must have worked out the true cause of Haas's transformation.

The silence down at the coffin works was broken by a trooper calling for a car. Another trooper was pulling open one of the big front doors of the building, flooding the courtyard with light.

"Bryce got him out," Dix said. He started off down the hill at a trot, holding his left arm out for balance, using his right hand to steady his gun. I followed at a distance, at a walk.

I stopped at the edge of the compound. They were bringing Haas through the front door. He wasn't handcuffed, but I didn't notice that right away. I was struck by how much smaller he suddenly seemed and by something about his face that wasn't right. Then I realized that the old man had used the time alone in his office to shave off his beard. He looked like everyone else now, any old man you might see on the street.

They put Haas in a car and drove him away. When the cruiser passed the spot where I stood, I backed into the darkness.

Thirty-three

I ASKED DIX to drive me to the county hospital. I wanted to see for myself that Krystal was okay. On the way, we stopped at the deputy's substation so he could pick up more allergy medicine. Several cars stood in the substation lot, state police and Sheriff's Department both. I mistook them for the ones I'd just seen depart from Rapture and decided to wait in the cruiser, having already said my good-byes to Emmett Haas. Dix was only in the building for a few seconds before he came out again, shutting the door quietly behind him.

"They've got Fallon in there," he said. "The sheriff's rushed back from his fishing trip so he could have his picture taken slapping on the cuffs."

"I figured you'd be squeezing into that picture yourself," I said.

"So did I," Dix said, keeping his voice low. "But when I saw Fallon, I came down with a bad case of the skin crawls. Let's make tracks. I can borrow some medicine at the hospital."

"Wait," I said and climbed out of the car. I would never confront Morell again outside of my bad dreams, not if I had anything to say about it. Confronting Fallon was as close as I would get. I don't know why facing a substitute bogeyman seemed so important to me just then, but the urge was enough to get me up and walking.

The big front room of the substation was almost full for once, but not so full that my quiet entrance passed unnoticed. Two men looked up at me, one of them the young state trooper who had mouthed off about the Ordained back in Rapture. He nodded to me and went back to doing what most of the others in the room were doing, which was listening to a scarecrow in civilian clothes—the prodigal sheriff—talk importantly on the telephone.

The only one who wasn't listening was the other person who had looked up as I came in, Steve Fallon. He was seated beside Dix's desk, within a few feet of the declaiming sheriff, near the center of the whole tableau but somehow not part of it. He wasn't wearing cuffs at that moment, only the heavy gold bracelet I'd admired earlier. He was smoking a cigarette, and a cup of coffee sat on the desk at his elbow. It wasn't exactly the rubber hose treatment, the treatment I'd expected cops to mete out to one of their own gone bad. Then it occurred to me that Fallon wasn't really one of their own. He was an outsider, an interloper from far-off, exotic Indy. His crimes satisfied the local prejudice against outsiders, which might have been enough to earn him the smoke and the coffee.

Or maybe he was already turning state's evidence, as Dix had predicted. I didn't hang around long enough to be sure. I didn't address Fallon, either, didn't ask him why he'd done what he'd done. I didn't think he'd tell me, if he even knew himself. Nor did I give him any catchphrase taunt to pass on to Morell in prison. It would have taken me hours to think of one. I just stood there, looking into Fallon's dark eyes and letting him look into mine. Not much of a confrontation by paperback standards, but it winded me.

I was experiencing what Dix had called the "skin crawls." It might have been the power of suggestion. Or it might have been due to a trick of the Keane memory, which had chosen that moment to replay Fallon's speech about drug dealers, the one he'd made in his Explorer as he'd driven me back from this very substation to Rapture. He'd called drug dealers "the soul dead," and those words were playing over and over in my head as I tried to stare Fallon down. I experienced one of those unprovable, unbankable insights that sometimes come to me when I've been up too long or drinking too much. I knew that Fallon had been speaking from personal knowledge when he'd used the phrase "soul dead," that he'd been leavening his lies with a tiny bit of the truth. And I knew that he was remembering that speech himself as I did, that the same phrase was running through his head, animating his skin.

At that moment, the sheriff put his hand over the receiver and announced to the room that Willie had been caught hitchhiking on Highway 50. Fallon looked toward the sheriff, and I backed out the door as Dix had done.

The county hospital was small and down at the heel, its vestibule linoleum so worn that you had to look in the corners to find its original color. No wonder Stanger had dreamed of building a replacement, I thought. Theodore Stanger Memorial Hospital. I amended the name to Stanger-Bowden Memorial when I saw Krystal coming toward me down a long, underlit hallway. I met her halfway. She was wearing green hospital scrubs, and her hair was still wet from a shower. She looked like she'd spent the last two days in a spa.

"Is Prestina okay?" I asked as an opener.

"Relax, Owen. She's doing fine. She wants to talk with you."

"I thought . . ." I began and gestured vaguely at her scrubs.

A ripply smile broke out on her thin face, brightening it and the dark hallway. "You thought I'd operated? I just borrowed these because I couldn't stand those clothes of mine another minute." She looked past me. "I heard Deputy Dix was here."

"He's raiding the pharmacy."

"All the bad guys accounted for?"

All except the pilot of the Helio Courier, I thought as I studied her. I'd given Dix the partial registration number I'd memorized, but I hadn't heard whether anyone had traced the plane. I never would hear. But I knew Krystal wasn't interested in the plane or even in Willie. Her smile looked freeze-dried now. It was the smile she could call up on cue for a sagging patient, I thought, a smile designed to hide what she was really feeling.

"Fallon is a bum," I said.

"I know, Owen. Believe me. I've had two days to reflect on that. I'm not mourning for him. I'm just embarrassed I was taken in so easily. I'm still a sucker for someone who treats me decently. Even after years of the Bowdens, I still carry that legacy from my . . . family. How long do you suppose I'll carry it, Owen?"

"That depends. How's your cholesterol?"

"Lower than yours," she said, punching me on the shoulder I'd wrenched in the plane crash. "Let's check Prestina."

We'd only gone a few steps down the hall before Krystal took up the subject of her legacy again. "This need to be loved is a gift from my father—not my family," she said. "I was afraid to say the word father just now. It gives me the shivers to think of him plotting to get back at me."

I knew those shivers, but I pretended otherwise. "Let him plot. He'll be in for a long time yet. Maybe forever."

" 'Stone walls do not a prison make,' " Krystal said. "Especially not for my father. Anyway, he doesn't need to lift a finger to screw me over. He's gotten that job done. He's the one who made me so desperate for a little kindness that I get misty over anyone who offers it to me. I was lucky with the Bowdens. They were genuinely nice people. But I can't distinguish the genuinely nice ones from the phonies. I can't control my cravings enough to tell a Bowden or an Emmett Haas apart from someone like Steve Fallon."

I dropped back a step as it came to me that Krystal hadn't heard the news about Haas. She didn't notice my reaction because we happened to be passing a nurse's station. Its sole occupant, an older woman working a crossword, asked Krystal how she was holding up, giving me a moment to catch my breath.

Shipe's room was a little way beyond the station. By the light of a monitor, I could see that her white hair was laid out across her pillow, that her big beak of a nose was pale and pinched, and that her eyes were closed.

"Asleep," Krystal whispered. "You'll have to come back. Will you be around long enough to come back?"

I didn't answer her. My mind was still full of the bad news I had to pass on. It occurred to me that Krystal would shortly be facing the same nasty job, and I took what cover I could from that.

"There's something you'll have to tell Shipe when she wakes up. When you think she's strong enough to take it. Emmett Haas is under arrest. He's one of the smugglers."

Krystal stepped past me without saying a word, going back down the hall in the direction we'd come. I waited a while before I followed her. I found Krystal behind the nurse's counter. The nurse was off somewhere, and the doctor was in her chair, her square shoulders rising and falling in time with silent tears.

I pulled up another chair and sat down beside her. Before I could reach out to her, she said, "What did I tell you? A sucker for a kind face." She wiped at her eyes with the back of her hand. "Emmett was my grandfather come back to life. Better than my grandfather. Kinder. More upright. My grandfather as I always wished he could be."

"Emmett really cared for you," I said. "He wasn't a phony in that respect. "He cared enough about you to help me find you."

"You'd say that whether it was true or not, Owen. You're in the Bowden camp. You're sitting there trying to think of the one thing that will make everything right for me. I knew people like you in medical school. They couldn't stand for anyone to be left hanging emotionally, even though that's our natural state. They made lousy doctors."

And detectives, I said to myself.

"Besides," she said, "for all we know Emmett had another motive for worrying about me. Maybe he saw me sharing his beach in Tahiti." She couldn't laugh the old man away. "Emmett," she said and wiped at her eyes again. "Why did he do it, Owen?"

I told her of Haas's midnight revelation, the idea that the Ordained had left their faith behind in Rapture Meadow, that he had dedicated his life to an empty sham. I expected more tears when I finished, remembering how drawn to the Ordained's faith Krystal had been. How drawn to it I'd been myself. I saw by the glow of the ubiquitous computer that her eyes had dried completely.

"Emmett is wrong, Owen. He's frightened and tired and wrong. The Ordained aren't finished yet. They may be a long way from finished."

I was still looking for tears in those steely blue eyes. I saw something else instead, something that lightened my heart. "Thinking of applying for Emmett's job?" I asked.

"Maybe," Krystal said, punching me again. "Or I may ask Brother Dennis to take it on."

"He'd like that."

We went to look for Dix. As we walked, I told Krystal where she'd find her truck and her license plate. She took that news so well, I considered telling her about the damage I'd done to her trailer. I was still considering when we reached the front door of the hospital. Beyond it, Dix was sitting on the hood of his car, looking up at the stars.

Krystal said, "You never answered my question about whether you'd be staying around."

I gave her a long look, and she actually blushed. "Okay, so I'm trying to play it cool," she said. "Is that such a crime? I'd rather you didn't rush off. I'd like you to stay for a while, period. There, I said it. Does that make you happy?"

"Yes," I said.

"But you're going anyway."

"I was thinking of driving down to St. Aelred's. Would you like to go with me?"

"If it's for your class reunion, I might be underfoot."

"It's just a visit. Brother Dennis thinks I need closure."

Krystal tossed her wet golden hair. "Closure," she repeated with a touch of disdain.

She was thinking about her commitment to the town of Rapture, if I was reading her mind correctly. That commitment had been about closure, at first. Now it had turned into something else.

"I'll go," she said, "just to keep you from getting too much closure. I think that stuff is overrated. It sounds like it's about letting go of the past, but it can be an excuse to drown yourself in it. That was Emmett's problem. He was always looking back. You have to look forward to stay alive."

"Like Dr. Prestina?" I asked. "And Commander Feasey?"

Krystal laughed. "Like you, Owen."

I didn't want to demote myself, so I didn't tell her how much time I spent in the past, how tethered by it I was, like Emmett Haas. I probably didn't have to tell her.

"Speaking of looking forward," Krystal said. "A new millennium will be here soon. Not the Ordained's millennium, but at least a fresh one. Doesn't that excite you?"

"Nearly to death," I said.

She took my hand. "If you don't get a better offer for the big night, come out to Indiana again."

I almost asked which one of us would get tied up this time, but I saw that—despite her joking tone—her offer was serious.

"We'll sit up in Rapture Meadow," Krystal said, "and face the millennium together. Who knows what might happen?"

"Who does?" I said.